PENGUIN BOOKS
Farewell Speech

Rachel McAlpine is the third daughter of Celia and the Reverend David Taylor and was born in Fairlie, South Canterbury. She has five sisters and four children.

Rachel McAlpine is the author of two previous novels, *The Limits of Green* (1986) and *Running Away From Home* (1987), both published by Penguin. Other works include four plays for young people and her *Selected Poems*. She lives in Taranaki and her interests include Tai Chi and making rag rugs.

FAREWELL SPEECH

Rachel McAlpine

PENGUIN BOOKS

PENGUIN BOOKS

Penguin Books (NZ) Ltd, 182–190 Wairau Road, Auckland 10, New Zealand
Penguin Books Ltd, 27 Wrights Lane, London W8 5TZ, England
Viking Penguin Inc., 40 West 23rd Street, New York, New York 10010, USA
Penguin Books Australia Ltd, 487 Maroondah Highway, Ringwood, Australia 3134
Penguin Books Canada Ltd, 2801 John Street, Markham, Ontario, Canada L3R 1B4

Penguin Books Ltd, Registered Offices: Harmondsworth, Middlesex, England

First published 1990
1   3   5   7   9   10   8   6   4   2

Typeset by Typocrafters Ltd, Auckland
Printed in Hong Kong

This novel is dedicated to a modest person with an awe-inspiring capacity to forgive.

Preface

Farewell Speech grew out of a long obsession with my great-grandmother, Ada Wells, and the suffragettes. It was only in the family that their names were mentioned. At school we were taught about the First Four Ships and the high country farmers, a history of Canterbury's élite. Yet in world terms their colonial activities were hardly unique, whereas when New Zealand women won the vote the news was an international sensation.

This modern silence about the suffragettes is reinforced by the people who knew these extraordinary women. Their public lives can be traced easily enough, since all their triumphs and wrangles were fully reported at the time, but not so their private lives. In our family the name of Ada Wells always touched a nerve; all reminiscences were coloured by intense dislike, admiration, embarrassment, resentment and pride. Violent, contradictory feelings are equally common among those who knew Kate Sheppard. As for my Great-Aunt Bim, I didn't even know she existed until my teens. There is still pressure to censor their behaviour and their views, to polish them into something orthodox.

The more I learned about Ada, Kate and Bim, the more I wanted to understand them. My mystification increased as I gathered more and more information about their lives. Only by abandoning research and writing fiction could I see them clearly. To write *Farewell Speech* has been to become all three.

I needed to hear them speak and so I gave them each a voice. They speak truths and half-truths and they deceive themselves, sharing the same old human urge to tidy up the facts. They do not tell a sweet, sensible womanly tale but it is their story and ours, and it feels true to me.

PART ONE

Chapter 1

BIM

Yesterday morning someone came to see me. A twit of a woman! She made me really mad! I've been brooding about that stupid woman ever since.

I don't know who she was and I don't care. She'll never come back here again, I made jolly sure of that!

'I'm interested in the women's suffrage movement,' she said to me. A fat sloppy sort of woman, skin like a pig. 'I'm doing some research on it.'

'Oh, are you now?' I said. 'Well, I'm interested in stopping this bank falling down.' I've had trouble with that bank for years and years. Planted it with ice plant but it still keeps falling down. All over my drive!

'I wondered if you might be willing to talk about your own experiences,' she said.

'How about doing something useful?' I said. 'Grab the other end of this bit of corrugated iron and help me jam it into the sand.'

She made a feeble attempt but she was useless, the iron fell down flat on the drive again.

'I believe your mother made quite a contribution,' she said, dusting down her piggy hands.

'If I bung a couple of stakes in front, that might work,' I thought. She followed me into the toolshed.

'I'm going to write a book about it,' she said.

'Go on then, go right ahead!' I told her. I found a couple of sticks and a mallet and she trailed after me back to the driveway. She started giving me a lecture.

'New Zealand women were the first in the world to win the vote.'

'Who do you think you're telling! I had Votes for Women on my porridge from the year dot!'

'Exactly. That's why I want to interview you, if that's not an imposition.'

'Get to the point, I'm a busy woman. Hold that straight, will you?'

I gave the first stake a good whang and it went in just fine. Pigskin jumped backwards. Never mind, I did the rest of the job without her. It looked all right. I felt a bit wobbly and went into the house to sit down. It wasn't a turn, I just felt a bit wobbly with the heat. When I came to my senses there she was, sitting in my chair at my table and plugging in a tape recorder thing!

'Would you like a drink of water?' she asked. In my own house!

'You want to hear about my mother?' I asked.

'That's right,' she said. 'You're almost the only one who can do it now.'

I hooted. 'They're all dead! Dead! Mother's dead and Chris is dead and Cos is dead — I've outlived them all! Nobody left to boss me around!' I've got the last word now, there's only me, me and my pumpkins and chooks and my old cats! Oh, I laughed and laughed!

She turned on the tape recorder. 'When did your mother first meet Kate Sheppard?'

That stopped me in my tracks. 'What's it got to do with her?'

Pigface popped her eyes. 'Why, everything, Miss Wells. Mrs Sheppard was by far the most prominent figure in the suffrage movement. In New Zealand, that is.'

'Do you want to know about my mother or don't you?' I asked her point-blank. She looked a bit scared.

'Of course I do! That's why I'm here!'

'Then stick to the point,' I said. 'What are you calling this book of yours?'

Got her! *The Sweet Suffragette.*

I exploded! 'There was nothing sweet about Ada Wells!' She went on about Kate Sheppard and I told her straight.

'My mother did as much as her!'

She didn't want to know about Ada Wells! Not on your life she didn't! I sent her away with a flea in the ear.

I sat in the kitchen fuming. I could see what she was up to. She wanted to start it up all over again, that hero worship of Kate Sheppard, just because she was the obvious one, the leader and so forth. That woman won't be happy till we're all on our knees kissing Kate Sheppard's foot, just like they did in the old days.

Kate Sheppard Kate Sheppard Kate Sheppard! That's all I heard for years and years from my mother and the newspapers and all the lot of them. On and on! How she was famous all over the world and what a good writer and a marvellous speaker and how the women loved her and the men loved her, and how she made the politicians give us the vote. I got heartily sick of the perfect Mrs Sheppard.

That was a long time ago, mind you. Must be fifty years ago she died. That was in 1934, the year after Mother. Nobody talks about her now, nobody even knows her name except for that bookshop.

It was all in the air, her fame, it just blew away. It's queer the way they've rubbed her name out. Every time the newspapers do a jubilee or a royal trip they sing the glories of the so-called history of Christchurch.

They're all very proud of themselves around here, even though nowadays the South Island is right out of fashion. Those people in the North Island seem to think they run the country, they're the be-all and end-all of New Zealand, they think we're just a bunch of country bumpkins down here in the South Island. It makes me so mad! It wasn't always like that, my word no, not in the heyday of Mother and her cronies! Mind you, there was always a difference between the city and the province. Christchurch and Canterbury were two different places altogether. One was full of wild women, the other was full of snooty farmers, beg your pardon, run-holders. Oh, I could tell a thing or two about Christchurch! They wanted to build a Brighter Britain, ha ha, they gave every place an English name and they put up a heck of a lot of blocks of grey stone. People think Christchurch looks quaint with its English cathedral and English courthouse and schools and university and even a loony bin built like a castle. Gothic! Gothic! Trying to bring the Middle Ages back, they were. That's not what Mother wanted! And we've got our sleepy little Avon River just like the English one, looping around all those show places and the daffodils and the blossom trees. And the nice view of the Southern Alps in the distance. Very pretty on the outside, Christchurch. But I know what went on behind those big pointy wooden doors, and behind those front doors in the upper-class suburb of Riccarton and the plain doors of St Albans, that's where we lived, that wasn't half as grand, oh yes I do, I know. I'm glad to be out of it. I like it here in New Brighton. It's all new here. I'm still living in Christchurch but it doesn't feel like Christchurch because I'm by the sea. Blow me down, why didn't they push the city out to the seaside years ago? Why did they keep pushing us further and further into the swamp?

But look here, this is the point, when the papers do their special issues about how wonderful Christchurch is, there's never a mention of the amazing Kate Sheppard, let alone my mother! It's always about the wool barons or some big brewery. I've never touched a drop of drink in all my life.

It makes you think. All that fuss, those years and years of work and all those things they did. All blanked out!

I had a bit of a lie-down but I couldn't sleep. When the heat of the day went off, I went out to have a look at my driveway. That blankety-blank bit of iron had fallen down, and more clay and sand all over the drive. Darn thing. And to make it worse, Stan turned up. I could do without him after a day like that.

'You again!' I said. 'What do you want this time?'

'Having trouble with your bank?'

'That's right, state the obvious!' He's so wishy-washy.

He prowled up and down and took some measurements and said, 'If you'll order the concrete blocks I'll make you a retaining wall. I could do it in a couple of weeks.' And he wrote down the number of blocks and so forth. I didn't take any notice. He was dreaming, he couldn't pour concrete, he's a boob and a weakling. 'I'll do it in a nice curve, and you can get the ice plants to trail down over the front.' Always worrying about what things look like!

'Stop fussing,' I said. 'I'll sort it out for myself.'

He took a box of fruit and veges into the kitchen and put it on the table. 'It's a good crop this year,' he said. So proud of his cherries! Anyone can grow a garden. He saw the business card that woman left. 'What's this?'

'A twit of a woman came round,' I told him. 'She says she's writing a book about Kate Sheppard.'

'There should be one about your mother,' said Stan.

'Don't be stupid! Nobody's interested in her!' I snorted.

'People don't give her credit. She did the best she could. She just didn't always follow through.'

I bristled! How dare he criticise her! 'Out you go! Out!'

He's used to my ways, I'll say that for him. I started to push him out the door but he was one jump ahead of me.

'You could always do it yourself,' he called over his shoulder. My word he can be vicious.

All night I thought about it and I got madder and madder. It's awful! To think there's no one left to remind the world of all she did! And in the end I got just about mad enough to do the bally thing myself.

Chris and Cos would die of shame if they knew what I was up to now. Because I've decided. I'm going to give it a go. I'll tell everything I know about my mother, the whole bang lot.

I can write, I'm no fool, whatever they say. Look what I've written already! Pages of it! It's just that my arm gets a bit sore. I've got a lot of Mother's stuff out of the dresser, newspaper cuttings and so forth, that'll make it easier.

I'm glad they're dead. I can give my version. Chris and Cos wrote her obituary for the *Press* and they made it all flowery. Here's a flowery bit:

'A cause might be despised, obscure, rejected, she not only helped it all the same, she helped it all the more, and in the dark and stormy days of unfounded truth, she was always to the front.' That sounds nearly like a poem, she'd like that.

Other people got even more carried away. Who on earth wrote this one? 'Her work was never merely on the physical plane: the whole experience of a full life shone with infinite gentleness in her face and flowed through her hands.' Here's a good bit — 'Standing alone in a cause was to her the natural outcome of advanced thinking. From the path of duty she never flinched, believing that spiritual forces in which she trusted implicitly were infinitely greater.'

I can't write like that. I'll say what she did and people can take it or leave it. Mother used that la-di-da language. That's where Chris and Cos got the habit. Always quoting poetry. Her mind was on higher things but she was as tough as old boots.

I might not call her Mother in this story, I might call her Ada. No, I couldn't do that. She might be angry if I called her Ada. But she's not here, she's dead! She wasn't a member of the Worldwide Church of God so she won't be there among the elect. Some people thought she was a bit of a saint, but there was no Worldwide Church of God in those days so she couldn't join. It's very strange that I am one of the elect and she's not!

I hate old age. I stopped going out to patients when I was eighty, I couldn't ride the bike any more after that. I get so mad when I can't do things. When I had the lumbago, that upset my legs, that crippled me. I think it's due to the back and I'd have given anything for some rubs. My own rubbing, I mean. I do what I can but I can't get round to the back. When I went out to the garden to do a little bit extra, it would ache all the way down and I simply shook with it, a horrible feeling. But the doctor came and saw me bending over the paths, and he said, 'Are you taking your heart pills?' So I went back to them and it's made such a difference. I don't go into town much now. But I go for a swim every day, put my coat over my bathing costume and walk over the sandhills to the beach. There's nothing like salt water, it's good for the whole system. I do love my swim. And it saves the hot water.

I mustn't wander off the point. Nobody's interested in my lumbago! Anyway here I am, I've started: I'm strong enough to do it. But now I'm going to stop. It's taken me two days to write this much! She was writing a book herself when she was ill, I saw it. I wonder what happened to that stuff she was writing? I don't think Chris got it.

Compared with Mother, Mrs Sheppard had it easy. Never dried a dish in her life. Mother said every girl should have a training whether she was rich or poor. Kate Sheppard never trained for anything! I'm not criticising her but let's give credit where it's due. Ada Wells was a respectable woman, no hanky panky. Oh, she was quite a woman, my mother! And I was a thorn in her flesh till the day she died.

Chapter 2

ADA

When first the sea-going traveller espies the shoreline of New Zealand he will note —

No no no, that won't do either. I simply don't know where to begin!

Miss Wilhelmina Sheriff Bain importunes me to write my memoirs, giving me no respite from her entreaties. As I am temporarily confined indoors, I have offered no resistance, for until I have conquered this indisposition it seems an appropriate thing to do. Quite misunderstanding the difficulties which beset me, she showers me with shameless and futile flattery, for it frets her to see me discard all my efforts of the previous day.

'All our lives we've depended on you for guidance, and you're such a wonderful writer,' she wheedles, eyeing me with those black button eyes, 'and the true history of our suffrage fight has not been written.'

'William Lovell-Smith wrote a perfectly adequate account,' I retort.

'A woman should write it!' She goes quite red when she's tussling with me!

I do not need persuading that it is my bounden duty and my destiny to write the history of our great struggle, and so help bring order out of chaos, thus making some small contribution to the more speedy advancement of a just society. But it is not as easy as she thinks! In the past few weeks I have begun from every logical basis, and time and again my hand has come to a halt after two or three pages. I am almost tempted to fall into despondency when I consider how feeble wraiths and my own mental weakness combine to obstruct my pen. What is it that corrodes my will? My dear St Bede must be sadly disappointed in me. He set the ideal example in so many ways, being the model historian; all my life I have tried to emulate his example in telling the truth to the aspiring multitudes, but now that the time has come when I should, I may, I must write the history of the valiant women of Christchurch, ignominious failure hovers ever near. Between knowing and doing the gulf is hard to bridge.

I have applied myself to many an ennobling topic, including the example set by my mother Maria, the Evolution of Culture that I have observed during the sixty-nine years of my life, and the transcendent wisdom of Rudolf Steiner. Each time my writing has proved lamentably unworthy. Today I thought I'd begin with a little geography lesson, a modest enough ambition, one might deem. Yet before I have written one sentence the task becomes all too arduous, especially when one reads the morning newspaper. The Disarmament Talks are doomed! That terrible War Debt, the nonsense of 'equality of arms', and now that madman Hitler with his million rifles.

'Write about your childhood!' Wilhelmina bids me daily. 'There's a lesson in that.'

That goes against the grain. It's a ridiculous idea. I'm only concerned with the future! But strangely, every time I pick up my pencil it is scenes from my youth that surge into my mind. Most absurdly of all, I even succumb to reminiscences of my childhood. I understand this is a symptom of old age and I resent it. I view with abhorrence the selfishness of dwelling upon one's own personal life!

Now I do not admit that Wilhelmina's advice is wise, but rather than sit here at my desk for yet another hour of frustration, I shall humour her. Perhaps if I begin writing in a wholly self-centred way, the teachings which I desire to convey will emerge convincingly as if from a parable. And there is always that wonderful writer's aid, the eraser!

I was born at Henley-on-Thames in 1863. I was the eldest child, favoured by my grandparents and my father. My mother had no favourites. She was Mary Becket Welch, known to everyone as Maria, even to her own children. Maria was a tiny woman, not thin but strong and vigorous and kind to one and all. Moreover, she was a lady, and she brought us up as ladies and gentlemen in spite of all obstacles. My father's name was very aptly William Pike, for he was tall and upright, pale and clammy to the touch. He called us his dear little chickens, and yet he was a Plymouth Brethren. His family had a coach-building business in Henley-on-Thames.

It is difficult to explain my parents, more difficult than writing about the Influence of Literature on the Education of the Race, for instance! Maria was stronger, and yet she deferred to Father.

Our mother Maria was a little bit proud of the fact that she was a Becket. One day she took me to a beautiful estate beside the river, where a huge lawn spread down to the water, dappled with shade from big old oaks. In the centre stood a mansion with white pillars.

'There!' she said with some satisfaction. 'Look at that! If we're going out to the colonies, I want you to know where you came from. This was your grandmother's home when she was a child.'

Maria showed me a brass plate set into the gatepost stating:

'Here St Thomas à Becket preached his last sermon before his martyrdom.'

I pestered her with questions, for until this moment I had always confused Becket with the wicked uncle who gambled the family fortune away.

'When he became archbishop he had to leave his family. He was called to higher things,' she said.

'Weren't we good enough for him?' I asked, waxing mightily indignant.

'That was seven hundred years ago!' said Maria.

Her answers disturbed me, for it seemed he regarded his wife and children as lower things to be discarded when he was singled out for advancement. Thomas à Becket was the first man to disappoint me.

The story reinforced the message I got from Father's church, the Plymouth Brethren. At nine I was a budding woman, obliged to sit at the back of the church and cover my head and lower my eyes in the presence of men. Women, Father explained very kindly, were evil; we were repulsive and yet at the same time fiendishly tempting. We were doomed to repeat forever the story of Eve, luring innocent men into the paths of sin.

The last time Father thrashed me was just before we left England, immediately after our last visit to our maternal grandmother. I did so love going with Maria to her mother's terrace house filled with polished furniture and velvet curtains and rich Oriental rugs. Grandmother Welch was short like Maria and wore slithery silk dresses and a cameo brooch. I was nine years old, and that day she gave me a red silk fan painted with a picture of two runaway lovers, by far the loveliest thing I had ever handled.

'Ada had better not keep the fan,' said Maria nervously.

'Nonsense!' said Grandmother. 'What's the harm in a fan?' She never understood Father's Plymouth Brethren ways. I rather disgraced myself with my eagerness to possess that fan, and in the end Grandmother and I triumphed.

I didn't flaunt it in front of Father, but once in our bedroom I pulled it out of my muff and fanned my little sister. Nell adored it but Blanche ran out of the room and told Father.

I knew what would happen. Father loomed up in the bedroom doorway, smiling and shaking his head. He never lost his temper. Events unfurled as they had to, step by step. He took the fan with one hand and my wrist with the other, and dragged me to the kitchen. The coals were glowing red in the range. Father threw in the fan and brushed his fingers against his black jacket as if to dislodge some noisome contamination.

He spoke in his usual loving tones. 'We won't have any of that women's muck in this house.' The fan flared up and crumpled in a skirt of flame.

'But it was pretty, Father!' I protested.

'It was only a fan,' said Maria. She was not quite united with Father on the matter of Hell.

Father's nails bit into my wrist as he spoke to me with deep sadness and affection. 'Little strumpet! A fan has only one purpose.'

'She knew no better!' cried my mother.

'All the more reason to teach her, dear. Whom the Lord loveth, He chastiseth. See, Ada, see the hot coals!' Their brightness burnt my eyes. Father pressed my wrist on the surface of the range and I smelt burning flesh. His kind, calm voice reached me through a red haze. 'And feel them! See your soul forever in the fiery furnace, feel your flesh burning for ever and ever and ever.'

'But why?' I whispered. I felt greatly disadvantaged by my size and my sex, and yet my spirit refused to accept that these disabilities were real. I believe I spoke from an incoherent urge to affirm my equality as a human being, small and female though I might be.

'Do not question the ways of the Lord, my little chicken.' Then he took me to the coal cellar for my beating.

Nowadays I do not condone frippery because it only makes housework, but I still can't see anything wicked about wanting a little prettiness. As I lay on the dirt floor one phrase reverberated in my mind — 'women's muck'. I found life very difficult to understand, although the situation was not new to me. It was not the first time I had been punished for the offence of being a woman, but if I were in danger of hellfire, surely so were Grandmother Welch and Grandmother Pike and our dear mother Maria. Perhaps Hell was for women only?

Of course I was used to being chastised; at the Plymouth Brethren school we were flogged for poor work or inattention, and that is perfectly natural, for a teacher cannot do her vital work if there are rebellious pupils in the room. However, the teacher did not love us, and Father did.

Still, I mustn't inflate the importance of this episode. I found strength in my mother's wisdom. 'There's always someone worse off than you,' Maria would say. I thought about street-urchins. I thought how terrible it would be if Father were a drinker. 'Use your willpower!' was another of Maria's sayings, a most useful one. I pressed my hand hard against the coal bin, fortuitously discovering that by making the pain worse one could almost make it better.

I did not feel degraded by the beating. On the contrary, I felt triumphant for my challenge had been accepted. A beating was in a sense the only victory open to me as a child.

Father decided on emigration when the Pike family coach-building business failed. He was afflicted by tuberculosis and Maria said the bankruptcy was no disgrace. (Nowadays of course one sees that as a symptom of the inevitable disintegration of the capitalist system.) We travelled on the clipper *Merope* as passengers, and that journey opened my eyes. The most exciting part was that the men were separated from the women and children. We saw Father only on Sundays! Maria blossomed. The Reverend Mr Cocks organised all sorts of social events, which Father forbad us to attend. He stayed in his cabin, for the Plymouth Brethren were not supposed to mix with anyone else. But how could we help it? It was a big ship full of passengers and immigrants with fifteen of us in a single cabin.

Most of the women were hideously sea-sick. A woman called Rosie was paid to clean the room but she was constantly ill with the motion of the ship. If Mother hadn't busied herself with the chamber pot and scrubbed the place out the journey would have been unbearable. Avoid people? Two girls in our cabin were just my own age and I simply loved those girls. We played word games and taught one another all the hymns we knew, while Maria looked the other way.

When three young babies died of diarrhoea, Maria promptly organised child-health classes for mothers. No one had ever heard of such a thing. Soon, if anyone was sick on our deck, they would call for our mother, who was well versed in healing treatments.

Of course there was no Plymouth Brethren preacher on board and consequently Sundays were very strange. We met Father straight after breakfast and sat together in a corner of the dining room while he read the Bible and prayed with an air of mournful resignation, 'Heavenly Father, protect these thy children from the evil influences that surround them.'

For two hours he would pray and lecture us all on keeping separate, after which we returned to our strange new world of women and children. We had so much fun away from the men!

I began having nightmares on Saturday nights. In that dark cabin permeated by the acrid smell of sickness and the rumble of ropes and wheels, I would force myself awake from a dream of Maria in Hell pulsing with flames, tearing at her clothes and hair, eternally boiling and burning. Restraining myself from screaming, I would sit bolt upright till I ceased trembling, then I would scramble across the shifting floor to where Mother was asleep with Blanche. I would stare at her until I was quite, quite sure she was still alive. It was a terrible thing to know she was eternally damned just for being kind to people. Oh, that was a cruel religion! Back in my bed I would imagine her voice in my ears saying, 'Ada, use your willpower.' But willpower couldn't keep you out of Hell.

This is far too personal. I, I, I! A clean page is called for.

I grew into a woman on that journey. For eight days Maria herself was ill, and then it was I who took charge in our cabin. I had more sense than some of the grown-up women, one of whom used to eat food with her hands! I did the washing and looked after my brothers and sisters. In the tropics we had to drag our mattresses on deck and beat them. I discovered I didn't like housework!

One day, Father's injunctions notwithstanding, I observed the Roman Catholic service; it was almost as strange as my first glimpse of African people to see them making the sign of the cross and kissing their rosaries. At the service were several kind and cheerful women and yet Father had constantly warned us against Roman Catholics.

Around the world we sailed, in that wondrous, heaving,

seething world of our own, drawn across the wild oceans by the mighty white sails of HMS *Merope*. Beyond Africa, beyond India, beyond Australia, circumnavigating the North Island of New Zealand and at last making landfall on the east coast of the South Island. We had sailed to the very limits of the earth, for to travel any further would have been to draw nearer to England again, a paradox which I found most bracing.

The experience marked me indelibly, as since that journey I have never held back, I have acknowledged no barriers, I have pressed my ideals to the very limit. Yet when we sailed into Lyttelton Harbour my feelings were mixed, for I could hardly imagine living with Father again. I kept thinking about my girlfriends and how I would miss them.

Christchurch was the infant city which became our home. Some of my family have established their domiciles elsewhere, but here I have remained ever since, apart from short peregrinations for definite purposes. I like to reflect on the fact that I have made my mark on Christchurch, and indeed on the nation as a whole.

But let me return to the time of our arrival, in 1873, when we rapidly found ourselves in difficult circumstances and I was obliged to do menial work whether I liked it or not.

Father bought a large gentleman's residence in Papanui, at 131 Office Road. It was on the edge of the old St Albans district, but we usually said we lived in Papanui. I preferred the mellifluous sound of the word 'Papanui', and it was the only suburb blessed with a truly New Zealand name. There was room to run a horse and a few pigs, and Maria planted magnolias and spindleberry bushes and a good vegetable garden. Within a year she was expecting another child; then Father's TB flared up, and when I was fourteen he went to a sanitorium in Timaru, one hundred miles to the south. Timaru was a seaside town, and the air was considered more salubrious for invalids. Doubtless Father made an effort to overcome the disease, but he could not assume a sufficiently positive attitude of mind. His failure affected us greatly for he was unable to earn a livelihood! Since the bankruptcy we had no income at all, and buying the house had taken all his capital.

Our mother did anything and everything to support us all. For years she took in washing, and I had to help. The house had five bedrooms, and one or two were always occupied by boarders. She did a good deal of nursing and massage and if some paid her, well and good. Every few months she travelled to Timaru to see Father. I thought we all got along very well without him.

Maria continued to have babies. In the seven years Father was away my mother had five infants, and also one that did not come to term. When I began my menses, Maria told me what are generally called the 'facts of life'. She made it seem very wonderful, and so it is. Nonetheless, when it became obvious that yet another baby was on the way, the facts assumed a new significance. These babies were not merely a product of God's will! By the time Father died, his wife had given birth eleven times. I remembered all his words about women tempting men; I watched her nurse little Ernest till he died of TB, and I blamed Father.

Naturally I did my part at home, but the centre of my life was the West High School. First I attended as a pupil, following which I spent three years as a pupil teacher. Whereas my income was forty pounds per year, the boy pupil teacher received fifty, which rankled with me as my marks were always higher. My salary was absolutely vital for the family, at times making the difference between eating and not eating. I learned how to teach from the headmaster, the Reverend James Cumming, a huge fierce man with a loud voice and a heavy hand with the strap. Five cuts for every spelling mistake — we learned! His pupils did wonderfully well at the universities, scooping the pool when it came to scholarships.

At the end of my third year I won a scholarship. What a thrill! A Junior Scholarship! It changed my life. Mind you, I had to fight for my education, for Father said it would make me arrogant and tempt me into laxity. In spite of Maria's doubts and Father's sorrowing letters, in 1882 I went off to the university to study for m̶[...] Latin, history, all the things I loved. I[...] examinations rather well.

In that year I was introduced to my hero, my[...] I recognised at once that he was my appointed [...] angel, and began my spiritual journey under his bene[...] guidance. He was the first to devote himself to the Englis[...] language, using it boldly to write down the truth. He alone made possible our inestimable treasury of English literature. Scholar, teacher, writer, historian, modest, brilliant and chaste, a man with no sins. So unlike St Thomas à Becket! After a day of lectures and an evening of mending or ironing, I sat alone over my notes and dreamed of Bede. I felt so close to him. I planned to graduate a double MA in English and history, and then to become a teacher-scholar like him.

But alas, a painful decision was forced upon me, for I had insufficient funds to complete my BA. One of my relatives claims I was the first woman graduate of Canterbury College. Wishful thinking! The Junior Scholarship is granted for only one year, giving a tantalising taste of higher learning only to whisk it out of reach. I had to leave; but Bede came with me.

After my university year I obtained a teaching post at Christchurch Girls' High School. I was twenty years old, and ever since then I have been a working woman.

)A

in my present state of health I find
own life than about Life itself and
the ... When I regain my vigour I shall
improve u... er with a dissertation upon the great
importance of i... y in the Formation of Character. In
the meantime I shall continue to set out the facts as I
remember them, leaving alternate pages blank for the inser-
tion of reflective homilies. Such additions to the text will, I
earnestly hope, convert this act of auto-biography into a
worthwhile project.

The Christchurch Girls' High School was a thrilling place.
The school was new, of handsome red-brick construction
with gothic windows. I loved walking through that imposing
front door into the foyer where there was always a huge bowl
of flowers on a polished table. Only the staff and prefects
were allowed to use that door, and even we had to step over
the gleaming brass doorstep. Miss Helen Conan was our
headmistress, the authentic first woman graduate of Canterbury College. Early in the morning I took the horse-tram up
Papanui Road to Victoria Street, whence it was but a
pleasant stroll across Cranmer Square to the school.

Not everybody was in favour of higher education for girls,
some people claiming that our female pupils did not have the
stamina of boys, or if they did it was a pity, for they would
work too hard and injure their health! Against such slippery
sophistry our staff was united, proud to be doing something
significant for the girls of a new nation, something to raise
them up. Education was the key! My own case shows this
dramatically.

When I was a child I felt myself cursed with huge ungainly ideas which I could express to no one. They were like monsters trapped inside my head, galloping round and round, all claws and ringworm. Having tasted higher education I now discovered conversation. At university and in the Girls' High School staffroom I could utter my ideas and develop them, deriving much pleasure from good-natured argument and discussion. I brought home my new notions with great enthusiasm. I had confidence, I bloomed! My sisters and brothers loved to hear all my news at the end of the day. Luckily, Father was far away, for his worst prophecies were confirmed in that I now knew his dogmatic beliefs to be at best narrow and parochial, at worst silly and vicious.

Looking back on those two years, it seems extraordinary that my path never crossed that of Mrs Kate Sheppard. Intellectually she is the superior of any woman I ever met, or any man for that matter. In Christchurch she stood out like a princess among the peasants, yet she certainly did not mix with the blue-stockings and nor I believe did she circulate much in society. I find it almost impossible to realise there was a time that Kate was not a part of my life. When we finally met it was as if I had lived in a mist, never realising that there was such a thing as the sun. Kate was the sun. But I did not meet her yet. If only I had, my life would have been very different.

By this stage the Anglican Cathedral had been completed, raising its bulk in the flat centre of the city, heavy and grey and shaded by Father's taboo. One day Miss Helen Conan called me into her charming corner room.

'I need you to take the girls to Morning Prayer this Sunday, Ada,' she said.

'With due respect, Miss Conan,' I replied, 'my religion forbids it.'

No other teacher was available, and the headmistress showed me plainly that it was my duty. Of course I was not really reluctant, for I was secretly interested in hearing the great organ and the choir, which were said to be quite wonderful. I set off eagerly on Sunday morning, walking all the

29

way into town, enjoying the fresh spring air.

It seemed all of Christchurch was packed into that
cathedral. Many pews were occupied by well-to-do people,
but the poor were also represented. The stained-glass
window over the altar was splendid. The boys' choir moved
me to ecstasy! Of course I had never entered a cathedral
before, even in England. The service ended with a triumphant organ voluntary as the colourful procession of dean
and priests sailed down the aisle, followed by the complete
choir in their crisp red and white robes.

Outside in the sunshine I supervised the departure of all
my girls, including dear Wilhelmina. When the last one was
despatched, a young lady in grey introduced herself to me as
Mrs Ballantyne, who was to become a lifelong friend. I was
about to go home when I heard the organ in the cathedral,
louder than ever.

'Is there another service now?' I asked Mrs Ballantyne.

'That's just the organist letting off steam,' she laughed.

'May I stay and listen?'

'Go ahead,' agreed my new friend. 'He loves an audience.'

Back inside I had the whole cool, strong building to
myself, except for the verger putting out candles and tidying
up. I had never even imagined a church so great! It was a
castle of goodness. The music played over me like beautiful
sunshine. At the climax it thrilled through my entire body,
causing deep vibrations in my very bones. When it ended I
sighed, and sat a little longer.

I heard a clatter and a tall, stringy man came flying down
the steps.

'What are you doing here?' he challenged me. His fair hair
stood out from his head in wild feathers, his face having a
reddish tinge. He exuded vitality — indeed, he could hardly
keep still.

'I liked your playing and so I stayed. Is that not permitted?'

'Humph! Do what I can with this organ,' he said
petulantly.

'Why, it sounds grand to me!' I stood up and he took my
gloved hand and kissed it.

'I've played on the finest organs of England,' he growled, squeezing my fingers before letting them go.

'You're the choirmaster too?'

'Riff-raff! Come and see the hurdy-gurdy.' He charged back up the aisle and waved me into the little cubby hole where the keyboard and organ stops were hidden. Although there was something thoroughly vulgar about him, I followed.

Three months later we were married. I had some reservations, but Maria was all in favour of Henry, Anglican or not. The night before our wedding I recited all his virtues to my sister Blanche.

'He's gifted, he has a mind, he has flair, he's different!'

'Different from whom?' Blanche inquired pedantically.

'Different from Father!'

'I'm sure he's not really erratic,' she reassured me.

'And I love his name. Wells! Mrs Wells!' I gloated. I still like that name far better than Pike. It was closer to Maria's maiden name. I wanted to be a deep well of clear water where others might find refreshment, a reservoir of the Water of Life. From Pike to Wells, I would be in my element at last.

'But what about church?' my sister worried. I said nothing, but privately I was attracted to the idea of joining the majority. That this demonstrated my immaturity I freely acknowledge.

Before the year was out, my darling Christabel was born. She was the joy of my life and she still is. I talked to her day and night. 'This darling girl is going to learn and learn and learn!' She had the loveliest nature, Chris, full of fun, always seeing the bright side. Right from the start we had so much fun together.

As soon as she could sit up I began reading to her. I read the tales of Hans Christian Andersen, *A Midsummer Night's Dream*, *Hamlet*, Tennyson — she loved them all! And as soon as she could speak I began teaching her Latin. At night after prayers I would say to her:

Hush, beating heart of Christabel!
Jesu, Maria, shield her well!

In the morning I would greet her like this:

Sleep you, sweet lady Christabel?
I trust that you have rested well.

But I'm running ahead of myself. The reason is simple, for I could sing Chris's praises forever!

My father never saw his first grandchild. He was buried in Timaru, and I did not attend the funeral because of my advanced pregnancy.

Now Maria mourned, as widows do. But no sooner had Father died than she left the Plymouth Brethren Church. Instantaneously! Instead she took the family along to St Mary's Anglican Church of Merivale. Underneath all that dutiful obedience to her husband she knew perfectly well what she thought of his religion. It didn't suit her at all! She believed in life, and so did I. As the choirmaster's wife I attended the cathedral services now, taking along little Chris. We both derived much inspiration from the music resounding in the vault of that great building.

Except that the choir was not performing very well. The boys had lost their discipline.

I must be tiring, for I perceive in myself an unfortunate tendency to write in short sentences, some of which moreover are even incomplete, and the sustaining of a full paragraph proves unexpectedly fatiguing. To write down conversations is an unusual exercise for me. Naturally I cannot swear that these exact words were uttered at any time, yet I believe like Alice that conversations are essential in a readable story, and the challenge is rather satisfying. Alas, I cannot fulfil her second injunction, for I am no illustrator.

'Henry,' I said one Sunday when he was carving the roast, 'those trebles were singing with their heads hanging down in their music this morning.'

'Don't you start!' He shoved a plate of meat at me. I was

growing used to his ways, which didn't mean I liked them. 'How do you expect a choir to sing in tune with an organ like that?'

'But, Harry, it's the best organ in Christchurch!' I tried not to upset him because of his asthma, but there were times when I simply had to express an opinion.

'It sounds like a dying hog!' screamed Henry. He threw down the carving knife and rushed out of the room. After a few minutes he returned as if nothing had happened and we ate our dinner.

I assumed these sudden exits were a way of controlling his temper and therefore his asthma. I tried to ignore them, although on his return he was sometimes more volatile than ever. Today, after tucking into his dinner heartily, he suddenly shouted, 'I've had enough, do you hear! I won't be criticised!'

'But, Henry, that's the first time I've ever found fault with your choir,' I pointed out.

'The dean, the bishop, the verger and now you! Nobody appreciates what I'm up against! They don't deserve great music!'

I just tut-tutted as I cleared away the plates. What can you say to a speech like that? He never made the slightest effort at normal politeness. Before we married I found this refreshingly honest but I eventually had to acknowledge that it was sheer boorishness.

The following day Henry came home in the forenoon and threw his music on the floor. I had just finished bathing Chris and was drying her on the table.

'Home so soon, Henry?'

For answer he picked a plate off the dresser and smashed it on the floor.

'You'll frighten the child,' I said. He went right ahead and smashed another. They were my favourite white china given to me by Maria, but I knew better than to mention that. I went and fed Chris in the bedroom.

Later I heard him playing the piano. Better, I thought. I went down to see what the fuss was all about.

33

'I've left,' he said. 'I've got too much pride to carry on.'

'But — what will we do for a living?' I asked. I'd never known anyone like him!

'There'll be parsons crawling on their hands and knees to me,' he declared. 'I'm the only organist in Christchurch worthy of the label.' For once he was right, as the vestry of St Michael's approached him almost at once. They conveniently forgave him a shameful betrayal, which had enraged them at the time. They had paid his passage from England, but within a year he had defected to the cathedral, taking half the choir with him! This delinquency notwithstanding, Henry returned to St Michael's, where he stayed for fourteen temperamental years.

We found a place to rent in Mays Road which was perfectly adequate. Henry acquired pigs and a horse and some hens in a burst of enthusiasm, only to pass the care of them over to me and Elsie, who was virtually the only help we had. Notwithstanding the considerable distance Henry had to travel daily into the city, from my point of view we were perfectly placed, Mays Road being positioned on the northern boundary of Christchurch. Although we were now domiciled virtually in the countryside, we were only a mile or so past Office Road. What a relief to be within walking distance of my dear mother!

Chapter 4

KATE

I wish to report that I am being bullied by a poetess. I was born in 1848, eighty-five years ago, but Jessie MacKay has no reverence for my great age and is actually threatening me with her pencil. I was christened Kate Wilson Malcolm and I agree to tell the story of my life for one reason only, to pass the time until Elizabeth McCombs returns to Christchurch after her first session in Parliament. If not for that, I would happily slip out of this world. No matter how fast I speak or what I say, Jessie writes down my words in her wonderful Pitman's shorthand. Twinkle, twinkle little star. Yes, I do believe she wrote that down! I don't think she's offended. She's a journalist, used to all sorts and conditions of men and women. I'm not so stubborn that I scorn her plan to keep me interested in life. I do see her point, that to sit in the sun and wait for Elizabeth, this is no way to live, even for the elderly. I can't help feeling proud that it's a Christchurch woman who has infiltrated the masculine world of Parliament at last. My friends here have done so much for the cause, it is very fitting that Elizabeth leads the way.

Christchurch! Oh, the despair with which I first laid eyes on you! Such a mess of mud and greasy clay and puddles and creeks overflowing. The closer we came, the uglier it grew. The only greenery was flax, which to my northern eye seemed coarse and rank. And the flatness! Everything was spread too thin.

I was twenty-one, and travelling with Mama, my brothers and my younger sister. Our eldest sister Marie came here to join her fiancé, George Beath.

'Dearest Mama,' she wrote, 'You must all come to Christchurch, I insist! George's business is thriving. Why, here's a whole nation of women in need of mittens and calico and scarcely a store in sight. George is so paternal with his staff . . .' In between panegyrics to her new husband, Marie sang the praises of Christchurch. The idea of its newness appealed to us all. Scotland held only sadness for us now, and Ireland was not much better. Yes, yes, all right, I'll tell you about my childhood!

My youth was split through with a trench as deep as Loch Ness. I had a childhood, and then I had my youth, my growing. They were separated by the death of my father and the width of Scotland. For I first lived in Islay, a tiny island off the west coast of Scotland. Look it up in the atlas, Jessie, don't pretend you know where it is. It's just a skip and a hop from Ireland, it reaches out two arms towards Derry. A chunky little island, all rocks and wind and ragged sheep and choppy sea. I made up a counting-out rhyme about my little sister Isabella:

> *Dizzy little Isy*
> *of the Isle of Islay.*
> *Isy isn't busy,*
> *You're not he.*
> *Isy mustn't grizzle,*
> *You're a she!*

Father gave it a tune and scored it with three-part harmony! We sang it round the piano in the evenings, along with the hymns he wrote. His name was Francis Malcolm and he was a lawyer. English law is constantly kowtowing to the past, but in Scotland lawyers were more like King Solomon than Portia. Father's job was to see justice done regardless of precedent. He said there was nothing sacred about history! I loved dinnertimes for then he discussed cases with the whole family. Grandmother Malcolm lived with us; she had a back like a broom handle. She'd travelled all over Scotland when Grandfather was Procurator Fiscal, settling disputes between the clans. We were never treated as ignorant children. We were all expected to think logically and even to read law books. Father knew such a lot; he'd even been to America. Mama usually played the devil's advocate. Her Irish background gave her a mischievous streak.

All of us went to the village school where we mixed with the servants' children as well as the laird's. I mention this because it was entirely different in England. The Malcolm family took it for granted that everyone rich or poor would get a sound education, but most of Christchurch had quite different expectations, being English.

Quite right, Jessie, drag me back to Islay.

As we grew older our schooling was supplemented by a tutor fresh from Oxford who filled our heads with all the latest ideas. Father sent away for every book under the sun. Ideas! They were meat and drink to us.

When he died, Isy and I went out of control, clutching each other, rocking and sobbing like babies though I was nearly thirteen. Our dear strong Father had gone forever! After some months of this, Mama stood us by the piano for a reprimand.

'Girls! Why did Father live?'

'To look after us!' Isy said indignantly.

'And what did he teach you?'

'To strive for justice?' I suggested.

'Yes, yes — and to live! You can't serve God if you're determined to die of grief. Throwing God's gift of life back in His face! The audacity of you!' She forced us to sing 'All Things Bright and Beautiful' and our mourning was at an end.

One day Mama told us, 'I've had a letter from Nairn. Uncle Jamie wants us to live with him.'

'What about our horses?' Marie wanted to know.

What about the black rocks and the white sea? What about the sheep and the wild grass and the hot brief midsummer sun? What about my school friends and Father's great library and our sturdy stone house sheltered from the north?

37

'We can't transport the whole island,' Mother objected.

'If you don't go to Nairn you'll go to Liverpool with me.' Grandmother's word was law.

We went to Nairn. We travelled by land following the length of that great gash of water, Loch Linnhe leading into Lake Lochy into Loch Ness. It was as if the sea split Scotland for us, linking Islay to Nairn. As the Red Sea divided for Moses, so the land opened wide for us.

Uncle Jamie's manse was large enough to absorb us all including our tutor. At first I found it gloomy. On rainy days it seemed like night in our panelled rooms, but Mama transformed them in her usual way. White embroidered shawls and oval mirrors and gleaming silver candlesticks enhanced what little light there was. Daisies or berries in white china vases lit up sullen corners, and Mama arranged our furniture so that each room was welcoming.

I found it very strange to have the sun rise from the ocean. 'Isy, you know how I got here?'

'I think so,' my little sister said drily, 'considering I sat beside you all the way.'

'No, Isy, I'm a great sea monster! I swam!'

> *I cut through Scotland*
> *With my long sharp tail.*
> *Neck in the crack,*
> *Tail in the lake,*
> *Splitting up the land*
> *From the Ocean to the Sea.*
> *Derry's just a swim away from Islay,*
> *Islay is a swim away from Nairn.*

So, Jessie, I have my poems too. I made that one up to mend the abyss in my life. I couldn't quite make it rhyme but we could skip to it.

'I don't want to tread on your toes,' Mama said tactfully to Aunt Anna, who did not appreciate any help with house, garden or servants. Mama resumed her role of devil's advocate, and again we had hot debates to season our meals.

38

'Jamie, I hope you don't expect us to attend your services,' Mama provoked him on the very first night. 'We'll have to find ourselves a proper Presbyterian church.'

'Jemima!' Aunt Anna was shocked.

'Ah, but we're a Presbytery as well as a Free Church,' Uncle retaliated.

'What does it mean by Free?' I asked.

Uncle's hot eyes gripped mine. 'It means free of the state and the Anglican Church, it means the congregation is free to choose their minister. That the people have some power in their own parish.'

'Now, Jamie, this isn't proper talk for the dinner table!'

Aunt Anna was overridden. Our talk ranged on and on, about politics and ethics, John Stuart Mill and Darwin, taxes, fishing rights, the rich and the poor and the problems of drink.

It seems to me in retrospect that the years with Uncle Jamie were one long, thrilling conversation, sharpened by his involvement with the real problems of real people. I'll describe a typical dinnertime. Aunt Anna would grumble that too much talk gave you indigestion, Mama would praise the apple dumplings, Aunt Anna would say Mama was looking tired, which was never true. She looked younger than ever, although nearly every day she rode around the countryside with Uncle Jamie on parish business. Sooner or later Uncle would claim that every social catastrophe was linked with alcohol; Mama would argue the point, but if we did likewise we would be sternly reprimanded.

'I hear gin is a powerful antiseptic,' I once said just for fun.

'Don't joke about it, lassie! It's a deadly poison!'

After the meal Mama would follow him into his study to try to revive his courage. For it was true, all around us were insurmountable social problems. We children found it hard to judge Uncle Jamie's moods. Aunt Anna was glad, I think, when Mama took over the role of comforter.

Uncle grew thinner year by year, battling for his congregation and he died suddenly at the age of fifty-two. This second blow affected Mama even more than Father's death.

It felt wrong to remain with Aunt Anna so we went home to Mama's people in Derry.

I worried about our mother. We couldn't shake her out of mourning. Our big sister Marie saved the day when she went to Edinburgh to study music and met Mr George Beath. Their courtship was brief and decisive. Within a year she had followed him to Christchurch and begun sending back these bossy letters saying Come! Come! Come!

There! I'm back to where I began. Marie found the words to draw Mama into life again. Our family embarked on the *Matoaka* for Christchurch; it was the right thing to do.

Chapter 5

KATE

Marie and George welcomed us into the house they'd built on Riccarton Road quite close to Hagley Park. It's still there, you know, Jessie, but it seemed very flimsy to me at the time, being made entirely of timber. It was obvious from the size of the house that my sister had taken our emigration for granted, for there was plenty of room for us all. Yes, we liked our new brother-in-law. George Beath was considerably older than Marie, but he was very kind and fatherly, and energetic too. On his instructions I'd bought dresses and bolts of cloth for his department store, and arranged for their transport on our ship. Fortunately he approved of my choices!

On our arrival we joined the Presbyterian Church of St Albans. That was the principal Presbyterian church, because at the time 'St Albans' included half the city, the northern half. But Mama fretted; she thought the Congregational Church was more in tune with Uncle Jamie's beliefs. Before long we all changed our allegiance, even George. The Reverend Mr Habens had none of Uncle's fire but he did have integrity. We were obliged to worship in the St John's Anglican Hall and we were naturally very keen to build a church of our own. George took charge of the design and was forever poring over plans. His first design was like a fortress.

'In my opinion that tower is too tall by half,' I said.

'It won't fall down,' he promised quite unnecessarily.

'They're building a cathedral down the road,' I reminded him gently. 'We're not in competition. A Congregational church should be more modest, don't you think?'

From then on I kept a close eye on the design and as tactfully as possible offered suggestions. Eventually we built the most friendly, practical, graceful, sturdy little stone church in all Christchurch, the Trinity Church in Worcester Street. It was a joy to worship there.

But this won't do, my dear, I'm jumping ahead. The church wasn't finished till 1875 and much of importance occurred before then.

Mama never quite recovered her old *joie de vivre*, but a new reforming zeal emerged in its place. As soon as we were settled in home and church, she insisted that Isabella and I start working for the cause of Temperance. She became a woman with a mission. I don't pretend to know all the secrets of the human heart, but I believe it was by way of a memorial for Uncle Jamie. Our two brothers were exempt, because when they weren't studying, they were helping George with his business. Mama took us to Temperance meetings in halls all over Christchurch. Our social life included many money-raising events such as concerts, church fairs, social teas and garden parties. Isy and I rather enjoyed all this. It meant we met all sorts of people very quickly, and got to know our way around Christchurch.

One fateful afternoon that first autumn we went to a garden party at the Ballantynes' beside the Avon River. We sat in the shade of a well-grown oak and listened to a string quartet playing Haydn among the roses. I found the cello player very disturbing; he was only seventeen with an arrogance out of all proportion to his age. He wore knickerbockers, whereas everyone else was dressed rather formally. He looked like a prophet strayed in from the wilderness with his dense dark hair leaping wildly off a high forehead. Now and then he raised fierce eyes and glared at me. I wondered what I had done to offend him! After the performance a short woman with a sweet motherly manner helped him pack away his cello and they left without eating or drinking. I was glad to see him go. At twenty-one I found it insulting for a beardless boy to stare at me so presumptuously.

We were eating pink ices when George introduced us to a very important gentleman. You guessed, Jessie! I agree, he was most satisfyingly mature!

'Mr Walter Sheppard is a city councillor,' George told us.

'How exciting!' I responded. 'Is it fun?'

The gentleman harumphed in a manner that was to become familiar to me. 'Not exactly fun, Miss Malcolm. I would call it a civic duty.' He was delightfully pompous and I teased him a little.

'How is the council going to rescue us from the Waimakariri River? Are you going to copy the Dutch?' I waved my hand at the mud along the riverbank, deposited there by the great flood. No no, Jessie, of course the Waimakariri didn't flow through the gardens of Christchurch! But when that mammoth river of the plains got out of control it naturally affected the placid Avon, whose source was all too close to the wilful Waimakariri.

Mr Sheppard's eyes lit up. He was on the Flood Control Committee and knew the ins and outs of every drain and stopbank. I was interested because good drainage means good health. Isy pulled a face and drifted off, but Mr Sheppard and I conversed for another half-hour. I remember discussing sanitation contracts, of all things! He was adamant that the pans belonging to public houses be emptied at least once a week and had pushed a resolution through the council to this effect. I found him extremely practical and kind, if not quite the most sparkling conversationalist in the world.

'I've heard that the land-barons have a stranglehold on local politics.' I was trying to divert him to a matter which concerned me more than outhouses. 'Will this city council control the purse-strings of Christchurch or is it a sham?'

He was both enchanted and startled by my interest. He was proud of his part in arranging a civic reception for the Duke of Edinburgh, and I found that rather appealing.

Isy chided me later. 'Oh, Kate, how could you talk to that stuffy old man for so long! I wanted you to play croquet.'

'He knows what makes this place tick,' I told her. 'It's

fascinating! Did you know that Sir John Hall was responsible for restoring the title of city council to Christchurch? Otherwise we'd only have a corporation.'

'How utterly enthralling!' Isy giggled.

'We are in a new colony, little sister, and the law is different and society is different. I don't like being ignorant. If we want anything done, we have to know what's what.'

'Fiddlededee!' said Isy.

That day caused ripples in my life. Twice in the next year I saw the young cellist. There's something very disturbing about a boy turning into a man, and he lodged in my mind like a piece of grit. On the other hand, we continually met Mr Sheppard at various functions, and he and I gravitated together as a matter of course. He was a widower, twelve years older than I. One day George called me into his study. 'Kate, my dear, Mr Walter Sheppard has asked my permission to pay court to you. How do you feel about that?'

This didn't take me entirely by surprise, for Isy constantly teased me about him. 'I think of him more as a friend, George.'

'Be fair! He's a good chap and he dotes on you. You can't string him along like this.'

'We don't flirt, George, we're not lovers. It's an intellectual friendship!'

'For you, perhaps. Now don't keep him waiting.'

I managed to keep the decision at arm's length for an entire year and a half. In the end I couldn't bear Walter's unhappiness. And Marie had her second child, which meant that Isy and I had to share a room. I wasn't used to that! Well, yes, it's perfectly true I had other admirers, but none of them stirred me any more than Walter.

He was no longer on the council, he didn't like the pressure. He knew everyone of influence in the town, but he had no idea of strategy. He was happier working as treasurer for the A&P Society and doing the accounts for Beath's and other firms. Walter was an Anglican of course. Before I met him he was a churchwarden at St John's, but he resigned after a fuss about the subletting of pews. This, I discovered, was his

44

pattern: he was completely honest, stood up bravely for what was right and proper, and when things got too hot he resigned.

He was a dear. When I married him it was a perfectly sensible thing to do. I learned a great deal from Walter and he was always kind.

Chapter 6

KATE

I think of the ten years that followed my marriage as my great sleep. I was like a racehorse being trained and groomed and exercised — but for what? I had no idea. It all seemed rather pleasant at the time, but there was an emptiness, a pointlessness which I have never known before or since. On the surface I was leading a busy and almost an enterprising life. If I told you the things I did in those years you might even be quite impressed. But I was useless, unused, and there is no greater tragedy. Of course I had to supervise my household, but before long I found Poppy, who took all those irksome duties off my hands. Wonderful Poppy, the best housekeeper in Christchurch!

My hunger for stimulating talk was not gratified by Walter. Let me give you an example.

'Three entrance gates and one exit gate are essential.' This was when the A&P Society was creating the show grounds. 'Then people can have re-entry passes.'

'A splendid idea, Walter,' I would reply.

'And we absolutely must have shade trees, and urinals in at least two places.'

'And a place for women to lie down,' I would remind him.

Through Walter I met lawyers and politicians and clergymen and scholars, yet every social occasion tended to degenerate into gossip or talk of drains. Soon after our marriage I made a bold decision. I started my Saturday soirées to which selected gentlemen were invited for the purpose of discussing interesting topics. The Land Question, Moral Aspects of Economics, the Evolution of Marriage, that sort of thing. We enjoyed ourselves vastly, and rightly or wrongly I lived for Saturdays.

Why didn't I ask any women? Jessie, you shame me. Apart from my own family I didn't know any educated women. A few had graduated from the University of New Zealand, but they were far too busy doing serious things to attend my frivolous soirées, or so I told myself. Any other women found me too serious, my opinions too bold, that was my reasoning. The truth is that I greatly enjoyed having half a dozen intelligent men all to myself for a few hours each week. It was partly vanity, partly thoughtlessness. And remember, I was still sound asleep.

We moved from St Albans to Madras Street in the centre of Christchurch, and I decorated the house. How I fussed over all that! Then, when I was twenty-nine, Walter and I sailed for England.

'Going home, eh!' As the *Rangitikei* sailed out of Lyttelton Harbour, Walter couldn't disguise his joy.

'Just for a while,' I said, watching the green indented coastline drift past.

'You'll like Bath,' he promised.

'My family is here,' I objected.

Walter assumed his sad pug face. 'My family is your family, they'll love you.' Oh, he meant well, but imagine seriously thinking his stodgy brothers and aunts could replace my whole vivid family! 'Once you've seen the doctors our future will be clearer.'

'True,' I murmured. I see no harm in telling you that after six years of married life Walter was very keen to have children, particularly as his first marriage had been without issue. For the hundredth time I wondered why I felt half-hearted. To be fully a woman was to be a mother; no matter what thrilling hypotheses about marriage were aired at my soirées, everyone took this for granted.

'Of course, a little baby would curtail your activities,' Walter said kindly. 'No more soirées when you're a mother!'

The journey was quite beneficial for my various tiresome medical problems. I read and wrote, and missed my gentle-

47

men. When we reached England, Walter's friends were so frightfully predictable that instead of forgetting New Zealand, I missed my life there even more.

In particular I missed Mr Alfred Saunders. He had no parallel in my acquaintance, and yet he typified what I liked most about the colonial people. You never knew him personally, did you, Jessie? How could anyone describe Alfred? He was in his late fifties then, but he could run rings around the young. He was a rogue member of Parliament, immune to party politics, a pioneer, miller, baker, farmer, educator, mesmerist, gold-digger, writer, breeder of horses and hens, trainer of wild steers . . . We met when he diverted the Ashburton River and set up a mill. He never sat still for long. As you know, Ashburton is all of fifty miles to the south of here, but unless Parliament was in session he attended most of my soirées. Did you know Walter had been a miller in the Old Country? That was one thing they had in common.

Imagine how I missed my friend as I took tea with the English gentlefolk. They were blind and deaf, locked in the past. Have you been to Bath, Jessie? It's said to be England's most beautiful city and yet it seemed dead to me.

'You must be so lonely in the colonies,' one elderly cousin sympathised. 'No kindred spirits! No history, no links!'

I began to suspect there were qualities in New Zealand that I had entirely overlooked, as I had overlooked the uniqueness of our Saturday conversations. What were they? The invisible problems, the invisible people of Christchurch? Had I been leading a Bath sort of existence there? What sort of life was a real life in Christchurch? I lay awake at night turning this over.

'I'm so proud of you, my dear,' Walter would say after every social occasion. 'They all adore you so.' I could not open my heart.

The doctors submitted me to tedious examinations but could offer no cure for my barrenness except for rest and peace of mind.

'Life is too strenuous in New Zealand,' Walter argued.

I visited my family in Liverpool and Scotland, but even

there I felt curiously dislocated. Where did I belong? After a year we returned to Christchurch. Walter sulked a little but he was very kind to me.

I found Alfred fired up about a great victory: all men over twenty-one now had the right to vote in national elections. What an uproar! Not just the property-owners, mind, but every man Jack.

'Alfred, you've done it!'

'One step on the right direction,' he corrected me. We both knew that the franchise was still a tangle of privilege, with men of property having several votes. 'Helped by my friends and some of my enemies.'

'What enemies? Everybody loves Alfred Saunders!' That made him smile, for he clashed with everyone sooner or later.

'Sir John Hall was a staunch supporter of the Bill,' he said from under those curly eyebrows. 'We worked together rather well.'

'You can't tell a book by its title,' I said.

'Tory!'

'So why are you still so cross?'

'Same old story,' he growled. 'We nearly had support for a clause which would have given women the vote! And that wretched Seddon led the opposition.' He took another gulp of cold water as if it were strong drink.

I soothed him, for this was one of Alfred's running battles. Can you believe, Jessie, that during my long sleep I never thought of it as my battle? I devoutly wanted women to vote, and I agitated on our behalf with every influential man who crossed my path. Yet I couldn't see how I could involve myself more personally, so I didn't try.

My little sister Isy married Henry May, and George gave him a branch of Beath's to run in High Street. When the Deans sold some land in Riccarton our family bought a good-sized block. Isabella and Henry built a house, and our youngest brother Frank began building too, with a young lady from Ashburton in mind. I visited Isabella frequently as their house was taking shape.

'Kate, you and Walter must build here too,' Isy said as we picked our way over the rough ground and stood on her verandah. The stunning mass of the Southern Alps stared us in the face, inflamed by the setting sun. 'We'll all be within walking distance.'

But Walter was settled in Madras Street.

'The city's so bad for your health,' everyone told him. 'The air in Riccarton is clean.' He really was an old fuddy duddy but I didn't press him.

'I shall design us a house just for the fun of it,' I told him. It was seven years before we winkled him out of the city!

Meanwhile he was still eager for me to conceive, and I began to feel like a failure. Now, Jessie, I'm going to tell you something that only two other people on this earth have known. Why shouldn't I? Those who consider me a wicked woman will have the pleasure of having their bad opinion confirmed. Those who regard me with adulation will doubtless find an excuse for my behaviour. I'm eighty-five. What use are secrets to me now? This happened over fifty years ago, when I was only thirty-two.

I used to visit the Hanmer Springs in search of health, particularly at the height of summer. The establishment was comfortable, the company congenial and the waters salubrious. One January I visited with a sharper purpose in mind. Human beings are creatures of habit and a certain gentleman from Napier was taking the waters, a distinguished gentleman whose name I shall not mention. He was urbane, intelligent, dark and shiny-skinned from the sun. We liked each other. At the inevitable musical evenings, I turned the pages while he played the piano. One afternoon we walked together along a forest path, and I confronted him directly.

'I hoped you would be at Hanmer this year,' I said. 'I think you know I greatly enjoy our conversation.'

A tree fern had fallen across the path and he held out his hand, helping me over. I did not disengage my hand, but stopped and gazed into his eyes, looking for signs of revulsion. There were none, although the gentleman was confused.

'Mrs Sheppard, we all adore you, and your presence makes a joy of January.'

Phrases! Compliments such as I received every day of my life. How could I convey to this subtle gentleman my most unsubtle desire? I chose bluntness.

'Mr A., I am here in the hope of curing my state of barrenness. Yet I am almost certain that my infertility is a consequence of my husband's condition, not mine.' I paused for a long while, still holding his hand. The gentleman's face paled, then went a dark red as he absorbed what I was saying.

'If I can help you in any way,' he said at last, raising my hand to his lips, which had a faintly purple tinge.

'I want a child!'

He looked swiftly up and down the path, and, finding it empty, drew me close. As he kissed me my heart pounded so noisily that the bellbirds' song faded away. I found my arms embracing him and my body greeting his most eagerly. Without words we walked through the forest to a secluded gardener's shed, and there on a dusty wooden floor I knew what I had never known before. Oh, Jessie, it was not just a child I had wanted all those years!

For a week I gave myself to him utterly, although he was not the man of my heart. Our time together was precious. He had a good wife, and I a good husband. When we said goodbye we agreed we should never meet again unless by accident.

He wrote me one letter. 'My dear Mrs Sheppard, I cannot refrain from writing just once to thank you for the most beautiful days and nights of my life. I have been to Paradise and my life from now will be lived in that knowledge . . .' I should have burned it at once, but I tucked it away among my other papers.

There! Are you disgusted with me? Oh no, you simply don't understand. Or do you? In October I had the great joy of giving birth to my only son Douglas. I cannot be sure that Walter himself is not the father. Perhaps the gentleman from Napier fathered my child, or perhaps he performed a different miracle, bringing me such an excess of relaxation that at last I was able to conceive.

But again I am jumping ahead in my narrative.

When I returned from Hanmer it was to find my mother weak beyond hope. It was a frailty of spirit rather than flesh, for she was only fifty-nine. I was overwhelmed with guilt, as if I had bought my fulfilment at the cost of her life. As I grew certain of my pregnancy, she drew nearer to death, and within three months it was over.

Her death shook me. Jessie, if you think people get used to bereavement, if you think that mourning is something that grows easier with practice, you are wrong. Losing Mama was painful. Mama was vivacity and grace, she was charm and wit and loveliness. She added spice to a life in Scotland which might otherwise have sunk into mere duty. She was luxury. I had lived my life with her flavour in my mouth. She had never quite adjusted to life in Christchurch. I suspect she never got over the loss of Uncle Jamie. When Father died, she transferred to Uncle her deep reason for living, for although she was the best of mothers, she was primarily a man's woman. She loved to flutter around a strong man, luring him to greater heights; that was the way she lived her life.

Her death threw me into chaos. She was the one soul standing between me and the gates of death. Now they were yawning in front of me. If I were to live only as long as Mama, I was well over half-way through my life. I retired from all social engagements and thought long and deeply about her life and my own. For all her influence on friends and family, what had Mama achieved? For all her brilliance, what changes had she wrought in society? She had lived as a handmaiden to men, and yet she had constantly urged me to live my life in the mould of Father and Uncle Jamie. 'Make the world a better place!' was almost the last thing she said to me. It was nothing new; again she was echoing the men in her life.

Red-hot in my mind was the episode in Hanmer. I began to see my whole life as selfish and wasteful. Thanks to my birth and upbringing I had a certain power, but I never used it except at one remove, by influencing men. Perhaps I had been a toy for men, but in return I had treated them as toys or useful tools.

I had never in my life doubted that I was a person, a valuable human being. It was the gentleman from Napier who helped me understand that I was also a woman; yes, specifically female. From this understanding there emerged another devastating insight. I gradually realised that, being a woman, I suffered from all the disabilities of a woman. I was like other women, I was not a unique being in my own right as I had always unconsciously believed.

Then I came full circle in my thoughts. I grew sure that if I wished to overcome the disabilities of being a woman it was simply not enough to behave as women had always done. Now, for the sake of Mama, who would hardly have understood the issue, I swore I would do my own work. No more discreet manoeuvring behind the scenes! I had regarded my soirées as a radical arrangement, potentially a force for change in society. Yet the opposite was true, for with my soirées I had been perpetuating everything I deplored. I was very like Mama. For her sake I would learn to take responsibility openly like a man.

I could not attend Frank's wedding in Ashburton because my confinement was close. Two days later Douglas squeezed his way into the world. I sobbed with relief to see my baby whole and wonderful. His timely arrival shook me out of depression and reinforced my will to work instead of play, to work in a way of my own. My long sleep was over.

Chapter 7

KATE

As a woman I had to work with women. Yes, I could see that. But where should I even look for these women and how could we work together? How can young people even begin to grasp the peculiar problem I faced? If a man wanted to achieve certain reforms, there were plenty of precedents and he certainly wouldn't be working alone. Men had institutions and clubs, men had the city council and political groups and Parliament itself. They had names and titles to give weight to their work, like President or Councillor or Judge. Even in the Temperance movement men were always the leading lights and nobody questioned the fact. But for a woman, the slate was blank.

I began close to home by initiating discussions in the Congregational Church, and when Douglas was three we started our Ladies' Association. It seems absurd now, Jessie, but Mr Hoatson was our president! Still, at last I had something to get a grip on, a group of women with a label and a purpose. As secretary I organised monthly visiting rosters, dividing Christchurch into districts and allocating each to a couple of women. Absentees were visited promptly and many cases of illness or need were discovered this way.

You seem a wee bit impatient, Jessie. So you want to hear about my 'real' work, do you? Open your eyes and your mind! Do not belittle my Ladies' Association, because that is precisely where I learned how to work with women on a national scale. The principles are exactly the same: systematic organisation, regular meetings to keep us cheerful and positive, and a clear attainable goal.

Working-class women had been all but invisible to me

before, and now I began to see how they struggled. All my activities multiplied and overlapped as I made myself useful in the church and in the Temperance movement. Before this time I had rarely come into contact with Maori women, although I heard stories that broke my heart. In 1883 a Young Women's Christian Association was formed, and I quickly became involved. Many girls came to the city in search of happiness, only to be overwhelmed by poverty and worse, and young Maori women had a double disability. We provided cheap accommodation and classes in domestic science, we set up a coffee and reading room at 128 High Street, and I took the Bible classes myself.

It was about this time that our family suffered a painful blow when my brother Robert died of a fall from a horse. It was very hard to accept. He was only thirty-two! To ease my grief I helped his widow and children and threw myself into my new-found work. Fortunately the one great event that made sense of my life was just around the corner: Mrs Mary Leavitt from Boston was coming to town!

We read in the newspaper: 'MRS MARY CLEMENT LEAVITT, a delegate from the WOMEN'S CHRISTIAN TEMPERANCE UNION OF AMERICA, will (D.V.) hold a series of GOSPEL TEMPERANCE MEETINGS IN CHRISTCHURCH.'

What an innocuous announcement for the bombshell that was coming!

Nowadays some people look sideways at the Temperance movement. They've no idea what things were like in those days! Fifty years ago the gin drunk by the poor was practically raw alcohol, and thousands were addicted to lethal patent drugs because you could buy opium over the counter in the guise of a 'tonic'. Most of the misery of women was connected with alcohol or drugs, so I was fully committed to Temperance.

When Mrs Leavitt came to Trinity, our church was overflowing. As she stood up my heart was with her. How could a woman address such a large meeting and not tremble?

'Good evening, ladies and gentlemen,' she began in that

clear, confident voice. 'I bring you greetings from America.' To my astonishment, the church suddenly rang with cheers! 'My theme for tonight is Money, Revenue, and Drink. Money is not evil! Everything on the face of the earth belongs to the Lord, and everything should be used for His glorification. Therefore money must not be utilised in the traffic of drink!'

Temperance meetings always attracted a number of rowdy drinkers because a good supper was provided. They generally sat at the front to provoke the speakers.

'What about the taxes?' shouted one old tramp, staggering to his feet and into the aisle.

Mrs Leavitt smiled delightfully at him. 'An old familiar argument: the Government earns revenue from the drink trade. Look again!' She read out some telling statistics. 'Now we see that the revenue raised by the sale of drink is only half as much as we need to house the criminals created by drink. Alcohol is not a source of revenue for the state. Quite the opposite — alcohol is a major reason why our taxes are so high.'

Her speech was punctuated by cheers and clapping. The red-faced drunk collapsed on the floor beside her and dozed off.

'He's happy!' yelled a working man.

'Happiness is rather different from a state of unconsciousness,' she pointed out with a smile. As she described hideous cases of poverty, illness and despair in our own city, even the drinkers grew silent. When she asked people to come forward and take the oath of abstinence, there was a rush to the table laid out with blue ribbon badges and pamphlets.

Our Ladies' Association provided the supper. This was the highlight of the evening, for now we met Mrs Leavitt personally.

'I am so ashamed that you were insulted in our church,' I apologised.

'I welcome interruptions from the inebriated!' she laughed. 'They illustrate the lecture.'

'You were well prepared.'

'Oh, they are quite predictable.' She brushed off my compliment and finished her glass of raspberry cordial.

As we circulated, I saw that Mrs Leavitt had already made the acquaintance of dozens of Christchurch women.

'Mrs Smith, good evening! And Mrs William Smith!' She greeted a stout old lady in black who seemed nailed to her chair, and then a dear little nut-brown woman holding a plate of sandwiches for her mother-in-law. Mrs Leavitt moved on, swallowed up by a swarm of admirers.

'I've heard much good of you,' I said to the older Mrs Smith, who was a formidable name in Temperance circles.

'You're the woman who entertains men, I believe,' she said coolly.

I turned to the younger woman, and for the first time clasped hands with Jeannie Smith.

After this meeting I joined Mrs Leavitt's retinue. From the Baptist Church to the Oddfellows' Hall, wherever she spoke, there I was in the audience. I studied her oratory keenly. She used statistics, history, anecdotes, parables, music, wit and charm to persuade her audience. Her emotions ranged from fiery conviction to the sweetest amusement. She never shouted, yet was always audible. Half her audience came out of curiosity, for a woman speaking in public was a freak; they stayed to applaud.

In every lecture she referred to that extraordinary organisation, the Women's Christian Temperance Union of America. At last came the lecture that particularly interested me: 'Woman: Her Duties and Responsibilities.' My sister Isabella and I arrived punctually and found the hall was empty. We spent ten uneasy minutes before a few more women joined us.

Mrs Leavitt surveyed the tiny gathering tolerantly. 'When I speak of the evils of drink, the people come in their hundreds,' she observed. 'When my subject is Woman, they all stay home. They're frightened! Never mind. A small group of brave women can have a mighty influence.'

Impressed by her positive approach, I looked around the little group hopefully. Counting two on the platform, there were exactly eleven of us!

'I hold that no one has the right to limit woman in the exercise of her faculties.' I felt a stirring in my heart. 'I am not here to teach insubordination. I simply claim that we do possess an immortal soul.' We had all encountered men who believed the opposite! 'It is argued that women ought to be wives and mothers, and so they should. But how can we manage that in Massachussetts, where women outnumber men by seventy thousand?' Isy and I burst into laughter along with the others. 'Some people say there are things a woman cannot do; for instance, that women can never be judges. Now, only one man in a thousand makes a good judge. Yet nobody urges that no man should be trained for the bench. Think of this, ladies: how many men can make an eatable angel cake or turn out a wearable bonnet at their first attempt? Not many! Yet they could do these things if they were trained, and so can women do many things if trained. Man's intellect is broader, but woman's is finer and more delicate . . .'

She articulated so clearly and wittily just what I had always believed that the hairs on the back of my neck stood up in alarm and delight.

Afterwards, as we shared a light supper, I asked, 'Mrs Leavitt, what shall we do? I agree with all you have said, but we are tied with a thousand ribbons. Wherever we turn, they tug us back till we are all in a great tangle.'

'I can answer that very briefly. Do everything! Save the children, rouse the dead church, spread the facts, influence the law: do everything!'

'Yes, but how?'

'Organisation is the key!'

'But what goal should take precedence?' asked Jeannie Smith.

Our visitor didn't answer at once, but looked around our tiny group as if seeing us for the first time. 'You have such a chance, starting from the very beginning, to get it right. If it were my decision, I would say work for the vote. You must put the ballot in woman's hand to protect your little ones.'

None of us believed her! We all assumed the Old Country

would grant women the vote one day and the colonies would follow. Mrs Leavitt backed her inspiring talk with practical strategies. She came and went like an angel through New Zealand. In her wake she left a string of branches of the WCTU.

'I really don't see the point,' said Walter. 'There are so many Temperance groups already.'

'Yes, where women just make the supper and raise the money. In the WCTU we'll do everything!'

'You won't achieve a thing without men to give you a hand,' he grumbled.

'I suppose that is the point,' I said.

Chapter 8

KATE

'Walter, it's high time we built that house in Clyde Road,'
I said one evening. 'A city residence is no place for a five-
year-old boy. Douglas needs fresh air and room to run
around. I want him to grow up close to his cousins.'

'This air is no fouler than the good Bath air I breathed in
my youth,' said that husband of mine as usual.

'Yes and look at you! You look like an old man, and you're
not even fifty!' I tried to keep Walter young but it was hard
work.

Our piece of land was prepared in advance with gently
contoured lawns and azalea gardens. I designed large, airy
rooms with bay windows and generous fireplaces. We were
fortunate in having George Beath in the family, because
through his department store I got all the new furnishings
that made the place pretty and colourful. I made sure that
the staff had good quarters, and that kitchen and scullery
were convenient; the whole household moved with us. My
wonderful housekeeper Poppy and our new outdoor man
Derry made the move seem comparatively simple.

As I took Walter on his first tour of the garden, I
remember Duggie was having great fun throwing a ball and
running after it. Our conversation as always was rather like
the game he was playing, with more dropped balls than good
catches.

'There are daffodils in the lawn,' I told Walter. 'You'll like
that, dear.'

'What's this peculiar thing?' He pulled at a young cabbage
tree.

'Leave it! This is my patch of native forest.'

'You silly goose! What's wrong with English trees?'

'Do you approve of the lawns, at least?'

'Nothing beats a nice terrace house.' In spite of all his protests, I believe he did grow to appreciate our colonial villa.

You remember that house, Jessie? It soon became a hotbed of political intrigue. The very first meeting we held in my new drawing room was momentous. We'd been pottering along nicely, so I thought, our Legal and Parliamentary Committee of the WCTU. Apart from me there was young Ada Wells, Lucy and Jeannie Smith, and Isabella, who only had to cross the road.

Ada was newly married with a baby girl, but that certainly didn't limit her activities. She was quite lovely at that age, Jessie. Swallow your prejudice and listen! She was strong in the mouth and chin, and that was nicely balanced by a high forehead and the most expressive eyes. Ada was much shorter than I, but she had an attractive figure, she wasn't dumpy. She had such a proud way that it took me months to realise she didn't have two pennies to rub together. In those early days she did her own dressmaking. If you looked closely, the frogging might be a little bit skew, but she carried it off, indeed she did! Although she was only twenty-three, she was a proud, intelligent, forceful woman. She was the most wonderful secretary, utterly reliable. Oh, I enjoyed Ada in those days! She was so eager to learn and so grateful.

All right, all right, I'll change the subject.

Let me tell you about that particular meeting at Clyde Road, on a Saturday morning in March. We sat around the big walnut table; Ada's baby and Jeannie's toddlers were with Douglas in the nursery. Ada read the minutes of the last meeting, written in her brisk, eccentric hand.

'Mrs Wells reported that there was still no response to the committee's petition to Parliament seeking to ban the sale of alcoholic liquor to children, and to prohibit the employment of barmaids. Miss Smith moved that the committee follow parliamentary —'

'How much longer is this to go on?' Isabella interrupted.

'It's five months since we sent that petition,' said Jeannie. She was pregnant, and could be counted on to keep track of time.

'Shall I send another telegram to Mr Saunders?' suggested Ada.

'Alfred says he's up against a brick wall.'

Round and round in circles until we turned to the next item on the agenda. It was a most unsatisfactory meeting.

At noon there was a knock on the door.

'That's William,' Jeannie said, glancing anxiously out the window. 'He's on his way home from the printing factory.'

To my knowledge I had never met William Smith, though I had heard a great deal about the man. He was the husband of Jeannie and the favourite son of Mrs Smith, and the brother of Lucy and Eleanor and Annie Smith, all good strong women who worked hard for Temperance. I found it hard to understand why his sisters chose to live under one roof with William and his family. My own family was very close, but we preferred to raise our children in our own individual houses. William Sidney Smith was the only man in a houseful of women and children, and I was not pre-disposed to like him. I felt his sisters should lead a more independent life. Even the youngest, Eleanor, was over twenty.

'Poppy will show Mr Smith into the parlour,' I said crisply.

'Oh, that would never do!' Lucy exclaimed. 'William insists on punctuality!' Her square face lost its usual stoic good humour and she was distinctly alarmed.

Jeannie lumbered to her feet. 'I'll speak to him,' she said, but I pressed her gently back in the chair. 'Must we all run around like chooks just because a man throws some wheat on the ground?'

Lucy and Jeannie exchanged guilty glances. 'You don't understand, Mrs Sheppard!'

'Oh yes I do!' I sailed outside to the front steps, where William Sidney Smith was checking his fob watch with some irritation. He was very broadshouldered and upright, and although he'd just come from town he wore country clothes, tweed plus-fours and a Norfolk jacket.

'Mr Smith?' I held out my hand and he took it briefly.

'Mrs Sheppard.' Like that, a bald statement of fact! No compliments or polite phrases from this man! 'Are you holding my family to ransom in there?' This was not meant playfully, I assure you.

'Do come in. Our business is not quite wound up.'

As his eyes hammered into me, I recognised him from that long-ago day at the Ballantynes', when a young man glared at me over a cello. These were the same furious eyes, now set in a heavier face. The beard was shaped and the hair thick and orderly, yet I clearly saw the young man within. I didn't like the man, yet I had to keep on the right side of him. The sou'west wind was tossing shadows all over the path. Somehow in the tension of scrambling leaves, that man slipped under my shadow.

'Then I'll join your meeting,' said William Sidney Smith.

'That wouldn't be proper,' I told him.

'Allow me to remind you I'm a member of the WCTU.' I knew that, and it didn't please me. It was certainly not my decision! What was the point of having a women's union if men could join? Luckily, only one other man had chosen to do so. 'I take a great interest in your proceedings. If not for my encouragement, Jeannie and Lucy would never have joined.'

'Nonsense. They have minds of their own!'

'I wish that were true,' he said sorrowfully. I could have kicked him.

'If it isn't true, that's surely because a man has robbed them of their choices,' I said as blandly as I could, and ushered him into the drawing room, where he automatically sat at the head of the table.

'Mr Smith, would you please hand me those papers?' I asked him sweetly. 'You have taken the Chair, no doubt inadvertently.'

He pulled a letter out of his breast pocket. 'I cleared your post office box on the way. From Parliament.'

We all sat bolt upright at that, I can tell you. Ada, as

secretary, held out her hand for the letter and read it aloud.

'Dear Ladies —'

'Ladies!' Isy nearly choked. 'Don't we have names?'

'Dear Ladies, The Petitions Committee has read your petition on the sale of liquor to children and does not consider it appropriate to present the petition to Parliament at this session.'

'Having sat on it for months!' Isabella fumed.

'And what a horrible sentence,' sniffed Ada.

'How dare they!' I felt faint with rage. I'd never felt so angry in my life! 'How dare they!'

'I don't understand what they mean,' Lucy said.

'They're throwing it back in our face,' explained Isabella.

'Oh no, my dear sister,' I said, as the truth slowly dawned on me. I was experiencing the spiritual equivalent of one of Christchurch's famous black frosts, dark sky, icy heart. 'It's infinitely more insulting than that. They can hardly be bothered to lift the pen. They obviously haven't even read our petition. I dare say they only deigned to write these three lines because Alfred Saunders pestered the life out of them.'

'Man to man!' Ada said sardonically.

'And what have they said? In so many words they tell us to go and hem a petticoat!'

'But what can we do?' asked Lucy, all confused.

I wasn't confused. I had been confused for years but now the truth was obvious, and already my black frost was melting into a wild rage. 'We are nothing to these stupid, lazy, slippery, vicious politicians. Nothing!'

Jeannie looked anxiously at her husband. 'Should we wind the meeting up?'

William Smith said quite crossly, 'Not on my behalf. Carry on!'

Ada referred to the agenda. 'We were going to discuss equal pay.'

'Blow equal pay!' I burst out. I seized that poisonous letter and screwed it up and hurled it into the fire. A red point flared and it quickly blackened into ash. I grabbed an armful of other papers and threw them at the fireplace. They fell all over the floor, and I wanted to heap them all on the flames but my sister pulled me away.

'Kate, what on earth are you doing? You've spent years gathering that material!'

But she couldn't put out the bonfire in my heart. 'Bother equal pay and widows' pensions and barmaids and the liquor trade! Blow them all!'

There was a silence full of doubtful eyes. Then Isabella asked in a very quiet voice, 'You're not giving up, Kate?'

I laughed aloud. I hardly recognised the sound. 'My modest, womanly plans have just exploded, and Parliament itself has put the spark to the gunpowder!'

There was another painful silence, then Ada piped up. She understood exactly what was going on. 'If only we were making the laws!' she said. She was ambitious, that one! She was one jump ahead of me.

'One thing at a time, Mrs Wells,' I said.

Now look out, Jessie! Here comes a poem, a remembering poem. I can never get them to scan properly like yours, but I seem to remember them just the same.

Up to this moment I always received
Whatever I wanted: a husband, a task,
A baby, a house. I may have been peeved
But I never had rage behind my womanly mask.

We waved our hankies and posted our petition.
Our facts were all correct and our minds were keen.
They overlooked our plea and by this omission
We are as nothing, we simply cannot be seen.

Do we have minds? Do we have souls?
Let us stop wheedling and whining and begging
*   for charity.*
Cast our fathers' crusts and pennies on the coals
And fight our way through fire to perfect parity!

Now meekness burns away in a blinding flash!
My blood is bubbling, I am incandescent!

A glorious rage is glowing in the ash
And I am bold and huge and delinquescent.

Who else knows the startling delight of rage?
Ada of mighty ambition and thinking eyes.
How terrible to meet it at this age!
How wonderful to burn away the lies!

Ada the girl of ardent devotion,
Ada the girl who is bending the bars of her cage,
Ada is beside me in my initiation
To the Heaven and Hell, the glow and the growth
  of rage.

Chapter 9

ADA

I am so relieved to read that the prospect of Hitler's becoming Chancellor is now remote. (The gerund demands the genitive.) I can't get it out of my mind, the way his Stormtroopers dipped their flag in the blood of their comrade. My word, that man can sway the crowds! Sometimes I feel my life has been lived like a good speech; introduction, challenge, opposing arguments, a climax and finally a good rousing up of the audience so that action follows inspiration. It's not enough to resonate! I come now to the challenge.

When the famous Mrs Leavitt preached in Christchurch I was far too preoccupied to attend, for this was when Henry left the cathedral and we were all in disarray. Although I approved of Temperance, I never felt it was the single solution to all the world's ills, and neither did Kate. I was drawn to the WCTU when I realised they had wider aims. One afternoon when Henry was being particularly obnoxious, I put on my hat and coat and walked out the door.

'Where are you going?' he called after me.

'To a meeting of the Women's Christian Temperance Union,' I replied, with every word in Italic Script.

My destination was a building in Worcester Street, midway between the Congregational Church and St John's Anglican Church. Inside and out it was adorned with Temperance posters. On a simple platform sat ten women, while dozens more were seated in the hall, the starkness whereof was softened with greenery and flowers. After a hymn and a prayer, a series of women gave their monthly reports. I listened, but I could barely move my eyes from a single strange lady on the stage. What can I say about a woman who impels you to gaze at her even when she is silent and still? Foolishly I rehearsed in my mind some lines from *Christabel*.

> *I guess, 'twas frightful there to see*
> *A lady so richly clad as she —*
> *Beautiful exceedingly!*

Indeed, I was greatly perturbed, and not just by her unexpected elegance. She had a radiance, a sweet grace that was like iron. She was listening so actively, with such intelligence. 'This person is lit from within,' I thought. Every other woman seemed to fade from my vision. I even felt myself clouding over, and I was generally held to be the strong woman of my family, almost one might say the father! I discovered my own softness; I felt a craving to take advice of this dazzling woman, who at last was introduced as Mrs Sheppard. The name was not unknown. Her voice was not loud, yet it penetrated for the hall was absolutely hushed. Absurd, the attention we gave to a report on letters posted and received. She spoke in an educated English accent with just the faintest trace of Scots. I immediately felt assured that here was a great teacher, the hour and the woman appearing simultaneously, each respectively explanatory of the other. Her voice was like a flute ringing in the forest.

Oh dear, oh dear! What am I writing? St Bede, guide my hand, I am but your servant. One could hardly call this history! Imagine descending to the description of personal mannerisms. I must push on with the factual record of our work.

Mrs Isitt closed the meeting with a prayer, and refreshments were served on a trestle table. I had one desire only, to get close to Mrs Sheppard. I waited nervously while a stream of women flowed round her. She was gracious with them all, even a very shabby girl with dreadful skin. I was hovering at the edge of the magic circle when a new group of women approached, apparently intent on carrying her off. Mrs Sheppard reached out to me across the throng.

'Don't go!' she said to me. 'You have something on your mind.'

Foolishly I looked down at the hand clasping mine. The skin was white and delicate against my own, and her touch was warm.

'Mrs Sheppard, I am Ada Wells.'

To my astonishment she said, 'I've heard of you. You're the girl with the golden tongue.' I had no idea what she was talking about. 'Miss Helen Conan said you have quite a way with words. How can I help you?'

'I want to help you!' I burst out. 'There's so much to do, and your way is best!' I was not at my most articulate and she quirked those shapely eyebrows.

'My way? I'm not sure what you mean by that!'

Her admirers buoyed her up with laughter, as if they all had a wonderful secret.

'I mean by changing the law. Your committee is the one that can improve the lot of women.'

Mrs Sheppard smiled and slipped her arm through mine.

'My dear Mrs Wells, if you've another hour at your disposal, come with us. We're about to have a short meeting upstairs.'

As if in a dream I was drawn into the Legal and Parliamentary Committee, just like that!

Meetings! After a lifetime on boards and committees the word now has rather different associations, but any meeting with Kate in the Chair was a joy, it was heady stuff! I came away from that first gathering with my allegiance locked not to the WCTU but to Kate Sheppard. I flew home six inches above the earth, knowing I had found a purpose in life. This was what I was born for! By supporting Kate in her ventures I felt I could change the world. I was only twenty-three.

I brought assets. My handwriting was rapid and clear, and I had the ability to sift essential information from long-winded speeches and lively arguments. I learned quickly and I had orderly habits; I became an excellent secretary.

I was happy! Only one problem worried me. I was expecting my second baby, although Chris was still in her pram.

How could I help create a new world for children if I was personally adding to their number year after year? I kept apace with the correspondence and I never missed a meeting, but I lived in dread of failing in my duties.

'Are you coping, Ada dear?' Kate inquired one day when I may have revealed my fatigue.

'This is all very well,' I said in a burst, 'but what about the next baby, and the next one and the next!' Surely these radical women would know what to do. Maria wouldn't help me. She was my own mother but her answer was no answer at all. If Father hadn't died she would be having babies still; it was disgusting. Maria said I was well equipped for mother-hood and that was that.

I looked over my minute book at Jeannie Smith, whom at times I found quite exasperating.

'Jeannie, are you going to have babies forever?' I readily concede that this was overstepping the mark.

'I'm happy now I've got my little Hilda Kate,' she cooed, turning to give the pram a wiggle. Everybody had to admire her Hilda Kate! She had lost one daughter, hence the removal of the Smith family into the healthier air of Russley Road, since when she had brought to birth three boys in four years before this new baby girl.

'Seven children! Isn't that enough?'

'Eight,' Jeannie corrected me. 'Counting little Hilda Martha, God rest her.'

I thought it was vile of William to keep giving her babies, but one had to respect her loyalty.

'Let's get back to business,' Kate said tactfully. However, after the meeting she drew me aside and instructed me on the prevention of conception. I was so grateful! She even gave me a hygienically packaged sponge and personally attached a string.

'This is so simple,' I exclaimed. 'Why doesn't every woman use it?'

Kate sighed. 'Not everyone approves, not even in our own little group. Isabella and I keep rather quiet about this.'

I admired the way she managed her own life so well, with

70

only one son. Her Douglas was about five and a very sweet bright boy. He was well looked after by his nanny, attending nursery school during the day.

Thus far I have failed adequately to describe Kate Sheppard. I shall now do so in a rational, scientific way. She was tall and slim and moved with consummate grace. She had the most lovely wide-apart blue eyes, fly-away eyes. Her hair was soft and wavy, a light brown with sunshine caught in it. She was fond of wearing lavender and mauve and soft greys, and lace and cairngorms. Thanks to Beath's department store, Kate was always elegant — never fussy but — oh, this is useless! She was a princess, a goddess, what more can I say? And I was her handmaiden.

To please Maria I named my second baby Alma Lucy Blanche, all family names. By the time she was two the child was nicknamed Cos. Chris was always asking 'Why?' and her sister always answered 'Cos!' Even then, one was of a spiritual bent and one had her feet on the ground.

Soon after Cos was born, Kate made the momentous decision to go for the vote. The vote or nothing! One bright blue spring day she and Isabella and I travelled down to Ashburton to talk with Alfred Saunders. I took my baby of course, but otherwise we left our duties behind. Kate's man Derry whistled and we three sat in the sunshine, singing in time to the horse's trotting hooves.

Kate had such a lovely voice! She sang with the Riccarton Glee Club.

'Oh liberty, oh liberty!'

Her soprano trilled up like a skylark soaring.

'Now I'll sing you "The Three Dreams". It's fresh in my mind.'

After forty-seven years it is still fresh in my mind, too.

'Here's one that William wrote —' I shut this one out of my memory.

'Kate, teach Ada the sol-fa system!' Isabella urged, so we rode along singing do-re-mi-fah-sol-la-ti-do. My husband had nothing but contempt for the sol-fa system and William Smith was the first person in New Zealand to use it. It may have been appropriate for a glee club, but Henry expected every singer in his Motette to read music and that was that.

One of the nicest things about this outing was that for once we were free of the Smith family. Not a single Smith was riding in that cart! Oh, I loved Jeannie of course, and everyone respected Lucy as a tower of strength, but once I was in Kate's circle there was no getting away from them. William Sidney Smith was the centre, and everywhere I looked there were Smiths — his mother, his sisters, his wife, his children. He started the glee club, he even sang duets with Kate. I feared that for all her strength Kate was sometimes in danger of being gobbled up by the Smiths.

We travelled on and on and on, straight and flat. The plains are so exceedingly flat!

Alfred and Rhoda lived in a simple house not far from Ashburton. They came out to greet us, both in their usual rather crudely constructed clothing, though one quickly overlooked their appearance. Alfred had a mop of wild curls and a broad, spreading beard. After all their ups and downs Rhoda seemed rather to have lost heart, but Alfred was always kind to her. Well over sixty, he was as vigorous as a boy. He showed us all over the small farm. Draught horses were his great love, huge, shaggy beasts. He urged us all to climb on board! I followed the example of Kate, who sat astride, and I thought I would split up the middle. It was strangely exciting to be so high above the earth. I let my horse walk quietly, being too cowardly to trot, but Kate and Isabella had learned to ride as children. They cantered around the paddock on the monstrous animals laughing aloud. Kate's hair flew out of its pins and lifted in the air like downy wings.

Rhoda made no allowance for our effete city tastes, serving no tea!

'I feel quite deprived,' I admitted at the dinner table.

'Tea is poison,' said Alfred sternly. Otherwise their diet suited me very well. I like simple food, though I prefer my vegetables cooked.

The purpose of our journey was to discuss our strategy

with Alfred, who had been involved in politics for decades.

'Now, Alfred, how am I to persuade you to lead our fight in Parliament?' Kate said as Rhoda handed out slices of red-currant pie. 'What infallible argument have I overlooked?'

'I'm not your man, Kate. I'd do your cause more harm than good.'

'Alfred, you're a legend in the House,' protested Kate.

'Precisely, I'm a circus freak. And women's suffrage is bound to be seen as a huge joke, even without my assistance.'

I bristled. 'That's outrageous!'

'It's a fact. How many people take it seriously? A handful, no, a teaspoon of people!' He spoke truth, for even within the WCTU we formed a minority so tiny it was almost invisible. 'The whole country will sneer and deride, and then I'll get angry and disgrace you. No, you want a man of dignity, a man who never forgets his manners, a gentleman. You want Sir John Hall.'

Kate shook her head in amazement. 'He's supported by the land barons! He's a Tory! It doesn't make sense!'

Notwithstanding our misgivings, we knew that Alfred was very astute, and eventually Kate was persuaded that Sir John Hall would be the ideal advocate. In the course of his long career Sir John had been Mayor of Christchurch, Leader of the Opposition and even Premier.

After dinner Alfred fetched an old pamphlet from the side-board and gave it to Kate. After one glance her lovely face relaxed into joy.

'Oh thank you, Alfred! I have so wanted my own copy.' Her hands trembled as she turned the pages. 'Did you obtain this from Femmina herself?'

Alfred tutted. 'Stop fishing, my dear.' They settled into the old sofa side by side while Rhoda cleared the table. Kate made her own rules; propriety was a movable feast for her. I excused myself, retiring to feed the baby and settle her down.

I was lying in bed when I heard Kate and Isy talking excitedly in their bedroom next to mine. I felt quite left out. After a time my door opened and Kate entered, her hair tumbling down behind her, clad in a dressing gown of white silk. Beneath it I glimpsed the softest Brussels lace.

'Oh, Ada — I have to show you this!' She sat on the end of my bed and read aloud: ' "An Appeal to the Men of New Zealand by Femmina . . . Our women are brave and strong —" '

'What appeal?' I asked. The candle lit her cheekbones most beautifully.

Kate began teasing me and I felt almost honoured. ' "How small a matter seems the simple concession here pleaded." Have you guessed?'

'I give in!'

'She was asking for the vote! All alone, anonymously, secretly, seventeen years ago. Listen: "We have statesmen . . . Champions from among these men will step forth and fight the good fight for those fettered weak ones who can only think and suffer." '

'We may be fettered but we are not weak!'

'Don't you feel the link? We're bound together, we belong!' Kate's eyes shone.

'I belong to — to women,' I heard myself say.

'And to this country — do you feel it?'

No, I didn't. Not at that stage. 'New Zealand is just where we happen to be,' I said. 'But there are women all over the world.'

'Oh, I know this almost off by heart. Listen, Ada. "But why is New Zealand only to follow? Why not take the initiative?" Oh, wonderful Femmina!'

On the way home we saw Alfred's mill. I was amazed at the waterworks.

'Surely that water is going uphill?' I wondered.

Isabella laughed. 'Not even men can make water flow uphill.'

Once back in Christchurch, Kate made her approach to Sir John. I cannot imagine anyone more utterly opposite to Alfred in every way. He was smooth and self-controlled. The perfect gentleman. That's not an insult, either! In no time Kate had him eating out of her hand.

I must get Bim to buy me another bottle of ink. Moreover, while the occasional very short sentence can be used to emphasise a significant point, I have found myself at times overlooking the fact that longer sentences, judiciously modified or embellished with subordinate clauses, are far more appropriate to the development of logical argument.

Chapter 10

ADA

Whereas Kate was determined to attain one goal, namely the female franchise, my conscience was incessantly troubled by destitute widows, neglected children, factory sweating, sickness and ignorance, and always over the horizon the smoke of war. Whenever I drew attention to these multifarious evils, Kate would remind me of the task in hand. We were now engaged in a battle that would take six years to win. Nothing would have pleased me more than to serve her cause alone, but a multitude of problems reared up.

First and worst, I found I was again with child. My method of prophylaxis had failed almost immediately when Henry discovered the device and cut it up with a pair of scissors, after which his marital approaches could best be described as punitive. He was not pleased to be presented with another daughter, and unfortunately there was something missing in Bim from the start. She had an odd look about her even as a baby. She has never said anything original in her life, but endlessly parrots me and Chris. It is nerve-racking of course but I've done my best with her. The wretched truth is that she lacks the normal feelings of the rest of humanity.

Maria, my mother, had set up a nursing establishment offering Professor Kirk's treatment, namely massage and various forms of hydrotherapy. There was soon a regular throng of paying customers coming to her house in Office Road. (N.B. This topic is not strictly relevant just here.)

Exerting herself assiduously, Kate wrote clear and copious letters to Sir John and Alfred Saunders and to the other branches of the WCTU. We were all delighted when she was appointed National Franchise Superintendent, which placed her in command of the troops nationwide. I assisted with the correspondence, but that third child really did limit my involvement. Sometimes I felt almost angry about it. If only I had managed my life like Kate's! She travelled and gave lectures and wrote articles and still found time to learn Esperanto, and establish the Christian Ethical Society, which held wonderful debates on such topics as marriage, economics and euthanasia. Unfortunately it was now clear that I must become a breadwinner. I weaned Bim at four months and began teaching again, this time at St Albans School.

Oh, it was frustrating, teaching all those young raga-muffins and vagrants! It was so hard to achieve standards when their parents were all on the move, liable to rush off to the goldfields at any moment. I wasn't well. Eleven months between babies is simply not enough. I had a few minor triumphs, but it was a battle all the way with the headmaster and the school committee. We were six teachers in a single room with five hundred pupils. Not only was it cold and draughty and very inconvenient for physical education, but I was obliged to listen to the headmaster, Mr Speight, teaching his unfortunate pupils in the sixth stand-ard. That man! He had no idea! No matter how fully I advised him, he was wedded to the benighted pedagogical method of drumming dry facts into reluctant heads and never mind any understanding. I persuaded the committee to put up four large curtains, but they weren't soundproof! Education should be an adventure! Through the dreary daily recital of English kings and dates I would grit my teeth and think of Kate. Throughout the four years I spent in this institution my head was booming with voices. Mr Speight's loathsome nasal voice, the pupils chanting, my voice, Kate's voice, Sir John's voice and the voice of the vile Mr Fish, MP.

'Twelve ones are twelve, twelve twos are twenty-four.'

'On what conceivable principle do you claim to group women with the insane or with children?'

'This is a drawing of a dandelion. Stem, calyx, stamen, pistil.'

'I beg to introduce the Female Suffrage Bill.'

'But now unrobe yourself; for I

Must pray, ere yet in bed I lie —'

'Oh, oh! Poor unfortunate women! They are being used by the temperance fanatics. We cannot make people sober through bigotry!'

'I beg to move this amendment: that "Person" includes Female.'

'Stitch, stitch, stitch.

In poverty, hunger and dirt . . .'

Yet I could have managed quite serenely if not for Bim. From the time she could crawl she was always prone to cause trouble. Always when I got home Chris or Cos would have some tale of woe which required all my reserves of energy to put right. I often felt my real life was lived with Kate at our Saturday meetings, and at the meetings we arranged with synod and the literary clubs and any group at all who would debate the great reform.

Sir John was continually putting our case in Parliament by means of motions, amendments and Private Member's Bills. 1890 was election year, and Kate organised the entire country so that every candidate was questioned on his views. One evening she and I went to Sydenham Hall in the poorer part of Christchurch.

'I will stem the flow of immigrants,' said the Tory candidate for Lyttelton, 'I will clear the prostitutes off the streets, and I will serve the interests of my constituents.' So much blah!

(I must watch my language: no slang! And I have certainly been overusing the exclamation mark!)

Kate stood up. She looked very impressive and very womanly in her grey velvet suit with a lace cravat. I wore my best crêpe dress with a little brooch, bearing in mind her warning that we should avoid looking 'mannish'.

'Sir,' she said sweetly, 'does that include the interests of your female constituents?'

He leered at her, the fat pig. 'I'm always ready to help a

lovely lady.' The hall erupted into laughter, but Kate didn't turn a hair.

Now I stood up and produced my pencil and notebook. 'Always ready to help a lovely lady.' Articulating his words with clarity, I recorded them in my notebook.

'Do you think women should have the vote?' Kate persisted with a charming smile.

'The fact is, dear lady, women do not want the vote. I've asked my wife and she tells me so, and therefore it must be true.'

'Women do not want the vote. I asked my wife, et cetera.' Repeated deadpan, his words sounded rather sinister, causing the candidate to twitch his collar.

'If we prove that women do want it,' said Kate, 'then will you support the measure?'

'Of course I shall!' The man was distinctly nervous now. 'Anything to please the ladies.'

I repeated his utterance loudly and wrote it down. The hall was briefly hushed, then with Kate I left the hall, brandishing the notebook on high. Cheers and boos followed us out. Yes, there were moments when I was useful.

The next year my life followed the same pattern, teaching all day, supplementary tuition with the girls at home, organising the household, Motette rehearsals and concerts and occasionally aiding Maria with the massage, all of which was peripheral to my real life, my life as a suffragette. Now we began gathering signatures for the first great petition. I never missed an opportunity.

There were occasions when I felt excluded from Kate's sphere by men. Men! When she won a page of the *Prohibition-ist* for the WCTU, that was a great coup, for now our message was disseminated throughout the nation. I felt very proud of Kate's debut as journalist. It was William Smith who printed this paper, who else? Consequently, Kate spent long hours at the printing works. Oh, it was all quite respectable, with Lucy usually on the premises doing the firm's accounts.

The feverish correspondence with Parliament continued unabated. Sir John and Alfred were like rivals in love, both wanting Kate's undivided attention. Alfred peppered her with intimate, hectic telegrams and letters, Sir John wrote with perfect self-control but with undisguised devotion, and as secretary I read them all. Before long they were at each other's throats. They were such perfect opposites that I began to think of them as two sides of a single person, Sir-John-Alfred, conflicting internally, with Sir John manoeuvring among the rocks of Party Politics and Alfred taking everything personally, rushing headlong at every target.

'Put not your trust in Princes or Premiers,' warned Alfred.

'I have the honour to be, madam, your ladyship's obedient servant, John Hall.'

'What paralysed me at first was Sir John's vile unmitigated treachery. I was boiling over with indignation and yet determined not to make a fool of myself.'

'I think the fact made a considerable impression in the House.'

'Thus endeth the last chapter of Sir John. Regards truly, Alfred Saunders.'

Kate was a positive genius the way she handled her two knights-errant, whether soothing Alfred, cheering Sir John, sharing gossip with Alfred or planning strategy with Sir John. Holding them together for six years was a miracle of diplomacy.

'Whom do you prefer?' I asked her one afternoon at the WCTU rooms in Latimer Square, where we were proofreading a pamphlet. It was entitled 'Ten Reasons for Supporting Women's Suffrage', and five thousand copies were to be printed by William Smith. 'Sir John or Alfred Saunders?'

She gave me a curious look. 'We need them equally. What would one be without the other?'

'But as a man, as a person?'

Kate put down her pen and strolled to a window overlooking the square. 'Those trees are turning colour already,' she remarked. In other words, let us not pursue this topic.

I couldn't leave it alone. 'Sir John has the social graces.'

'And who suggested involving him in the first place?'

'Yet Sir John stands for everything we want to overthrow!'

'He has a mind of his own,' Kate corrected me.

'He's a man without passion,' I suggested. Kate flushed very slightly. I missed nothing, I tracked every movement of every corpuscle, but I did not wish to arouse her displeasure and so we reverted to the job in hand.

I niggled over this for rather special reasons of my own. It was apparent that her husband was by no means Kate's equal. No one is wholly self-sufficient, and I saw a vacant space into which Sir John or Alfred might easily step, or so I thought. For Kate's sake and for the sake of the cause, I wanted to pre-empt any such disastrous development. She herself was too pure to perceive the risks inherent in her situation. Invariably and deservedly, Kate was surrounded by men and women who adored her. This, combined with the very public role she now played, made her most vulnerable. For this reason I felt it was my duty to become indispensable to her comfort, to protect our leader by assuming the position of the person most loved and relied on. With this obligation ever in the forefront of my mind, should I therefore try rather to resemble Sir John, or Alfred?

She was more light-hearted with Alfred, but intuitively I thought I should align myself with Sir John, perhaps because he was the more formidable character. He certainly had more influence and he was much more like St Bede. It was not an unnatural ambition, for I recognised within myself some of his qualities. But I have an Alfred within me too. Even now I sense him there, raging and growling to be let free. His ultimates and absolutes, his impulsive urge for vengeance, his wild temper have grown all the more ferocious for being locked away. He constitutes no less unwelcome an influence on my character than Thomas à Becket. Yet in later years I discovered something most strange about the real Alfred, to wit, that he suppressed a gentle love for sixty years. He too had his Sir John of self-control and selflessness, and this was the daimon he hid from our sight.

I had far less time with Kate than I craved, and I made the most of every minute. I constantly bestirred myself to be perfect for her. She herself was inimitable, as playful and passionate as she was discreet and gracious. She had no need to suppress any side of her being. Her judgement was perfect and yet she was utterly spontaneous. I competed with Sir John, hoping to obviate an inappropriate and perhaps scandalous invasion of her private life. As it turned out, I was looking in quite the wrong direction.

Let us get back to the story of the suffrage fight, steeped now in treachery and trickery. Our opponents, the liquor lobby, would stoop to anything! When Sir John unrolled that first petition of ten thousand signatures like a carpet, Parliament was impressed. But then our arch-enemy Mr Fish threw our allies into disarray with a devilish plot, and the Bill was thrown out. We were all disappointed. Then Kate became ill, and I was under pressure at school.

It began as usual with a reprimand from the school committee. I smoothed it over but they persisted in their attempt to remove me from my post. The headmaster and all his corporation were determined this time I should go. I resisted as long as possible but in April I resigned.

The very next morning I went to the WCTU rooms, where I found Annie Smith, another of William's sisters, adding up some figures.

'Do you know where Mrs Sheppard is?' I asked her. 'What a lovely day!'

Annie's face warmed up. 'She's at the printing works,' she said.

'How's Jeannie?'

'Near her time, but cheerful as always.'

This was Jeannie's tenth pregnancy. I concealed the revulsion I felt at this endless whirl of births and all those people crammed into one cottage like rabbits. Four adult women, one man, and all those children! It was not impecuniousness that obliged them to live in a slum, it was a positive choice on the part of the tyrant. Westcote seemed to me like an egg farm, and a most unsanitary one at that.

Still, nothing could depress me on this wonderful day and I tripped around the corner to the printing works in Manchester Street. I went upstairs to the office, hearing the clatter of the printing presses out the back. There was Kate, peering over a page set in cold type or whatever they called it.

'Do you approve?' William Sidney Smith was asking.

'Yes, I'm glad you used those capitals. Capital work!'

Kate was in a frivolous mood. She held out her inky hands and I seized them with joy. 'Ada! What are you doing here?'

'I have resigned!' I said triumphantly.

'Making a virtue of necessity?' William Smith could be so sarcastic.

'I am at your disposal, dear Kate!' I said firmly. 'Now we shall see some action!'

Kate laughed aloud.

'That will be nothing new,' said William quite super-fluously. 'Mrs Sheppard has the whole country on its heels.'

'I know what Ada's capable of,' said Kate. 'You'll see, William!'

Thank goodness he moved away to deal with a workman. Kate showed me the page which was ready to print.

'Look, it's all about you!' she flattered me, reading out bits. ' "Is it right that while the loafer, the gambler, the drunkard, and even the wife-beater has a vote, earnest, edu-cated and refined women are denied it? Is it right that an educated woman can be trusted to teach a school, and yet not be trusted with a vote that is given to the boys she has educated?" '

'I'm not a teacher any more,' I pointed out.

'Surely you didn't give in?'

'There is another factor,' I said obliquely. Kate's eyes dropped to my waistline.

'Oh. I wondered.'

'Never mind,' I said gaily. 'These things happen.'

Kate was really puzzled now. 'But last time you were so disturbed!'

'Last time it kept me from my suffrage work. This time it frees me from school teaching willy-nilly. I can help you now!'

'But the money?' We were good enough friends for Kate to broach this subject.

'I shall help Maria with her patients. Meanwhile I'm at your service.'

And so we began the last big push for the vote.

Chapter 11

ADA

I meant business, and Kate could see it. We formed a habit of meeting at her house every morning when Douglas was at nursery school. The children and I were staying with Maria in Office Road and it wasn't a long walk to Clyde Road. There we planned strategy and shared the burden of work.

'First of all, a Women's Franchise League,' I announced right away. Thanks to our public education campaign we had more and more supporters, of whom some were atheists and some imbibed the occasional glass of ale. For these helpers a separate organisation was mandatory. 'I'll book a hall and then I'll start writing letters.'

Kate was pleased. 'Quite right. We've been lagging behind our sisters in Dunedin. Now come outside, I've got something to show you.'

Leaning against the side door was a spanking new black bicycle. Kate climbed on board and gave me a beautiful demonstration.

'George has imported one hundred of these,' she called out, crunching through the dead leaves on the lawn. 'Isy and I have got the knack of it.' She dismounted with remarkable grace. 'This is yours, Ada.'

'Oh no!' I exclaimed, worrying about the cost.

'It's my gift! Imagine how you'll dash around town! And the iron horse eats no hay and asks no fare,' Kate continued, irresistibly.

I climbed on the seat, using the verandah steps. I learned to pedal and steer with Kate running along behind holding the saddle. Inevitably I had my first fall, collapsing into a pile of leaves. Kate was yards away!

'You let go!' I accused her and she laughed.

'Lots of times! You've learned to ride the iron horse!'

Within a week I was using it daily. We were the odd ones out until Kate started the Atalanta Club for women cyclists. On fine Saturdays we sometimes joined their club trips to Brighton or Sumner — with our petitions in the basket! I became accustomed to people staring at us, and they grew accustomed to the sight of women on bicycles. I must confess I found that peculiar awareness of my legs somewhat disturbing at first.

An admirable vehicle for gathering signatures, the bicycle conveyed me to woollen factories and shoe factories and candle factories where women worked ten hours a day for two and six a week, with noisy machines, awful lavatories, ten minutes for lunch — all manifestations of why we needed the vote. I received much abuse, but I received many signatures too. I never went anywhere without my petitions. They were rolling in!

One day I entered a drugstore in Cashel Street, little knowing it to be a veritable den of lions. I was waiting for the lady assistant to serve an elderly man, when a young spiv bounced in and waved a piece of paper at me.

'Sign the petition, ma'am? Votes for women!'

'Take that thing out of here!' said the apothecary, a rat-faced man of the worst type.

'Why's that, sir?'

'It'll break up happy families, that's why!'

We called that Argument Number Four, after 'it's unnatural/monstrous/mannish' and 'women don't want it' and 'the chops will be burnt'.

'Pardon me, sir, this is right up your alley,' the spiv said with a broad wink.

'Sir' read the petition and smiled; he dipped his pen in the inkwell.

'But only women are meant to sign,' exclaimed the lady assistant.

'That's all right,' chirped the young man. 'You can sign yourself Mary Murphy.'

Then the customer butted in. 'What's wrong with you lot? Give the women the vote and they'll shut the pubs!'

'And no more little blue bottles of bliss for you, my man,' agreed the other chap, tapping the medicine bottle.

The old man was confused. 'What does it say?'

The druggist was writing names, laughing to himself. 'Mary Murphy. Sally Evans. Annie McGough. Susan Billings. Lady Barker. Lady Hall . . .'

I read the words aloud over his shoulder. ' "We the undersigned beg to record our belief that it is unlawful and unChristian to give women the right to vote in elections." '

'That's not fair!' the young woman protested.

'How much do they pay you for this, young man?' I asked.

'Seven shillings a hundred,' he said brazenly. 'Want to sign?'

'I certainly do!' I seized the papers and simply ran out of the shop! Kate was most impressed with my presence of mind, and glad to have plain evidence of the liquor lobby's treachery.

(Of course I do not claim those were the exact words uttered in this memorable adventure, but it was rather fun reconstructing the dialogue! This morning I seem to be writing with more rapidity than correctness. These new nibs that Bim bought are probably the reason my pen is racing ahead. I can see my sentences have been rather loosely constructed, but I feel that can be justified when writing conversation. Later I can bring a bit of spit and polish to the style but in the meantime I believe I shall just carry on.)

Forgery or no forgery, the liquor lobby had no hope of matching our petition. Kate had heaps of signed forms on the floor of her drawing room, and the heaps grew taller and they multiplied. We began pasting them together in a long roll, hardly able to keep pace with the influx of parcels from all around New Zealand. On the first of July we had a telegram from Sir John, telling us it was time to despatch the petition.

'What's the final count?' Kate asked Lucy as we sealed it inside a sturdy brown cardboard box made by William.

'Nineteen thousand two hundred and eighty-four.' Lucy knew her numbers!

Kate's man Derry drove us to the port of Lyttelton, where we personally put it on the *Penguin* for Wellington. We performed miracles of organisation, and all without telephones or trains or buses. I have always maintained that only perfect organisation makes possible perfect freedom.

'We're bound to win this time,' I said to Kate on the journey back from Lyttelton. The stars were out and we were bundled up against the cold. It seemed we were unbeatable and inseparable.

'It's more than a petition,' Kate said. 'As an educational device it's worked beyond my wildest dreams.'

'It's strange that the more converts we win, the more vicious grow the insults.'

'Not strange at all. At first our enemies thought they could laugh us out of existence, but now they see we are dangerous adversaries.'

We had done our work, and now it was over to Sir John and Alfred. I moved on to my next chosen task, establishing the Canterbury Women's Institute with the aid of Professor Bickerton.

Now that was a radical body if you like! We took the vote for granted and were planning to use it to the full. We studied the laws of the land and clarified our opinions on the Divorce Laws, the guardianship of children, the Communicable Diseases Act, wages for women, education, prisons — everything. Kate was all in favour and joined us on the committee. For once the boot was on the other foot, for I was the president for years, while she took a back seat. The CWI was my baby; I think Kate was favourably impressed.

Speaking of babies, my next child arrived in September, just as Bim went off to school. It was a boy this time. Henry was quite tickled, and for me at least it was a novelty. We called him Stan. He was born easily.

Not so the great cause! Endless stonewalling ensued. Our distress mounted month by month. Alfred's feud with Sir

John blew into horrible proportions. The two Maori members were now with us, but as Alfred put it, 'It looks as if the franchise will be wrecked by the excessive artfulness of some of its nominal supporters and the extreme simplicity of others.' There was a lot of nonsense about party loyalty and postal votes, all stirred up by that double-dealing Seddon.

One afternoon in spring Kate opened this telegram: 'It is all right unconditionally accepted you have got the franchise. I shall be home on Sunday, hoist your colours high. A.S.' We all hugged and threw our handkerchiefs into the air!

Not half an hour later, the telegram boy delivered a painful blow. 'A sudden split has occurred at last moment and we look in a worse predicament than ever. I was deceived in what I last telegraphed. Govt deceived me. A.S.' The cause was lost.

I bicycled to Kate's house the following forenoon early. Poppy told me Kate was still in bed — unheard of!

'Will you tell her I am here?' Poppy showed me into Kate's bedroom. It was the loveliest room in pale greens and mauves, but Kate was very low. I sat beside the bed. I felt her pain: her eyes were dark and her skin so pale.

'Have you a headache, my dear?'

She looked at me in despair and said, 'Heartache! Are we really such monsters? Simply to want a say in the government of our own country?'

'You're no monster!' It was unthinkable.

'Yet what have we been called almost daily for the last six years?'

I ticked off insults on my fingers. 'Unwomanly, unsexed, immodest, indelicate, fanatics, sluts, blue-stockings, shrieking sisters, coarse, vulgar, hysterical, busybodies and freaks.'

'Exactly, they call us monsters!'

'It's only a word, Kate! Think what they mean! A monster is simply something too big to grasp.'

'But freaks and half-men!' She couldn't get it out of her mind.

'Myopic slander,' I said. 'They'd say the same if an angel came to call.'

'But we are women!' She was almost talking to herself. 'When Isy and I were children we were — oh Ada, I do miss the sea! Do you know *The Little Mermaid*?'

Of course I did. 'No self-respecting mermaid would swim in the Avon,' I said, trying to jolly her out of this.

'Mermaids don't have souls, you know.' Kate turned to me, her eyes brimming. I put my arms around her and she sobbed. 'Just because I've only got one child! I'm a woman! I'm a woman!'

I couldn't bear to see her in this state. I went to fetch some household items from Poppy.

'I'm going to give you a rub,' I said.

Her face was buried in a lace pillow. Pulling back the bedclothes I gently turned her on her back. She lay stiffly, as if her legs were joined together, as if she really were that mermaid stranded on dry land with only fog to swim in. The room was warmed by a coal fire. I covered the upper part of her body with a blanket and slipped towels under her legs. Then I got to work on those feet and legs. At the first touch of my hands she winced.

'Sore? Just accept it, Kate. I have to make it worse before it's better.' Everyone has their weak spots which are the very parts most in need of rubbing. Little by little she relaxed and those beautiful legs reflected a sweeter state of mind. I worked upwards from the feet, as usual.

At last she said, 'My stomach, Ada. Rub my stomach.'

I was reluctant, for a stomach rub can be most painful. I resolved to rub very lightly. I raised the soft nightgown and revealed her most secret part. Monster? I thought with a mighty wrath. This is the sweetest, most essential woman. I most earnestly desired to rub away all the pain of those tumultuous years. Softly I moulded the muscle of her belly till the tightness relaxed. Her nightgown twitched higher as if by accident, and, following what I thought were her wishes, I attended lovingly to her. Though in her forties, she had full, firm breasts.

Massaging my friend was utterly unlike rubbing Maria's clients. I had longed to rub Kate many times when she was tired and strained, and always she had resisted. Normally I feel quite separate from the patient; now I rubbed as I breathed, my touch was as light as breath, as rhythmic, as right. Kate's strawberry nipples rose at my touch and I was afraid.

My hands continued but my soul stood still. I was stupefied by the impulse I felt; it took all my discipline to suppress it. Kate willed me to continue till her tension was released. When I detached my skin from hers it was like flaying myself alive. I could not remain to sponge her with acetic acid, although without this the treatment is not complete. I pulled the bedclothes over her and fled the room without a word.

I stumbled to her drawing room. I stood in the centre, unseeing, appalled at the thing in my heart. Was it evil? How could I know? I searched for a name, a label. I rejected all except 'love'. Rendered half insensible, I wrestled with my very self, or part of me. Was there a mermaid in me? Were these the feelings of Alfred Saunders when his eyes alighted on my Kate? How could something so sweet be unnatural? I fell to my knees in confusion and silently cried out to St Bede. He came, he nearly always came when I called but he was too benign. Punish me! I begged him. O my teacher, teach me! He refused to punish me or to teach me.

At last I suppressed the sensuousness that had almost engulfed me. I sat at the desk and blindly sifted through the correspondence. I would not allow myself to think 'This is her desk.' I thought only, 'This must be answered' or 'This is not urgent.' When Kate's housekeeper looked in, I offered an adequately convincing representation of myself as honorary secretary.

'Mrs Sheppard will be here soon,' said Poppy. I thanked her automatically.

When Kate entered the room her cheeks were rosier. She was wearing a favourite dress of mauve with a little shawl-collar of Irish lace and carried a big vase crammed with snowball blossom. She put the vase on a walnut side-table, artfully fluffing up the great balls of sweet white flowers. The room was lit up and scented.

'There!' Kate said. 'You have soothed my body and the flowers will soothe my spirit. Let's get on with it. How shall we word the next petition? We must decide at once so that William can print them immediately.'

I was overwhelmed with relief. Whatever unwonted passion I had suffered, she evidently had not been similarly afflicted. Our friendship would not be poisoned if I kept my feelings under control. I took my cue from her, and noted all her instructions.

So the campaign resumed and rolled on. Kate refused to tolerate any sign of despair.

'Our defeat is most trying,' she wrote. 'To sit down and mourn, however, would be worse than foolish. Let us work with extra zeal and energy until our majority is so large that the Legislative Council dare not reject our petition, and the country will know that we mean it!'

Extraordinary woman! She even published a satirical piece which made fun of her deepest pain. Within days we were laughing about it!

'Dorlesky says you call women angels, and you don't give 'em the rights of the lowest beast that crawl upon the earth. And Dorlesky told me to tell you that she didn't ask the rights of an angel; she would be perfectly contented and proud if you would give her the rights of a dog. A dog ain't called undogly if it hunts quietly round for its bone, and wants its share of the crumbs that fall from that table that bills are laid on. A dog won't have to listen to soul-sickening speeches from them that deny it freedom and justice — about its bein' a damask rose, and a seraphine, when it knows it hain't: it knows, if it knows anything, that it is a dog.'

After that when we were accused of being monsters, or unwomanly, we would meet each other's eye and think, 'Undogly!'

Kate travelled up and down the country winning new converts and raising the spirits of all. At such times I remained in Christchurch holding the fort. I could not afford to leave the children or to abandon my patients. And to tell the truth I felt it was safer.

Our struggle for the franchise was loud and public and often verbally violent. My struggle with the urges within me was just as intense. Many times I locked myself in the wardrobe while I prayed to Bede and argued with him. For he continually forgave me! I did not want forgiveness. I wanted clarity, I wanted instruction, I wanted discipline! Really, I told him one day, I'm better off saying my tables than coming to you for help! This method of self control is frequently efficacious. When he failed me I found myself speaking the wrong words:

> Her silken robe, and inner vest,
> Dropt to her feet, and ful in view
> Behold her bosom and half her side —
> A sight to dream of, not to tell!
> O shield her! shield sweet Christabel!

Christabel! The precious name would draw me back to my domestic duty. Chris was a joy. After such struggle I would clasp the child in my arms and kiss her. Innocent love! She was doing so well at school and at her music, and so was Cos. Stan was not a difficult boy. I had much to be thankful for. But why had I called her Christabel? I wanted something better for her than marriage. She was only a child.

Our third petition was successful, although Kate had to be on the alert to the very end. Our enemies even attempted to prevent the Governor from signing the Bill!

The joy, the relief, the excitement of winning our struggle! Letters and cablegrams from all over the world — recognition by world leaders — the false fawning of old enemies — the mealy-mouthed new friends . . . and a sudden loss of closeness and purpose in life. Oh, there was much to be done, mountains to move! For years we had shared this single driving, inspiring goal, and now it was replaced by rows and rows of mountains to move, one thimbleful at a time.

With that I could have coped. But my dear Kate, my angel, drained by the struggle, was ill. And worse, worse,

worse — how could I live with the knowledge? She was leaving.

$$12 \times 0 = 0$$
$$12 \times 1 = 12$$
$$12 \times 2 = 24$$
$$12 \times 3 = 36$$
$$12 \times 4 = 48$$
$$12 \times 5 = 60$$

Chapter 12

KATE

Now, Jessie, you don't want the old story of getting the vote, do you? As Mr Pember Reeves said, we simply asked the men and they gave it to us. It did take seven years and sixty thousand signatures and a thousand thousand pamphlets and letters and lectures, but we won. We could afford to be gracious about it. I allowed myself just one little jibe to a journalist from the *Graphic*.

'It certainly is not pleasant for a woman who advocates what she believes to be right and just to be called a "shrieking sister". But it is rather amusing, too. It seems such a boyish thing to drop reasonable argument, and call people names. We have always been told that it was women who could not reason, so that when men break out in this absurd manner, it seems very funny. Of course, we could retort with "beery brotherhood", or some such expression; but we have refrained.'

Yes, that gave me a little satisfaction! I freely admit we were not all of us perfectly logical ladies throughout the campaign. Ada was inclined to get carried away at times. I made allowances, knowing that in her personal life she had urgent, immediate need of certain reforms, such as the right of married women to have economic independence. She kept my feet on the ground.

We had a grand celebration in honour of all our friends, particularly Sir John Hall and Alfred Saunders. My husband was in a fine mood that evening.

'Happy it's over?' he asked Jeannie, beaming all over his face.

'My word, yes,' said Jeannie. 'Now I can spend some more

time with my family.' All the children were there that night, even the toddlers.

'Quite right too,' said Walter.

'I'll be glad of a rest,' Jeannie confided. She had that special look on her face.

'Not again!' Ada blurted out.

'I have two families, and this is one of them,' I said, reaching out to clasp hands with Ada and Lucy. 'I'll miss you all.' Walter had been trying to drag me away for the last year.

'Booked our passage,' he announced. 'Going in March.'

'You'll be there for the World Congress — our woman in London!' said Lucy.

'But you're coming back?' Ada protested. 'We have so much to do!'

I looked at William, dour and handsome as always, dominating the group by silence. I can't remember what I said to Ada. It was all rather complicated. Walter took me and Douglas home in a cab full of flowers.

Letters poured in from all over the world — not many of them in Esperanto! No, English was still the common language. The most touching letter of all came from Nelson.

I was at the printing works editing my Penelope page when William entered the little room I was using. He gave me a letter in an elegant hand, and turned to go. The writer's name meant nothing to me but when I read the first few lines I cried out, calling him back. He stood behind me and read aloud over my shoulder:

'My dear Madam,

'My heartfelt congratulations on the attainment of our object — the female Franchise. I say "our" for I have desired it earnestly for fifty years, and I have secretly worked for it since 1868. I have endeavoured to keep it before the public eye — being fortunate in possessing a friend who was the proprietor of a newspaper —'

I turned and met William's eyes. Yes, that's right! The letter was from my heroine, Femmina, revealing her identify at last. I felt an immediate strengthening of my bond with her, for I too was fortunate in my friend.

'But as my late husband was bitterly opposed to this reform — all has been done anonymously. He was a good and learned man but prejudiced. John Stuart Mill advised me to form a league, but my hands were tied — I am an old woman now, but I thank God I have been able to register myself an Elector and I now look forward with hope.

'It has long been a comfort to me to feel that stronger hands than mine were carrying on the great work — doing it openly, fearlessly, not as I ever did — like a mole. How I would have been cheered had I known you in my past life of soul's loneliness. I wish I could tell you the story of my life, and how I have suffered under men's unjust laws. I shall follow you in my thought — it is to me as though you gathered up the dark threads of my life's efforts and move the web in bright sunshine . . .'

I put my head on the desk and wept like a tree in a tempest. I wept for Mary Muller, who as Femmina had been my inspiration for long years. I wept for all the years I had had to be strong for all women, even for women stronger than I, for years of being surrounded and yet alone. William pulled me to my feet and pressed me close. Those tight arms were like steel round a barrel, they kept me from bursting apart as I wept and wept and wept. I'd never thought him capable of such compassion.

At last the storm subsided and at the exact moment he released me. I blew my nose and tidied my hair. Neither of us said anything. The moment flew out the window. Thank you, Jessie, perhaps a glass of water . . .

No matter how tired I was, there was work to be done. There were only three weeks for women to register as voters. William printed piles and piles of registration forms, not trusting the Government to do it in time. One last mammoth effort, meetings all over the country, and women turned out to vote en masse. So much for those who bleated that we forced the vote upon poor helpless women against their wills.

Before leaving Christchurch I wanted to spend as much time as possible with the dear friends who had shared the battle years. Ada continued to visit me every week; it was a hard habit to break, and why should we? She gave me regular treatment for my cramps with her healing hands. We plotted a programme of law reform.

'Ada,' I remember saying one morning as we sat on the verandah in the sunshine, 'we're facing a Hydra, you know.' We had drawn up a list of unjust laws as long as my arm, starting with the vile CD law. 'As we slice off one head of the monster another one grows in its place.'

'But we educate in the process,' Ada reminded me. 'The more we ask, the more we gain.'

I looked out at my lovely garden that I would soon be leaving. The little stream was running low in the heat. Ada wanted us to attack every clause of every unjust law.

'Why not have one grand spring-cleaning?' I said. 'Ask for a single Act that sweeps away all discrimination?' It was a wonderful, simple vision.

'Sir John does not agree.' It was almost as if she wanted to prolong the battle.

I laughed aloud. 'He says it is beyond the intellectual capacity of Parliament to understand this simple notion.'

'Granted the stupidity of men,' Ada said, 'if you want a single goal, make it the election of women to Parliament!' If I had known this project would take the rest of my life, I might have given up then and there.

I felt a little sad to be parting from Ada. I had watched her grow from a girl to a woman.

'I've a small gift for you, Kate,' she said shyly on our last morning. I was touched: she'd made a tapestry in a camellia design. 'Now you won't stay away too long? We can't carry on forever without our commander!'

I embraced her warmly. 'Dear Ada! I do need a holiday, you know.'

'That's all it is? A holiday?' she pressed me. I couldn't answer. I was so exhausted I could barely think beyond our departure.

Once on the ship, Walter became quite possessive, fussing over deck-chairs and rugs and lemonade, never leaving me alone unless I begged him. I spent as much time on deck as possible. When I managed to shoo Walter off to play quoits with Douglas, I often found myself thinking of Westcote, where Jeannie and William lived. My last visit was vivid in my mind.

Derry drove me out there, collecting Douglas from school on the way. Walter didn't come, he liked his comfort! It was a hot dry day. Along Riccarton Road we trotted, past Church Corner and into Russley Road where we met a flock of sheep going to the stock-yards. We pulled over and waited till they passed.

'On the island of Islay, Duggie, a flock of fifty sheep was considered large!' I laughed.

'Will we go to Islay?'

'We'll go to Edinburgh, dear, and Nairn. But Islay! It's the end of the earth.'

'Father says Christchurch is the end of the earth,' he said sagely.

'The earth is round,' I said, and we jogged on towards Westcote. Even from a distance it looked an idiosyncratic house. William had a way of adding rooms and sheds *ad lib* as the family multiplied. Compared with my beautifully symmetrical home it was lop-sided and confusing. Once a four-roomed cottage, it was still tiny compared with our Clyde Road house, but it had a lot of rooms!

Annie and Jeannie met us in the drive, and Derry took in our bags and a box of oranges. We waved him off in a cloud of dust.

Win was never far from her mother Jeannie. She came forward to greet us in that stiff way she still has. At fifteen she was already a great help in the house and garden. I don't need to tell you that she was always just a wee bit — well, she was never destined for higher education, though she did do a course in orcharding.

'I have made a cup of tea,' she said. Jeannie took me in by the hand and Win served us very nicely.

'So refreshing!' I said. 'And, Win, your griddle cakes are delicious. What a jewel you are.' She blushed with pleasure.

It always took me an hour or so to get used to the sheer
number of people in that house. We sat in the dining room,
a smallish room with a very long table and a fireplace big
enough to roast an ox. William's three sisters were always
busy. Lucy was working in town at the printing works,
Eleanor had a music pupil and Annie excused herself to milk
their cow. The children came and went constantly, for
Jeannie was the centre of their world. She was heavy with
the next baby, let me see, that must have been Colin, who
was her eleventh and last. Sometimes, I confess, I wonder
how Nature decides which women are fit for motherhood. It
wasn't a perfectly natural event in my case, for I had to go
out of my way to achieve it. Others like Jeannie are almost
continuously pregnant, and that doesn't seem fair. Neverthe-
less, for every child Jeannie had a patient ear, a sensible word
and a soothing touch. There was mischief but no naughtiness.
Jeannie was something of a miracle as well as my good friend.

'Is one of the children missing?' I asked eventually, when
Douglas had run off to the swings with Ken and Hubert.

Jeannie smiled. 'Edgar's living with his grandparents now.
He's working in town, you see.'

'That's kind of Mrs Smith.'

'Oh, it's no extra work for Eleanor Phoebe,' laughed
Jeannie. 'She hasn't done any housework since her forty-fifth
birthday. She lay down on the couch and said to her family,
"That's it! I've looked after you for twenty years. Now you
can look after me!" '

'So she does have a sense of humour?' I wondered.

'She was perfectly serious, I assure you.'

'I'm forty-five. Perhaps I should do the same thing.'

'You don't exactly wear yourself out with housework,'
Jeannie said drily. 'Now, shall we take a turn around the
garden?'

I excused myself, being a little tired, and Jeannie frowned.
'Are you still having those pains?' She fetched a couple of
bundles of dried herbs and told me how to make them into
a curative tea. I wrote down the instructions, since I was not
skilled in such womanly arts.

At five a prickly excitement ran through the household. Annie made the children wash their faces and change their pinnies. Win bustled round setting the big table. Macie put a bunch of flowers in the centre, and Eleanor brought out William's slippers. When young Ken was tidy he was sent to the gate to keep a look-out for the workers returning from the city.

'They're coming! They're coming!' You'd think it was royalty at least. I went out to meet them with Douglas.

Lucy looked tired. Westcote was a full hour's walk from Church Corner, which was as far as you could go on the public coach. As we entered the house Annie took her brother's coat and hat, and Lucy gave hers to Win. William was ushered in to 'his' chair in the front room, where his slippers were waiting. Macie came hurrying in with a bowl of warm water and a towel, and the two workers washed their hands. Then Win brought in two bowls of clear soup. I disrupted the ritual.

'May I have some of that lovely consommé please?' I asked Win.

She glanced at Jeannie, and hurried out to get another bowl, although I had not earned it. The others slipped away and William, Lucy and I sat in the front room together, peacefully talking over the day. At precisely six o'clock, Win knocked on the door.

'Dinner's ready, Father,' she announced.

William took his place at the head of the table, indicating I should sit at his right hand. Lucy was at his left, and the littlest children down the other end by Jeannie. Eleanor played a chord on the piano and suddenly the whole room sang:

> *Thank you for the world so sweet,*
> *Thank you for the food we eat.*
> *Thank you for the birds that sing,*
> *Thank you, God, for everything!*

Three times the grace was sung, the first time in unison,

the second time in four-part harmony, and finally with a descant by two of the girls.

As we sat down Douglas whispered to me, 'Mr Smith has got his own choir of angels!'

I caught William's eye and smiled at him, and the fourteen of us began the first of five very simple courses. The little children got quite fidgety as the hours went by, but they were not permitted to budge.

'Are you going to Professor Bickerton's lecture on *Walden* next week?' I asked William.

'Are you?' he asked. 'Oh no. You'll be gone.'

Lucy's face dropped. I didn't want sad talk so I quoted a favourite passage that might cheer everyone up. ' "Time is but the stream I go a-fishing in — I would fish in the sky, whose bottom is pebbly with stars!" '

'Maybe you'll catch a red herring,' said Jeannie.

'Oh, Thoreau is downright seductive,' William said disapprovingly. 'His view may be austere, but his language is sensuous.'

'What will Bicky say about his view of reformers?' I was determined not to hear a word about my leaving.

'Our motives spring from constipation,' William said ironically.

'Don't take it personally, William. Thoreau would be quite at home here, living off the land, getting water from a well.'

'Wouldn't you say he's implicitly a reformer himself?' We knew each other so well, William and I, that our thoughts flew from mind to mind with only the barest of verbal assistance.

'Who is?' asked Lucy, lost between Thoreau and Professor Bickerton.

'Explicitly!' I began. Out of the corner of my eye I saw little Hilda Kate playing with her spoon and giving her mother meaningful looks. She wanted her pudding! So I finished my last potato and Win and Macie began to clear the plates. 'What he deplores is the tinkerer, hacking at the branches of evil instead of striking at the root.'

'If you haven't struck at the root of evil I don't know who has,' William said warmly. That was one statement the whole family could follow. I felt rather uncomfortable under that row of admiring eyes.

'Now tell me — isn't Westcote a little Walden?'

'Hardly,' said William. 'Solitude is not a feature of life in Russley Road!'

Win put a slice of boiled raisin pudding in front of me and Lucy passed the custard sauce.

Chapter 13

KATE

It was the first time that I had stayed a whole weekend at Westcote. Their rhythms were like a hammock, awkward to clamber into at first, but quite soothing once you relaxed. On Saturday morning Jeannie and Win took a turn around the garden to plan the day's chores. I was *de trop*, and once I'd seen the roses, William summoned me for a stroll. I had slept in the girls' bunkroom, and I saw their row of mattresses on the floor of a little shed!

'Aren't they cold there?' I asked with a certain guilt.

'Not in March!' William led me to his boundary where the beehives stood, and over the neat gorse hedge we watched three racehorses doing their paces round a training track. Imagine, the puritan Smiths living next door to a racehorse breeder! The sky was striped with wrinkled clouds, frizzing at the edges like my hair when it was freshly washed.

Neither William nor I ever alluded to the time when he had embraced me, but since that moment there was always a fine web of feeling drifting between us and around us. My arms were as light as butterflies. On such a sunny, windy day, there was a chance they would catch in one of those floating cobwebs.

All right, Jessie, all right. Our departure: I'm getting to it.

'Addington is an odd word, isn't it?' I said to William apropos of nothing, and triggered off another hour of talk. Later, I wanted to save this moment and so I wrote a poem.

> *Full blown roses petition the bees*
> *And Queen and workers vote for the roses.*
> *Their votes are posted in the humming hives*

And William scrutinises with his owning eyes.
Multiplication is what happens to our lives.
I see the hard political necessity
Of adding hundreds and thousands to our ranks.
This winning mare with shiny flanks
Goes galloping over the blue-scraped sky,
White feathers streaming from her mane,
Generating clouds and foaling up on high.
Once she has joined the celestial majority
She finds she can never be single again.

We all went to the Riccarton Methodist Church on Sunday morning. Jeannie took pride in the honest wooden building, having worked mightily at fund-raising. Walter came to collect us all; I wasn't up to the walk. In the congregation were the Ballantynes, Cannons, Broughtons and Taylors, and there were horse-trainers, stable hands and jockeys, labourers and tradespeople. I felt quite at home. The singing was a treat! Eleanor played the organ and William conducted the choir which included half his family.

We parted in the church grounds after the service.

Our tiny family, Walter and Douglas and I, returned to Clyde Road. The emptiness, the silence were quite shocking. I was silent too. It seemed my lovely house was dead. It was built for meetings of the WCTU and the Franchise League. I felt too tired to breathe life into it and less unhappy to be leaving.

We joined the ship in Wellington, where I was honoured by a small gathering of women. I read bewilderment in their faces.

One young woman gave a speech that was almost bitter, speaking as if I were gone already. 'We have entertained an angel unawares and treated her like a scullery maid. Mrs Sheppard is leaving and that is our rightful punishment. I pray that the women of Great Britain accord her the honour she deserves.'

It was perfectly absurd and I told them so. 'Ladies, if I look a little pale tonight, please do not assume responsibility!

Blame the forces of Nature, for we had a very rough crossing of Cook Strait.'

In Sydney, Perth and Ceylon the ship was invaded by delegations bearing exotic flowers and fruits. Once I overcame my surprise I accepted their tributes on behalf of all New Zealand women. They prepared me for my reception in Great Britain, where I was given a heroine's welcome, and I began to grasp the real magnitude of our achievement. All delegates to the World Congress were warmly welcomed by the Lord Mayor of London, by Lady Henry Somerset and Lady Aberdeen, by Miss Frances Willard, by the great, the noble and the blessed. Even so, I was specially honoured. I remember, for instance, standing on the platform in the Queen's Hall before an audience of thousands — when all at once they rose en masse and waved their white handkerchiefs! After the Congress I gave lectures in England and Scotland and grew quite used to that ocean of handkerchiefs, and to the roar of cheers.

I feared growing swell-headed, Jessie, and do you know how I overcame this? I pictured my friends alongside me on the platform, Ada on my right hand, for she humbled me most. I have always been a privileged woman, even a spoiled woman, and the last thing I deserved was admiration.

From the moment we arrived in England I found myself in great demand, advising on tactics and dealing out courage. I walked, I talked, I smiled; I was living proof that women could achieve the franchise. I hate to say this, but I received additional adulation purely because I was a normal woman, wearing a dress, moving as women are expected to move. One reporter gushingly called me 'the sweetest, neatest most womanly woman one could hope to meet'. Some hoped, some feared, all expected that I would sport a hearty beard and hornrimmed spectacles and coarse tweed trousers, and shriek like a banshee.

Our domestic arrangements were only partly satisfactory. We took Douglas to a school in Surrey, where he was very happy and very popular. Walter and I took up residence in his old place in Bath. Dear, oh dear! He was so proud of it.

It was a large apartment not very far from the cathedral. I thought the building quite hideous, a great stone blotch that couldn't decide whether to be Gothic or Norman or modern. Still it had a pleasant outlook over the river and a park with the traditional tide of daffodils, a cramped and corseted version of Hagley Park. His friends and relatives came to visit and he enjoyed the newspapers.

'Walter, could we exchange our apartment for something on the ground floor?' I asked him one day when his gout was playing up and I wasn't at my strongest.

'Stuff and nonsense! It's good exercise,' he blustered. If we'd had a house with its toes on the ground I might have felt more at home.

At first he accompanied me on my excursions, glowing with pride at all the praise. But then he got the sulks.

'You are coming to Bristol with me aren't you dear?' I asked.

'All these meetings are the same. What's the point?'

'Oh, come now,' I chivvied him. 'The people are different!'

'I like the people of Bath best,' he said, and that was that.

I could partly understand his feelings as the meetings were chiefly for women. But Walter was representative of a thousand other husbands, giving support even when he really didn't understand all the fuss — he deserved credit for that. What's more, Walter was responsible for our greatest source of fund-raising, the refreshment tent at the annual Agricultural and Pastoral Shows. But there, he didn't want to be thanked. I came home from Bristol a couple of days later, encumbered as usual with bouquets.

'How was it, my dear?' Walter looked up amiably from his *Times*.

'Wonderful,' I said. 'I learned a lot. As usual they expected me to have horns and hooves . . .'

'Very nice, dear. And now look here, I say, I want you to see the specialist in London this week.'

I was willing enough, although I postponed the operation until the end of the year.

After the event Walter seemed positively pleased to have me laid up. He fussed round the cook urging her to concoct me little treats. His sister found us a capable nurse, but I longed for Ada's magic fingertips. I could almost imagine them soothing the scar when it itched. Oh, England! I hate even the memory of that time, looking out the window through perpetual drizzle at those bleak winter trees and that mushy lawn. It irritated me to see the Avon flowing sluggishly below me and to know it was not my Avon! Even spring failed to delight me; the daffodils reminded me of home.

The mail from New Zealand was cheering. Our plans bore fruit when our oldest member went to the national WCTU convention in Wellington, on a special mission. The sea trip to the North Island was quite an adventure for her! She was the perfect ambassador, and succeeded in convincing the convention that we needed our own magazine. All the same, Lucy wrote that there was much opposition to the idea. 'It's too soon, it's not necessary, we can't afford it, etc.' We won through! It was so exciting to receive that first *White Ribbon* off William's press. I had been appointed editor and was posting off my editorials and articles and news from Britain, but I could hardly oversee the whole process from the other side of the world indefinitely.

In Douglas's summer holidays he and Walter and I made the promised journey to Scotland, combining it with visits to new friends like Lady Aberdeen. I hoped that Scotland would heal me, Scotland where all things still seemed possible. England was so rigid. But my home-coming was tinged with sadness. I'd lived longer in Christchurch than in Scotland now, and Christchurch was home. Islay was a dream of sheep and white-caps. Nairn had changed in ways I did not like. Christchurch beckoned me home.

Meanwhile, Lady Aberdeen was urging me to establish a National Council of Women in New Zealand, and I was corresponding with Ada and Lady Stout on the matter. As the weather cooled down in Britain things were coming to the boil on the other side of the world.

Ada sent me hot news from the CWI. 'We are organising a Women's Convention for next April, with delegates from every political group. Imagine, Kate, all of New Zealand's most radical women gathered together in one place! Please be home in plenty of time . . .'

Lucy sent me similar messages about the *White Ribbon*. They needed me!

'I must go home,' I said to Walter for the hundredth time.

'We are home.' Oh, he was impossible sometimes!

'It certainly isn't my home!'

'I couldn't live in Scotland, dear.'

'Oh, don't be ridiculous. We've lived together in Christchurch for twenty-three years.'

'Don't you like Bath?' he said pathetically.

For once I lost my temper with him. 'Bath is England. So final and so smug! I'd rather have a place that's being invented, changing!' I couldn't make myself understood; we were too far apart on this. His precious ring of houses was a barricade against change.

'If something is perfect,' he said mildly, 'there's no need for change.'

'If the English make something "perfect", they repeat it ad nauseum! There's no room to move — oh no, I do not like Bath, Walter. It's the embodiment of everything I do not like.'

Walter made a little joke. 'I suppose you prefer the graceful proportions of Westcote?'

In truth, that higgledy-piggledy cottage was closer to my heart. 'Westcote fits no category. It's not locked into this vile English class system.'

'Don't tell me there's no class structure in Christchurch! The chimes will never be stopped for a cousin of Ada Wells.' It was an old quip dating from his city council days, when Lady Barker demanded silence for her cousin lying ill at the Clarendon Hotel and the Post Office clock was silenced.

'Of course there is! There are the Griggs and the Murphys and there always will be. But there's also a vacuum where people can meet.'

109

'You haven't recuperated properly yet,' he quibbled.

'If you're so concerned about my health take me out of this horrible climate!'

'At least let Douglas finish the term at school.'

'Oh, sit in your Bath and stew!' I said. 'I'm going home.'

I bought our passages and Walter gave in grudgingly.

That was a joyful arrival! I was back among my old friends who knew me as a human being, not as a symbol. I was Kate once again and not Mrs Sheppard the suffragette. Nobody touched my cloak and expected to be healed. Here were just my friends and family, expecting me to roll up my sleeves and get on with the job.

Chapter 14

KATE

You were there, Jessie! Wasn't it thrilling? To sit at those huge polished tables in the Provincial Chambers as if we were a real governing body? Bring me the photo from the mantelpiece. Yes, that one — the very first National Council of Women. Don't we look old-fashioned in those high necks and leg o'mutton sleeves! Ada had taken her skirts up several inches, but she was the odd one out. There you are in the back row, looking rather startled I always think. There's our one and only Maori member, although nobody ever drew attention to the fact. That would have been considered bad taste, because we thought the Maori race was dying out.

The WCTU did a lot of work with Maori women, you know, and we had a column in Maori in the *White Ribbon*. But in the NCW we simply assumed that all women belonged together, because the law ground us all down equally. Ever since the franchise work I have known what race of people I belong to. It's the race of women, the woman race. I couldn't tell you even now whether I feel Scottish or British or New Zealandish, but I do know I am a woman.

Don't laugh it off! It was a great achievement, discovering the race of women. Surely you felt it too, that pride in belonging?

Look at William's mother on the left! Just like Queen Victoria, making sure we don't get up to mischief. I'm in the centre, perching with a most temporary air. And dear Ada in that schoolish dress with her head on one side — listening for worms, I called that. You can see how her face was a perfect oval, can't you? Not that beauty is important of course. Ada's sitting at my feet, leaning against my knee, and young Clara Alley beside her. Remember how they called us the Parliament of Hens, and Clara the pretty little chicken? Do you recognise Wilhelmina Sheriff Bain on the right of Ada? My word, those bright eyes! See that young brain buzzing!

Lucy and Eleanor weren't delegates, but they were there. We didn't see much of Jeannie that week. She said she had enough on her plate and I have an idea it was all a wee bit too radical for her.

We really began with a bang! You read your splendid poem, 'The Women's Battle March'. Yes, Ada made sure we had some culture, first poetry and then art. Some of us visited Mr Van der Velden in his studio to see his masterpiece, 'The Sorrowful Future'. He gave us a lecture and Ada was quite carried away by the sad little girl facing poverty and exploitation. She convinced us that the painting should be bought by the state, but the next day one of our older members claimed she had misheard Ada's motion, not having her ear trumpet in place, and we used that as an excuse to quietly reverse our decision. Of course the real reason was that Ada had overstepped the boundaries of good sense. It was not for us to tell the Government what paintings to purchase.

The original idea was that Lady Stout should be president of the National Council of Women, but somehow it turned out to be me. I think everyone knew that Ada and I would be doing all the work, and they didn't see any need for a figurehead, which was rather an English notion. As it turned out, Anna Stout took umbrage later on at some of our activities. I didn't care what label they gave me as long as I was able to work at the centre. Ada was unanimously elected secretary. I can see her now, her hand flashing over that minute book, only stopping when she wanted to say her own piece.

The country was astounded to discover what we had in mind.

'That a minimum wage be established by law.'

'That the conditions of divorce for men and women be made equal.'

'That our treatment of criminals is not satisfactory.'

'That the land of any country belongs to the people.'

'That capital punishment be abolished.'

'That the age of consent be raised to twenty-one years.'

And for our grand finale: 'That absolute equality be the law of the land for both men and women.'

Jessie, are people interested in these things nowadays? Do you think they care? Or am I just a lone mermaid singing to myself on a rock in the middle of the ocean? Yet this was surely the most influential group of women ever to band together in New Zealand. As Ada said, it was 'the beginning of child welfare, old age pensions, better conditions in orphanages and the destruction of bumbledom in general — it was those meetings that sowed the seed of progressive ideals'. The country was startled to find that we women had clear ideas about legal matters, and could speak eloquently in a formal meeting. There I go again, singing to myself. I'll change the subject.

After the excitement of the convention it was back to work. Ada came to Clyde Road on Tuesday mornings to deal with the NCW correspondence. It became our custom to begin these sessions with a massage.

'It is your first duty to regain your health, and not just for selfish reasons,' she argued persuasively. 'Your loved ones depend on you.'

I was happy to submit. Ada's treatment was not superficial, but spiritual.

'A perfectly healthy person is unconscious of being hampered by a body,' she said as she warmed the olive oil and closed the bedroom windows.

'I'm not certain I would like that,' I admitted, although my body was the site of all my various aches and pains.

'All dis-ease,' Ada continued, warming towels by the fire, 'is caused by obstructions and poisons built up in the system.' She tucked a large warm towel under me. 'With any person but you I might suspect some sin or negative thought which needs to be expiated.'

'Do you never lose heart, Ada?'

She shook her head. 'That is simply not permitted.'

'How do you stop yourself?'

'I lock myself in a closet and close my eyes. I deliberately bar the door against all base thoughts and commune with the source of life. Now hush. Put your mind in touch with Power, Truth, Peace, Righteousness, Beauty, and Joy.'

Some people complained that Ada's rubbing was painful, but with me her touch was perfect. It was as if we were one being, pure spirit. Relentlessly her fingertips found out the impurities in my system and kneaded them into a palpable knot. The natural electricity in my body built up and up until it was discharged in a shudder which wracked my frame. Often tears would flow and wash away the ugliness within. For she was quite wrong to admire me as she did. I was far from perfect.

After our health session I dressed and before tackling the letters we shared a pot of weak tea.

'They've asked me to be president of the Women's Christian Temperance Union,' I told her casually one morning. 'Not just for Christchurch but for all of New Zealand.'

'Then take it!' she reproved me. 'Think of the influence!'

'I've refused higher honours than that, Ada,' I pointed out with some amusement. 'If the World Congress had their way I'd be conducting the franchise struggle for the entire world.'

A haunted look crossed her face. 'Weren't you tempted?'

'Not for a moment. It seemed a most unwieldly task.'

'I would have helped you.' She was so dedicated.

'I prefer to tackle challenges that I can win, don't you?'

'I don't think I know the difference,' Ada said. 'I want what I want, and that's what I fight for.'

'I shall plead ill-health to the WCTU so I don't offend them,' I decided. 'I want a sharp focus. I'll concentrate on the NCW and *The White Ribbon*.'

Don't you think *The White Ribbon* was a marvellous name for a magazine? William Smith set aside one room in his printing works for our use. We looped white ribbons around the walls. He thought this very frivolous! Never was a newspaper set up with clearer goals. In fact, we had one goal only: absolute equality for women.

Alfred Saunders had lost his seat in the House. One afternoon William showed him into our office with a very long face.

'Alfred!' I rose and grasped his rough brown hands. 'What news of the by-election?'

William fetched another chair and Alfred sat down heavily, looking every one of his seventy-six years.

'Lost out by eleven votes. They don't want an old fogey like me any more.'

'You're an institution!' William protested.

'A dinosaur,' Alfred contradicted him. He looked around at the ribbons festooning the walls and his old grin came back, the one that changed his face from a grumpy dwarf's to a jester's. 'Just as well I'm leaving. I don't like the thought of women in the House, not even you, Kate.'

'It's only fair and right,' I argued. 'And it will happen.'

'The best MPs will grant your every whim,' he said tetchily.

'How delightful!' I teased. 'That'll be a change.'

'It's not good! Parliament is the place for rigorous argument. And how are you going to deal with the likes of Mr Fish?'

William exploded. 'That vile man! His language!'

'No doubt if he had to deliver his insults face to face he would modify them somewhat,' I answered quite serenely.

'No no, you don't want women in Parliament. I've got a better solution: an Upper House composed entirely of women.'

'Oh, Alfred, don't be absurd. That's pie in the sky.'

For once Alfred didn't answer me back. He slumped in his chair and I fetched him a glass of cold water. I was somehow not surprised when he told us quietly, 'Rhoda's not well.' I felt a great sympathy. Alfred relied on her so much and was the kindest of husbands. 'Not all women want to be a help-meet,' he said oddly, and Ada chose that moment to arrive with her Home Page.

I couldn't see any connection between Alfred's last two remarks. He seemed unwilling to explain, so William began talking, perhaps to give our old champion a breathing space. It was the most dislocated conversation, and for once I simply listened.

'But that is what women are for,' said William. 'Help-meets. And the right to enter Parliament is simply the last, inevitable step in making women fitting mates for men. Men don't want useless dolls, we want intelligent, informed, responsible, useful helpmeets.' Although his sisters were unmarried he still considered they were on the earth to help a man — namely William Sidney Smith!

'Men will benefit greatly when women get into the House,' said Ada. 'The husband of a Member of Parliament will indeed be a privileged man.' I had a pretty good idea what Ada really thought of men, for she sometimes implied we'd be better off without them! But even Ada could hardly say that out loud in public. 'Women are not dominated by the demon of greed,' she continued. 'Our concerns are for the welfare of every age group and either sex. The whole nation will profit and therefore men will profit.'

'Oh, Ada, old friend,' said Alfred, finally drawn into the discussion, 'why dress up your wants in white robes? Isn't it enough to say you are human? I hate to hear you begging for our approval. You have the right to live for yourself alone.'

'But Alfred, men need women,' William said with authority.

'I can see that,' said Alfred. 'But do women always need men? Some women prefer to live without men, and why shouldn't they?'

It was Alfred, not Ada, who spoke on behalf of women. Where did he get this understanding? Was he thinking about his wife? I kept silent, watching my friends. What led them to utter these particular ideas, and to hide others? They were all following private paths of thought, and so was I, for my own domestic life was balanced precariously on the edge of a cliff. I was amazed that we four people could have worked together so closely for so long.

Alfred and I went down the stairs and out to the cab stand.

'Give Rhoda my love,' I told him, and kissed his cheek right there on the street, much to the shock of the passers-by.

Back in the office I read Ada's Home Page. Today her subject was smallpox. 'The pores of the skin must be opened, and the abdomen, the source of fermentation, must be cooled . . .' Her column was immensely popular. She knew so much and she was afraid of nothing.

'I quite agree about compulsory vaccination of babies,' William was telling her. That amused me; Ada didn't care whether he agreed with her or not! 'It's a form of torture for the poor. But is it strictly accurate to say a week of your treatment will remove all danger? I shall alter that "will" to "should".'

'You'll do nothing of the sort. You're not the editor!'

I was tempted to let them fight it out but as usual I intervened.

'William?' I nodded at him and he left us to it. 'Ada, dear, could you try and be nice to William?'

'I am nice! But I won't lick his boots.'

Oh, I loved those times! The smell of the printing ink, the sound of the press going hard at it, and the first copy drying in front of our eyes. I even enjoyed the spats between William and Ada. They were part of the excitement. We were a family again. Jeannie was in charge of our finance, and together we tramped the city drumming up advertising. Needless to say, Beath's took a regular half-page. Jeannie was also responsible for articles on hygiene. Sometimes she and Ada trod on each other's toes, and Jeannie was always the one to give way.

We all promoted sensible dress. One day my sister burst in my front door looking quite bizarre.

'Isy! What on earth is that?'

She twirled around in front of me. 'Divided skirt for ease of movement on the bicycle — just what you need, Kate! And no waist, no constriction round the vital organs. It hangs from the shoulders, see?'

'Very ingenious,' I said.

She popped me on the head with a big envelope. 'Here's

a paper pattern for your dressmaker.'

'You know perfectly well I wouldn't be seen dead in that rig-out, darling. I approve in principle, though.'

'And you'll urge every other woman to wear it.' She knew me well.

'If you can find me a version that looks pretty,' I suggested without much hope.

'Pretty for the men?' Isy taunted. 'One day you'll catch your skirt in a wheel and it'll serve you right!'

When she left the house was very quiet. On the whole I preferred the days I spent in the city.

What a momentous year that was! In the December issue Ada wrote a Christmas message that struck me to the heart.

> *Prove that in yourself is a fountain of joy.*
> *Do not give the whole thought to material things.*
> *Act upon the thought that the current of Love*
> *which never ceases flowing may find through you*
> *a channel . . .*

The current of Love flowed through me like the Waimakariri River in full flood. Eventually Walter decided to leave New Zealand; that was the inevitable culmination of our marriage. Douglas helped shape the decision. He wanted to finish his schooling at Christchurch Boys' High School, then go to university in England. That seemed fair and reasonable. The agreement cost me much anguish and yet I could see no other way.

Chapter 15

KATE

I missed my old teddy-bear of a husband. We didn't speak of separation as a marital condition but as a temporary arrangement. Walter's departure was noted as 'a visit Home', but all our friends knew the real state of affairs.

We lived in different elements. It was a wonder we blended so smoothly for so long, when he liked a bathroom and I liked the cold wild sea. I'm speaking metaphorically, of course, for we had quite a good bathroom in Clyde Road, and the sea was only four or five miles away. But Canterbury is ferocious — don't you agree, Jessie? A place of extremes, hot mad winds, clammy fogs, sparkling frosts. I've grown used to it. The town is become quite tame nowadays, but when I was young it was as raw as the weather.

Now I know what you're thinking: there I was in my beautiful white house protected from all hardship by my income and my servants — and I'm talking about life being raw! Yes, true, to all appearances I was no pioneer. I was what they called a 'womanly woman' with all the social graces. But that's not how I felt inside.

Douglas adjusted quickly to the new situation. He was well liked at school, and much involved in cricket and rugby and dancing lessons and the school debating society. At the end of the day we always had great talks and I would help him with his prep. He was a very delightful companion, a darling. He looked forward to going to England for university, after which I hoped he would settle in New Zealand.

On Sundays we went to Trinity Church, after which there was a family dinner at George and Marie's house, complete with news bulletins from Frank, who had moved to Rotorua and started an auctioneering business. Isy and I were still close but we were going our different ways, even before she went to Auckland. She helped to establish a Women's Club, and I had lunch there now and then to please her. But I didn't need a club: I had the WCTU and the NCW and the CWI, I had Jeannie and Annie and Lucy and always I had Ada by my side.

It was exciting to watch the maturing of Ada. She helped set up the Children's Aid Society for poor and neglected children. My own instinct was not to rush in and care for these children, admirable though that was; I wanted to start at the other end.

'If married women had a share of their husband's income,' I pointed out to Ada, 'half these problems would vanish overnight. The mothers could take care of their own children.'

Ada and I travelled together to the annual conventions of the NCW, to Dunedin, Wellington, Napier, Auckland and Wanganui. It was our job to decide on the major speeches. At first we spoke with a single voice, but soon we developed separate styles and concerns. Our longest journey was to Auckland for the 1899 meeting, where we stayed with Isy. Ada had a speech on 'Our Duty to the Unfit', and I on 'The Economic Independence of Married Women', elaborating on her speech of the previous year. We tried to read them on the last leg of our trip but the movement of the coach made it difficult.

'Ada,' I said, 'I'll have to introduce your speech. Do you think this is a fair summary? "Our duty to the unfit is to place them in positions of independence where they may develop character as well as provide for their daily wants."'

She looked quite worried. 'You haven't mentioned the equitable distribution of wealth, or the municipal factories.'

'Do you think the women of Auckland are ready for the ideas of Marx and Engels?' I asked her as we bounced along.

'Never mind if they're ready! We don't need the horrors of private industry here, thank you very much, not in this beautiful new country.' We were both entranced by Egmont, the lovely mountain receding behind us.

'Writing a speech is very different from writing an essay,' I mused as if to myself. 'Over the years I have learned a few tricks. I like to sweeten the pill with anecdotes, and I feel it is quite legitimate to begin and end with the masculine point of view.'

'I know your style, Kate! I call it the one, two, three approach,' Ada chuckled. 'I expect you have fourteen reasons why married women need an independent income, and a sound retort for every opposing argument.'

As a matter of fact I was trying to give her some hints, but Ada always felt she knew best.

When she addressed the NCW all my reservations were justified. I usually tried to answer the question 'Why?' Ada skated rapidly over the *why* and told us in laborious detail *how* we might achieve her personal vision. Her argument grew like a nest of ants. Her summary alone included eleven points. Free Kindergartens, Municipal Co-operative Industrial Farms, the sterilisation of unfit parents, the daily routine for prostitutes — oh, my head was spinning! Her speech was twice as long as mine. It was the quality of her mind endlessly to multiply. She could not stop, she couldn't put fences around her vision. I heard fifteen 'shoulds' in three minutes. Oh dear.

Yet Ada had the audience gripped. Her voice rang, her eyes shone with this wonderful certainty of hers! Sheer enthusiasm lay behind the proliferation of detail. Yes yes, some did find it irritating, but to me it was touching. She was thirty-six, yet she seemed so very young with all her ideals on display.

Yes, she was important to me. We did so much together. And yet there were problems because of her very constancy, her devotion. She couldn't get on with my other friends. With Walter gone I felt more and more like a rope, strained and fraying in an endless tug of war. What do I mean? Well, this sort of thing. One day I was in our office at the printing works with Jeannie and William. We needed a filler for page three, and we were all making suggestions.

'I think we should reprint this old poem,' I decided at last.

'Women's Work'. Jeannie and I gave it a comical reading, complete with curtseys and tragic faces.

> *What can a helpless female do?*
> *Rock the cradle and bake and brew.*
> *Or live in one room with an invalid cousin,*
> *Or sew shop shirts for a dollar a dozen,*
> *Or please some man by looking sweet,*
> *Or please him by giving him things to eat,*
> *Or please him by asking much advice,*
> *And thinking whatever he does is nice.*

At which point I couldn't help giggling. 'Sir, is this poem all right, sir?' I asked with sickly sweetness.

'Twenty-two lines,' William counted. 'And it still needs saying.'

'What a very nice decision,' I said. He was too serious for words! 'I'm just a poor helpless woman. You can tell from the bumps on my head.' I took Jeannie's hand and guided it over my skull.

'Oh oh oh!' said Jeannie. 'What have we here? Ladies and gentlemen, the largest Bump of Determination in the Southern Hemisphere! No wonder those curls won't stay put.'

I felt her friendly little hands leave my head to be replaced by William's. One big hand held my skull while the other one explored the famous bump.

'I think it's getting larger,' he announced.

'It's very tender today,' I said.

'Why's that, I wonder?'

At that moment Ada came in and she glared. 'I'm here now, I'll take over!' she announced imperiously, and knocked William's hands away. Her fingers began a massage which was more like a brutal assault. She couldn't bear anyone else to lay hands on me.

'No, Ada! I don't have a headache.' I removed her hands. 'We were just playing.'

I couldn't blame her for looking sceptical. William was

hardly a playful man, yet he always provoked the naughtiness in me. Jeannie was full of fun, but William couldn't tolerate her jokes except when I was present. We were three quite different people when we got together in our trio.

'Could I see you alone?' Ada pulled out some papers with obvious irritation, and William and Jeannie left the room. 'It's my Home Page. It's very personal this time.'

I sat down and skimmed through her manuscript. ' "How often are our children launched on the rude waves of life's sea with never a word in explanation of the wondrous meaning of sex . . . No thoughtful child believes the story of the cabbage or the stork . . . Oh, mothers! it is time to forbear this lying and betake ourselves to truth. And yet this simple duty seems hard to most of us, so terribly akin, from the perversion of our thought, seem sex and sin . . ." Why, this is excellent, Ada!'

'Not too daring?'

'No, it's wholesome and it's timely.'

'You can see why it had to be read in privacy.'

'Not honestly,' I answered. 'William can hardly set the type without reading it, can he?'

'It's a talk to mothers, not fathers,' said Ada tetchily. 'And it's a women's magazine. I find it very difficult working with William.'

I had noticed. 'Without William there would be no *White Ribbon*. Without William we might not even have the vote!' She knew very well that no other printer in Christchurch would have handled the jobs we gave him. I was about to remind her of the Scottish gentleman who called *The White Ribbon* 'a bomb in my suitcase' — but I remembered that this too had incited her jealousy at the time and was best forgotten. I resented having to censor my thoughts.

'Oh, come now!' she protested.

'Who printed our pamphlets? And the petition forms, and the registration forms? Who exploded Seddon's little plot over the electoral rolls? Who provides this office? Who wrote the history of the franchise?' I found it very tiresome reciting my little catechism yet again.

'Well, Kate, you know best.' That was as close as Ada ever came to an apology. She was a proud woman!

The time came that I had been dreading, time for my son to depart for England. The prospect filled me with utter desolation, but I took pains to conceal the fact from Douglas. He was fizzing with excitement.

'You'll come over and see me soon, Mother?' he urged me often. He did love me so.

'Of course, my darling, and Father will bring you back for a visit too.'

Fortunately, Alfred Saunders, newly widowed, was to travel on the same ship. He stayed with us the night before they sailed. He was in a state of hectic confusion, talking randomly about his life, from his childhood in Salisbury to Rhoda's death. His company kept me from weeping shamefully at the imminent loss of my sweet son.

After dinner Douglas was the first to retire. When he kissed me good night I almost disgraced myself. I turned back to Alfred who was settled by the fire as if he were preparing to stay up all night.

'Alfred! You are in a strange state. Are you sure this journey is wise?' Alfred's eyes evaded mine and I swear that for the first time in his life he looked almost sly. I sat beside him and clasped his hands. 'We are old friends,' I reminded him. 'You're keeping something from me.'

His weather-beaten face crinkled enigmatically in its frame of wild grey curls. After a little hesitation he told me the most remarkable tale, which strongly influenced me in making my own great decision.

'You know I adored my mother, Kate,' he began in a different, quite earnest manner. 'She was devout and affectionate, and made up in great measure for the tyranny of our father. As far as I'm concerned, she had only two faults. Firstly, she was tone deaf. And secondly, she gave us no guidance on the choice of our life partners.'

I sat up alertly in my chair. Alfred knew this would interest me in a most personal manner.

'We lived in the country, where we had little opportunity

124

to mix with people of our own age. The only young people to visit our home were parsons, and our many cousins. My sisters were constantly getting offers of marriage from curates! We had thirty-two cousins on my mother's side alone, and on high holidays we would all get together for a few days' celebration.

'My parents told us it was utterly forbidden for cousins to marry. Yet we were healthy, normal young persons, susceptible to the natural excitements of our occasional social life. Many of us fell in love. All the ingredients of the romantic novel were there, except for the happy ending. Our upbringing led most of us to loneliness and disappointment. Of the unhappy thirty-two, one-third never married, a few married very badly indeed, and scarcely any married well.'

'And you, dear Alfred?' I asked delicately as he paused for rather a long time.

He met my gaze, and in those dangerously honest eyes I read his answer. It was the story of my own marriage, a story of kindness and comfort, and no joy.

'Why are you travelling so suddenly to England? You must have booked your passage —' The thought was too crude to express: as soon as Rhoda's breath left her body.

'My cousin Sarah has had an operation. She was my childhood playmate, the one I should have married.'

'Was that why you left England in the first place?' I wondered.

'Only partly. I couldn't imagine ever being happy there. My father was impossible to work for, and angry if I struck out on my own . . .' He drifted into his thoughts.

'And now?'

'Now I know that those restrictions were wicked nonsense. I'm going to care for her, live with her, and marry her if she'll have me.'

I was so touched. I sat at his feet and put my head on his knees. I expect I was in an emotional mood.

'And all these years — do you regret them?'

Alfred was silent. My pent-up tears began to flow for him. A lifetime spent away from the woman of his heart!

When he reached England he married his Sarah immediately. He was nearly eighty. His story and his actions set me pondering over my own life.

Chapter 16

KATE

The house was blank without Douglas. I sometimes found myself wandering hopefully from room to room in a sort of daze. His absence forced me to confront my situation, my peculiar dilemma.

It was summer. That hot, bright Christmas was a cold dark time for my soul. I was not lacking loving company, of course, even though in Christchurch my immediate family had dwindled to my sister Marie and George and their children and grandchildren, and my brother Robert's widow and children. But family celebrations and visits to Westcote only heightened my anxiety. I wrote a poem about the torment I was going through. I couldn't get it to make sense, and no wonder.

> *Photographs in silver frames,*
> *Sweet mementoes and precious names,*
> *Teas and flowers without thorns,*
> *Trees and treasures on the lawns.*
> *I am served asleep and awake*
> *By Poppy and Derry and Cook.*
> *I rob them of their dignity,*
> *I pay them money to look after me.*
> *No wonder I am bemused.*
> *I am serving the unfit and the abused*
> *Yet I am being carried.*
> *I serve the women who are married*
> *Yet I am living alone and almost happy*
> *With only Cook and Derry and Poppy.*
> *I serve the poor and the small,*

Yet I am rich and I am tall.
It is for others that I endorse
A revolution in our country's laws.

To be the perfect servant of tomorrow
I have shouldered a private sorrow.
So that people hear what I have to say
I strangle in the knots of yesterday.
Knots, nots, knots, I lie in bed
Hearing a kind of madness in my head.

I am fifty-two and past my prime.
Will I be eighty before I climb
Out of the well, out of the bath?
I want to walk that broader path
I've been preparing all my life.
I am more and also less than a wife.
I can't even make myself a cup of tea.
Can I cook up a life that will nourish me?

Ada helped me a great deal, although unwittingly. Her Home Page always showed a terrible courage. I re-read all she had written, and often a sentence would grab my eye like a hook.

Despondency should be carefully avoided.
If ye know, happy are ye if ye do.
If life is to be intelligently lived by us, we must avoid getting into ruts as we would shun soul loss.
Until women throw off the chains that drag them down . . .

I was not myself. I hardly knew what these random sentences meant. I read them completely out of context. But some little voice in my head would call out, Yes! Yes!

But yes to what? What I desired I dared not utter even to myself. I knew, but did not know.

That year, 1900, the National Council of Women met in Dunedin. In my presidential address I suggested that we might be growing apathetic and selfish, but in truth I was addressing myself. I also spoke of illegitimacy. I felt this was one of the cruelest blows that could befall a child; no happy home, the mother taking all the burden, the father escaping all blame, and a legal stigma into the bargain. They accepted this part of my speech without any fuss. The explosions came later.

The week began mildly with an editorial in the *Otago Daily Times* saying my address was 'quiet, practical, moderate, perspicuous and lofty' and 'sound and sweet and wise'. I tell you this with some irritation. Why are the arguments not sufficient in themselves? Why must the journalist always respond so very personally? Yes, that includes you, Jessie!

As the convention developed, so did the excitement. There was the usual outrage over all those 'nasty' subjects, like illegitimacy and the CD Act. Then the married men of Dunedin arose in wrath to assure us they were not immoral, oh no! There was grave tut-tutting (again) over our policy of economic equality for married women and because we wanted women in the House. A journalist scoffed at the New Woman, preferring the old model who did not quote Emerson. But all this was tolerable. Indeed, it was only too effective in attracting the public.

The trouble arose when Wilhelmina Sherrif Bain gave her speech on Peace and Arbitration. What an uproar! The audience was like a box of explosives. At the first hint that war might not be a good thing, the shouting started.

'Tell me ladies,' railed one heckler. 'Are you praying for a British victory in South Africa?'

'Certainly not!' said Miss Sherrif Bain.

Ada stood up and tried to shout over the hullabaloo. 'I cannot pray for the success of the British and I cannot pray for the success of the Boers. They are both equally wrong.'

'Traitor!' somebody bellowed. 'You come to our fair city, you sit in our Council Hall, and you forget you are our guests!'

'Ship them out!' came the call from the audience. It was a fiasco.

The next morning we received a letter by messenger.

'Your paper on Peace and Arbitration and the discussion thereon have so astounded me as a loyal British subject, I positively refuse to take the chair at your meeting tomorrow night. I am, etc., R. Chisholm, Mayor.'

'Good riddance,' said Ada.

'We must explain,' I insisted. 'He wasn't even there!'

'No apology! We've done nothing wrong.'

'Ada, you were a trifle tactless,' I said carefully.

'We've always condemned war, that's our job!'

'But in wartime we must tread softly.'

'Oh, Kate!' Ada was so exasperated. 'Why must everybody, everywhere, at every time love and adore Mrs Kate Sheppard? Can't you tolerate anything less?'

I quietly absorbed her remark. Once again her words caught at my soul and helped me in my great decision.

We talked to the mayor to no effect. We wrote to the paper condemning war in general but denying we were opposed to the Boer War in particular. It was a slippery position and I resolved to take more care in future.

By the end of the convention I had made the decision that had been tormenting me. Ada was the first person I told. Her reaction was not sympathetic, and this was very illuminating for me. If my close friend had difficulty accepting my resolution, how much more persuasive I should have to be with others!

When we returned to Christchurch I felt more strong, more sure. I did not delay. After discussions with William I went to visit my big sister in Riccarton Road.

'How wise you were to marry George Beath,' I began when the maid had brought our morning tea.

Marie smiled. 'I take it you're not just talking of practical matters?' Her well-contented glance took in the drawing room, where everything was built to last.

'He's a dear, and you're well matched,' I said frankly.

'My only worry is his health. He's seventy-three, you know.'

'But you're happy?' I wanted her to be happy.

She glowed with satisfaction, *mater familias* incarnate.

'Now, Kate, you didn't come here to ask me that!'

I stalked around her room, toying with trinkets. Marie didn't push me but she didn't make it easy either.

'I've decided to go and live with Jeannie and William Smith,' I eventually announced, and watched shock, hurt and disapproval make chaos of her kind face. She led me back to the sofa like an invalid.

'Dear, I know you're lonely,' she said. 'Why not live with us?'

'You haven't got room.'

She spoke quite angrily. 'We've got three times as much as the Smiths! Kate, what is this? A communal experiment like Professor Bickerton's?'

'Of course not! At least — it's just what I want, Marie.'

She looked at me shrewdly. 'You? You alone? What about everyone else? What about me?'

I took her hand calmly. 'It really does concern just me and Jeannie and William, but I will feel much happier if you can accept it.'

She sighed. 'A thousand times in the past your views have horrified me and then, as time goes by, your views have become my own. But this! It's so dangerous! Think again! Think of Walter — think of Douglas! You will bring the most frightful scandal upon our heads, you must see that!'

I was so fond of Marie. She pulled her hand away and I could see I'd offended her deeply. She quizzed me and I did my best to justify the proposal. She kept suggesting alternatives until at last I had to tell her.

'Marie, there's more to it.'

She was very cross with me. 'I knew it! We won't be able to cover this one up!'

'I've never done anything immoral, Marie. But I love him and I'm tired of being brave.'

Marie sat in silence for quite a time.

'I've never yet managed to change your mind, Kate, but don't you think you owe it to us to think this over?'

I'd thought of nothing else for the last six months, and I told her so.

'It's my turn to influence you,' she said. 'I'm so afraid for you.'

'You can try,' I agreed. But after a month of argument I was even clearer in my resolve.

William, to my surprise, met with equal opposition. He chose the dinner hour to announce the plan. He simply put down his knife and fork and stated, 'Aunty Kate is coming to live with us.'

It was a blunt approach, but in fact there was no satisfactory introduction. No matter how cunningly padded, the message would still have clanged like a cracked bell.

According to William, the children clapped. They were thrilled! Then they took a look at their mother. Jeannie was utterly devastated. Sadly, William's sisters, among my most ardent admirers, didn't take kindly to the idea either.

'Where will she sleep?' asked Annie. 'We haven't got room!'

'There's plenty of room,' William said sternly. 'The boys can move out to the green shed for the meantime. I'll build a room out the front for Kate.'

'But she won't like it!' Lucy said. 'She's always lived in luxury!'

'Will she help in the house?' asked Win.

'Of course not!' William said.

'She's had servants all her life,' said Eleanor. 'There's no servants here.'

'You like Aunty Kate,' said William. 'You love her. And from now on our home is hers, and that is the end of the matter. Now, Doris, how many bunches of violets did you pick today?'

Doris looked nervously at her mother, who had not said a word. 'I picked seven, Father. They're in the bucket by the well.'

When William told me I said, 'But was that the first time you mentioned it to Jeannie?'

'There was nothing to discuss.'

I told myself it would be better for Jeannie if I were there to warm his spirit and challenge his authority and deflect his attention from her. He did not love her, and was cold to her in my absence. Possibly I may have been a little too ready to overlook certain other aspects, but I did have good reason to believe she would benefit from my joining the household. Even if her initial reaction was not a happy one, in the long run I was sure she would see the advantages.

Jessie? What's the matter? This is hardly news to you! Oh. What about Ada? Well, as I said, she was very upset. I thought you didn't like Ada? She came up with a hare-brained scheme for me to go and live with her instead. The very idea was quite terrifying. Anyway, if it was simply a matter of finding a congenial family I would have moved in with Marie.

But that's outrageous, Jessie! You're entirely incorrect! We were friends! Women don't love each other that way, or if they do, it's very very rare. Where did you get such a notion? Ada was the most disciplined woman I ever met. If she ever had an impure thought she would have suppressed it ruthlessly.

Jessie, it is very sweet of you to visit an old lady every day like this. I think we might give ourselves a rest for a week or two, don't you? No, I'm not ill, just a wee bit tired. Goodbye, dear. Win will show you out.

Chapter 17

ADA

For a time I abandoned the penning of this document, for the fear of being too plain and materialistic was giving me pause. My mind has been much exercised in seeking a way of causing the narrative to reflect certain great truths about life; without the inference of morality, how can any writing be justified?

In purely practical terms it is difficult to retract my words. It is too early in the autumn for a hearth-fire, and our wonderful modern gas stove is not a suitable place for incinerating evidence! If I throw the offending manuscript into the wastebasket, either Bim or Chris will certainly retrieve it; Bim for sheer perversity and Chris because she values all I write.

We were always considered dangerously explicit. I wrote one article about how babies develop, but I left out one vital aspect, viz., the father's gesture. It seems so trivial. He has his way and goes off on his midnight walk. Perhaps Evolution will render the human male obsolete, and not just in his procreative role.

I have trouble using the word 'God'. Christ is the great inspiration; we can all be Christ in our time. I believe this world is a spiritual world, and that Love beats at the heart of things. It is here in this room, in its plain furniture and pretty curtains, in the holiness of simplicity. For 'God' I now substitute more accurate names such as the Over-Soul, the great All-Spirit or Evolution.

Kate has prayed to God the Father all her life.

In the meantime I shall have to leave what I have written. I'll talk to Wilhelmina when I'm better. She'll know what to do.

I am on the verge of feeling almost disheartened. I do believe in Evolution, I believe the Spirit of the Future is here already. Yet in Germany Hitler has got what he wanted, he's Chancellor now. After all he's said and done! With his million rifles and his whips! There'll be a bloodbath — there's no hope of Disarmament, not now. And the League of Nations has refused to give women a voice on their council. I see all I have done being undone. And yet all these troubles have their purpose, for they must force people to see that Domination through Love is the only possible solution. I do believe, I do, but it is hard.

Our next great triumphs were the NCW and *The White Ribbon*. They are well documented. *The White Ribbon* and the Conference Proceedings are there for all to read.

It would have been more proper for Kate to come to me.

Our friendship was wounded at the Dunedin NCW meeting. But not killed, never killed.

'I am moving into Westcote with the Smiths,' she said.

We were alone in the council rooms before the emergency executive meeting. Mrs Williamson was entering the room at that very moment. I was astounded and not just by what Kate had said. Her timing! Did she want to discuss this in public? Or did she think that bald declaration was sufficient?

O shield her! I thought. She wasn't used to living without a man.

When the six of us were present Kate took the chair.

'With reference to the unfortunate events of yesterday,' she began with a terrible blandness, 'Mrs Wells and I have tried to appease the mayor. It is now clear that we should have vetted Miss Bain's speech before the public reading.'

I was smouldering. 'Mrs Sheppard, it is virtually the same paper you read at Wellington two years ago! The council approved of it then, and it has merely been updated. Why the change of policy?'

There was a cool silence around the table before Kate replied.

'Public sentiment has changed along with world events. This is not the right time to preach pacifism.'

'There is no more appropriate time!' I objected.

'I've prepared a public statement: "The council as a whole does not share the pro-Boer sentiments of two of its members."'

My eyes clashed with Kate's. 'You are throwing young Wilhelmina to the wolves!'

'I see it as peace-making,' said Kate.

I could hardly believe my ears. 'I don't care if ten thousand mayors take offence! War is always wicked! This is a betrayal!'

Nobody answered. What could they say? They were wrong! When I finished speaking, Mrs Williamson cleared her throat importantly. 'Mrs Sheppard, may I raise a second matter?' Kate nodded, casting a nervous glance at me. 'Miss Christina Henderson, BA, has agreed to stand for the post of honorary secretary.'

Of course I was not offended.

'By all means let us have Miss Henderson,' I declared warmly. 'She will benefit greatly from the experience. And please do not nominate me this year for vice-president or for any other executive position. My work on the Charitable Aid Board is too demanding.'

I was applauded and later Kate made a very pretty speech of appreciation.

In the late afternoon I positively dragged her into a corner. 'What is this nonsense about Westcote?'

'Hardly nonsense, Ada.'

'Come to me!' I cried. 'You must!'

'My dear, I could never live with Henry,' Kate said.

'Then he must go. It is done!' I could barely live with him myself.

'I want to live without servants,' Kate niggled. We both hated relying on domestic help but it was hard to find an alternative.

'We could rent a flat,' I said. 'I can cook. Chris and Cos are wonderful company. And Bim is not too bad at cleaning.'

Kate look distinctly uneasy. 'I particularly want to go to Westcote.'

'Then we'll take a country cottage and see Jeannie and Lucy every day!' I cried. O shield her, I thought! I must shield her from her own dark thoughts and from that terrible man, that Svengali, that brute!

'I belong in the Smith family,' said Kate. 'They call me Aunty Kate.'

I lost my dignity. I pleaded with her, I clutched her hands.

'Kate, Kate! Don't you see? People will think the worst! Oh I know you have nothing evil on your mind my dear —'

She quoted my own words back to me — my own words! 'It is a truly doleful fate to have no mind of one's own, Ada.'

I began to think her mind was deranged.

'Kate, have mercy! Our first Member of Parliament must have a name as pure as the sea!' She looked at me most oddly. I could see it was a new thought and I pressed it. 'Don't sabotage our work! You are born to enter Parliament, to conquer the men. You can get whatever you ask — it is only a matter of time!'

'I ask permission to lead my life in my own way.'

'But it's your destiny! Anyone in New Zealand will say the same. You are the only woman perfectly fitted for this great duty.'

'Then you will have to perform it in my place,' she declared.

She never budged from this appalling decision. Within weeks she had sold the house in Clyde Road and was living in that miserable leaky hotch-potch of a cottage. The haste with which she acted spoke volumes — it was the behaviour of a tormented woman. She never seriously considered our living together — she was too weak-willed. When Douglas left, she found herself without chains and it frightened her. She rushed to replace them with links of granite, she bolted them in place. I blame William Sidney Smith of course. He had a most uncanny, vicious power — he was surrounded by cringing women — it was thoroughly unhealthy — three sisters, a wife and two adult daughters as well as all the children. The boys left home; they rebelled! He was the only man in the nest — none of his sisters married and none of his daughters. He wouldn't allow it, he wanted his harem intact! Oh I don't mean that literally, of course, but they were all his slaves and now Kate, proud perfect Kate, the uncrowned Queen of New Zealand had been sucked into his whirlpool. I could never see the attraction of William Smith. He had a superficial masculine appeal I suppose, being very upright, very handsome and commanding in his manner but he never had half the quality of Sir John Hall. He was not a gentleman. And such a humbug, preaching feminist ideas and treating his womenfolk like vassals! He had always coveted Kate — he stalked her for years before springing the trap. Now she was in his private zoo along with his other unfortunate specimens.

I date my supreme commitment to the cause of Peace from this time, for our clash in Dunedin was not a coincidence. Under his influence Kate began losing her nerve and pandering to the warmongers. When it became clear she would do her reckless deed no matter what the cost, my thoughts took a new turn. If she would not fight for Peace, it was my duty to fight twice as vehemently. I swore that nothing would compromise my hatred of militarism. We shared every other goal as before but we grew further and further apart on this issue.

I tried not to condemn my dear but in truth my sadness went bone deep — not for myself, of course, but for her. It was a tragedy. All Christchurch was buzzing and hissing. Every conversation turned to the wickedness of Mrs Sheppard. Her true friends swore there was nothing sinister in the arrangement, conventional people were deeply suspicious, and her enemies had their heyday! For years and years the scandal raged, flaring up whenever anyone spoke out on Temperance or on Women's Rights. She damaged our cause beyond repair. It was not just her own hopes of reaching Parliament that she destroyed — it was those of all women! Here we are, thirty-three years later, and it still hasn't happened. As long as she lives, our enemies have the ultimate weapon.

Kate took it all in her stride.

I witnessed one attack myself. I was walking along Manchester Street with my Home Page, wanting to intercept Kate as she arrived at the office. A dozen men were waiting on the steps. Kate and William always came to work together and as they approached, the group became restless. With impermeable charm, Kate beamed at the hostile gang.

'Here he is!' one bully yelled out. 'The man with two wives!'

'Knickerbocker Smith! The man with two wives!' They shouted on and on, the same horrible words. Some of the conversations recorded in this document are only approximations of the words which were said at the time, but these remarks I can confidently report verbatim. William glared and Kate smiled serenely.

'Get him! Tar him and feather him!'

I was appalled! But Kate sailed through those brutes like a ship with the wind behind her. 'Good morning everybody,' she said, showering them with perfect courtesy. I was more shaken than she was. I had to have a cup of tea before we could get on with our business. I was so sad for her. The woman adored by thousands, reduced to this!

'Has this happened before?' I asked.

'It happens,' she said. That was all.

'But those men should be arrested! They were threatening your life!'

'Why punish them?' said Kate calmly. 'They're only doing what they're paid to do. Somebody else has put them up to it.'

Oh, I grieved for her! Fortunately I had much new work to occupy my mind. That is the way to deal with grief: stamp it out by serving others.

When I followed Mrs Black on to the Charitable Aid Board I felt my work was an offering to Kate, a triumph that I laid at her feet. The men treated our ideas with scorn. We stubbornly persisted and were back on that board year after year. Our work was so frustrating. We saw at close quarters such awful misery, and yet we had no power to attack the root cause of the problems. That power was deliberately withheld from us by the men on the board. All we could do was alleviate the distress of the poor women who applied to us for charity.

My pity was especially aroused by the hopeless fate of the illegitimate child, whereof many sad cases came to our notice. Unable to impress upon the board the urgency of the problem, Mrs Black and I called a public meeting on Social Purity and spelled out what should be done.

'Illegitimate children should have equal legal status with those born in wedlock and should bear the name of the father,' I told them.

'How are you going to manage that?' The speaker was very skeptical and there was laughter.

'A qualified officer will be appointed to ascertain paternity,' I began and the same vulgar man interrupted.

'A fat chance you've got!'

'Mrs Wells, what if the father is a married man?' a young woman with a pinched white face asked. I was not disconcerted by the ominous implications of this question.

'It may seem hard on his wife but it should be done. Every law is hard for someone, and the married woman now has her remedy. Things could hardly be worse than they are already!'

'If a husband keeps his amours to himself, the wife should be content,' interrupted one stout woman. 'So long as he doesn't bring her into the house and sit her at the table!'

'Hear, hear!' Really, Kate's foolish move made life difficult for me at every turn.

'It is only right that a wife should know if her husband is unfaithful,' I affirmed. 'I come now to point number nine: legal detention for the parents of more than one illegitimate child if they neglect them.'

After a lively discussion the meeting endorsed all our motions unanimously. Sometimes I felt I could persuade a public meeting to stand on its head and sing 'Dilly Dilly Duckling'.

My life did not consist entirely of meetings, of course. I spent a good deal of my week working with Maria at Office Road, for she had more patients than she could cope with.

The income was essential for our Leipzig fund, and in 1902 I travelled to Germany with Chris, settling her into the Leipzig School of Music. What an adventure! I found a good little boarding house, met all her teachers, stayed with her till I was sure all would be well. The German language came easily to us both. It was thrilling to be in the land of Goethe and Beethoven. I went to concerts almost daily, and music filled my soul to the brim.

When I was tempted to fret for my life-work in Christchurch I locked myself away and meditated. Time and place fell away and I made great spiritual progress. I hope my reader does not deduce that I am boasting. It was the guidance of my dear St Bede alone which made possible this advancement. I needed all his support to retain Hope in the face of a most agonising discovery: my beloved Germany was riddled with militarism. Soldiers everywhere I looked! Even civilians seemed to be marching. Militarism was a poisonous spider spinning its web over all the land. Germany was my heart-home, and at the same time it was a vision of Hell.

A wonderful opportunity came my way when a certain Rudolf Steiner gave a series of lectures on Life and the Cosmos, humbling us all by revealing a spirit greatly evolved. I was thirty-nine and he was forty-two, but my soul was still in kindergarten, whereas he had the wisdom of aeons.

Since that first encounter I have followed all his teachings and acquired every book he has written, most treasured among which is *The Meaning of Life*. He reinforced my confidence in a new Heaven and a new Earth.

Germany embodied our most hideous possible future, and also our source of salvation. Germany reminded me of Kate. She contained the Cosmos, yet in Kate there was no middle ground.

It was hard leaving Chris, but I knew she would study well and make friends and live healthily. On my way home I visited Alfred Saunders and his new wife in England. Despite infirmity they were both well content. Alfred was getting around on a tricycle!

I don't think I mentioned another perfectly sensible plan:
I could have moved into Clyde Road with Kate. She loved
that house and there was plenty of room for all of us.

Chapter 18

ADA

Before I took Chris to Germany, St Michael's had finally lost
patience with Henry and dismissed him. He accepted the
position of choirmaster at Durham Street Methodist Church.
A rather nice cottage in Chester Street was provided. I
wasn't happy to move so far away from Maria, but needs
must. We were back in the middle of town, near Christchurch Girls' High School and the cathedral. In Christchurch there is no such thing as a new start.

I saw Kate often. Together we attended the conventions in
Wanganui in 1901 and in Napier the next year. I planned my
trip to Europe around those dates. The subject of Peace was
delicately avoided. I spoke on the Influence of Literature on
the Education of the Race in Wanganui, and Jessie MacKay
tackled the touchy Domestic Servant question. I concen-
trated on inspiring my audience. It was grand to steal Kate
away from the gossips of Christchurch, for in other centres
she was adulated as before.

My Napier speech was quite a surprise to Kate. I had
polished up my style, aiming for a resonance that matched
the lofty sentiments I wished to express. My topic was
Culture. I was rather pleased with this section:

'The pagan faith that might is right must give way to the
new ideal that it is the bounden duty of the strong to lift up
the weak hands and to strengthen the feeble knees, and thus
fulfil the law of love and thereby teach that right is might.
Such a change of consciousness means the ascension of the
state, which seems to be the plan and intention of Evolution
that knows no stay but acts in obedience to an eternal
impulse to move forward.'

If only I could reach such heights in my present writing! In those days I could sustain a single sentence for half a page. One's sentence structure is quite a good guide to one's health for it requires considerable energy to maintain a serious thought with appropriately elevated vocabulary beyond three or four subordinate clauses, particularly if they precede the main clause.

As I spoke, I watched Kate's face for the approval which brought such joy to all. I could no longer be sure of her every thought and feeling. My work on the board had impressed on me the hideous effects of heredity especially in the case of illegitimate children. Wretched girls had wretched sickly babies and criminals had criminal children. But I cannot express my views more eloquently than I did at the time!

'At present the morally, mentally and physically Unfit in tens of thousands still become parents. As the sacredness of human life becomes realised a thousand bonds of law and of false belief will be broken, and parenthood will be regarded as the holy thing it is.'

I was determined to introduce the subject of Peace one way or another, and just as Kate was doubtless sighing with relief, I launched into the final, most rhetorical phase of my speech.

'That patriotism which would achieve its ends by force is a false and hollow mockery, whose way is by the palpitating anguish and the life-blood of fellow men; by the heart-breaking despair and woe of women; by the torture of little children . . . This patriotism is but a hollow haunting ghost, and its power can be but fleeting.'

Then, when all the waverers were either squirming or seduced, I rapidly changed the subject to one which would meet with universal approval:

'Perhaps in no respect is the culture of the individual more marked than in his appreciation of Woman. Does he esteem her as the help-meet whom God has given him, or does he think of her as his vassal and inferior?'

Ruskin and Shakespeare rounded off what I still regard as one of my finest speeches. (The complete text can be found by interested parties in the minutes of the NCW Convention of 1902 and could be purchased at the time for a sixpence.) As the applause rang out I beamed at Kate, who congratulated me on my eloquence.

The next convention was held in Dunedin. Kate's speech on Women's Disabilities was crystal clear, and a huge audience responded with great excitement. It was my honour to be chosen to make the official farewell speech to Kate, who was departing again for England. I intended a very poetical style, but when I saw her standing in front of the council, seemingly frail but large of heart, when I thought of the slanderous attacks she had to bear — notwithstanding the fact that she had invited them — all literary aspirations deserted me and I could speak only of how greatly she was loved, and how good and pure was her spirit.

She wished to see her son settled in digs near the University of London. But she was unwell, and disappointed to find she could not actually stay with him. She therefore returned to us quite quickly. If I had been with her she would have received proper care.

For three years Kate and I went to Europe on alternate years. In 1904 I took Cos to Leipzig and brought Chris back home. I was so proud of my talented daughters. Chris was a woman now, and we read the same books and had the most wonderful talks.

I was quite happy with the other children too. Bim seemed to have found her slot helping Maria with the treatments. She stayed at Office Road a good deal which gave me some relief. Maria was very tolerant and even claimed Bim was useful. At least it kept her out of mischief. We didn't see much of Stan, who was always biking across town to see his friends. By the time I took Cos overseas he was nearly thirteen. Our domestic life was almost settled. Of course Henry came and went but that seemed normal enough. As ever, my mother Maria was the source of our security. Remarkably, I have written little about her since describing my marrige, I think, perhaps because her strength was quiet and modest, yet she was the rock on which my life was founded. I saw her several days a week, catching the tram to Office Road to do my share of treatments. I enjoyed it! People say I have healing hands and if so, I inherited them from Maria.

Alas, she could not live forever. Seeing her almost daily, I barely noticed the gradual shrinking of my mother. She grew weaker, and I suppose Bim did more of the heavy work. Maria's presence embodied great wisdom and an enlarging sympathy for the weak, which fine qualities are inevitably interdependent and mutually creative. Her kindly spirit shone out like a lamp. There was no one who did not love and admire her. (I think I achieved that quite unobtrusively, the subtle interweaving of facts and spiritual teaching. Perhaps this document is not entirely without merit!)

Who would have thought she would end her life like this? Raised to be a lady, married to a Plymouth Brethren who would have locked her in a tower if he could, now she drew the sick world right into her home. She moved from idleness to isolation to a life of loving service. In Maria's life I saw the history and the future of the world. She lived out the Evolution of Society in a single lifetime and filled us all with soul-sustaining Hope.

How dreadful then was Bim's reaction to her death, screaming and howling like a banshee! I was so ashamed.

'Bim!' I shook her quite severely the day of the funeral when she started up all over again. 'How you insult your grandmother's memory! Do you really believe she has passed into darkness beyond God's ken? There is no death! She is in the light! She has plucked the rose of life eternal!'

'Oh! Oh! Oh!' That silly girl wailed in her grating voice and I shook her again.

'What would Maria say? There are others worse off than you, isn't that so?'

'I know but oh! Oh!' cried Bim, flinging her arms and legs around in that gawky way.

'Bim, we are about to go to Maria's funeral. If you are coming with us you will kindly remember that it is a celebration.'

Chris put Bim's hat and coat on her and helped her down

the stairs. She is always so kind, my Christabel. Merivale Church was full to overflowing with Maria's friends and admirers. It was a great joy to know she had gone to a higher service.

Maria had very wisely left the house to me. None of my brothers and sisters had need of it, since Blanche had gone to Australia, Nell and Kate were married, Will was teaching in the country, and Tom had decided to set up his own practice. Only my youngest sister Edith was with us in the big house.

It fell upon me to earn the family livelihood. Morally the Office Road house was mine, not Henry's, yet as my husband he could have claimed to be the legal owner; the law was still foully unjust in spite of all our efforts. Fortunately, I knew Henry would not dare to challenge Maria's gift. He fell out with the Methodists and drifted to St Luke's but now I could view his career with equanimity. Along with the house came the patients, of course, and Bim and I had our hands full from that day on.

Somehow I managed to combine the hydrotherapy with my work on the Charitable Aid Board. Maria's life and death was an inspiration and I was determined to show the usefulness of women on the board. Since Kate's move I felt more responsibility than ever.

Mrs Black was my only ally on the board. It was the Waltham Orphanage that concerned us most. The matron was a rough customer and yet I felt sorry for her because she knew no better. She took a dislike to one poor child and nearly killed him with neglect — and this was a state orphanage! We tried to keep the scandal from erupting. I succeeded in getting milk for the children's porridge, poor things, and bathrooms — but I couldn't stand over and wash them all myself! In the end Mrs Black and I were forced to demand a public inquiry. Indeed, we took the Charitable Aid Board to court, even though we were on the board ourselves. The inquiry went on for more than two weeks. We had a fine old fight. Bim kept all the newspaper cuttings; she was quite intrigued.

'What a pity it had to reach this point,' Kate remarked one day. We were meeting in the WCTU coffee rooms in Hereford Street. The place was very homely with its scrubbed wooden tables, and it was good to know that William Smith was not hovering near.

'If you were on the board it would never have happened.' We were both drinking weak coffee — playing ladies, I called it. 'They just don't like me and that's all there is about it. Not that I mind!'

Kate was staring into her cup. 'I've only got one life,' she said.

Yes, I thought, and you've thrown it away. 'You'd have charmed those men into positively wanting to improve the orphanage.'

'I doubt if Mr J. T. Smith is susceptible to my charms,' said Kate wryly. He was one of my most patronising critics, a former chairman of the board, and the father of William Sidney Smith. That gentleman's hostility towards 'progressive ladies' was certainly due in part to Kate's behaviour. But how could I reproach her? Her own life had been utterly spoiled.

'This orphanage is a lost cause,' I admitted in a regrettable moment of weakness. 'But it is possible — I know it is — for the state to care for its waifs and train them in useful work and wash away the stains! Think of Lorne Farm.'

I had searched the country for model homes, and I'd found one. It was clean, fresh, wholesome, with little rugs by the beds and a sweet, sensible matron, but when I spoke about Lorne Farm to the board they sneered at me.

Kate's lively eyes filled with compassion and she covered my hand with hers. 'Don't lose heart, dear,' she said. 'You are doing splendidly.'

I went back to the fight with renewed vigour. In the end Mrs Black and I were thoroughly vindicated.

Chapter 19

ADA

It is more than a week since I laid down my pen. I find it very puzzling, this reluctance to resume. There is no aspect of the last quarter-century of my life that I am unhappy to confront. On the contrary, they have been years of triumph. On the political side there has been drama and excitement a-plenty, whereas more privately, I have experienced spiritual fulfilment.

Why then this feeling that it is rather less than vivid? I have derived great joy from watching Chris marry and have children — Cos and Stan too, for that matter. Bim comes and goes, we put up with each other.

She said to me today, 'You should get on with that writing!' Inevitably she has found out what I'm doing. She spies on me, which I interpret as a mode of revenge. 'Don't stop now!'

So if today I resume my task, it is for one reason only, to keep her at arm's length. At least while I'm writing she doesn't come fussing and fiddling in my room. She respects the written word as a thing apart.

I was writing about the orphanage inquiry.

In the midst of the turmoil Alfred Saunders departed this earthly life. After Sarah's death he returned to New Zealand to die, and Kate and I often met at his daughter's home. She pushed him around in a kind of basket-chair on wheels. She loved us to visit him and talk of the old days. I was only forty-two, in my prime, and yet seeing Alfred and Kate always left me feeling tired.

I must be wrong. How could I have been tired at forty-two? Could this illness be polluting my memory?

Kate kept up a good front, never revealing her inner sorrow. Her visits cheered our old friend greatly, yet to see them together made me quite nostalgic.

Only two years after Alfred's demise, Sir John Hall followed him into the light. We were bereft of our two old champions, but that was no reason to mourn. There is no Death! I cheered their passing for they returned to God whence they came.

Shortly after the orphanage affair I was swept away into what, in the last analysis, must be regarded as my life-work. No More War! I was tragically wrong in thinking that after the Boer War militarism would put down its head and crawl away. On the contrary, the clouds of war have glowered over the world ever since. When Joe Ward brought in the notorious Defence Act in 1909 it was the last straw. He rammed it through the House just before Christmas. I expected better of him. We fought it with every weapon we had.

By 'we' I mean every organisation to which I belonged. In the CWI, which was still in fine fettle, we were battling as hard as ever for essential reforms. I should have written that in full: the Canterbury Women's Institute. The National Council of Women had disintegrated when Kate went to England. By 1912 I belonged to the Theosophical Society and the National Peace Council and, of course, with Mrs Elizabeth McCombs I'd set up the Housewives' Union. Now we all combined our efforts. We gave those Ministers a hard time!

But what was the point? What has changed in the world since I went to Germany and saw a rash of soldiers staining the land? Bim has brought in this morning's *Press* and what do I read? That the whole of Germany is seething with anger and hatred and fear! The Government aiming blow after blow at the nation's liberties — freedom of speech is dead — freedom of the press nearly gone — Nazi stormtroopers raiding the Catholics' printing works — the Nazis planning to march on Berlin on the fifth of March — oh, throw it away! Throw it away! Twenty-five years of life wasted on a lost cause! It makes me fume, it makes me absolutely boil with rage!

War! That man with his rifles and whips! Dragons of the prime that tare each other in their slime! There is nothing like bright and beautiful thoughts for the insurance of good health. No More War! It is my heart's continual iteration and yet war rages within me. The more I fight it, the more violently it flares up. I have told them and told them that war is wrong, that they must arbitrate, they must! There is a terrible blockage somewhere, nothing gets through. How can the human race evolve with such a blockage? Have I been praying to the wrong deity? Kate has always been content to pray to God the Father. There will be a new Heaven and a new Earth. She promised! I must tell Bim to read the Bible but stick to Labour.

I fought my way up to the city council on the No More War ticket. The Labour Party announced it very bravely: We Do Not Believe in War. It cannot happen because there is no belief. Alas for most of us, we are yet in the bonds of conventional thought. The Labour Party was limp in phrasing it thus. They should have said, We Do Believe in Peace! Thousands chanting the positive slogan! Thinking it loud and bold and strong! It is far too easy to lose a negative thought, it slips away like a fish. We fear to launch our frail bark lest we founder in a lonely sea. Hitler says he will retain control no matter what the cost. That wicked man, that brute! I will retain control as I have done for sixty-nine years. My father, give up the whip hand, let me advise you, for I have learned much. Do not give ear to the wily Becket. Bede is simple and wise and truthful and to be trusted and he is always by my side.

Why should I lose hope? I do not. This life is but a passing shadow. Beyond the veil is the white light of the Cosmos. When I join the Cosmic Spirit I shall strengthen it with bonds of iron. Every being who has lived greatly in this incarnation will greatly enrich the force of the Over-Soul. One more soul, one which has retained control will tip the balance. Hold tight, hold tight! Never let go like Kate.

$$12 \times 13 = 156$$
$$12 \times 12 = 144$$
$$12 \times 11 = 132$$
$$12 \times 10 = 120$$
$$12 \times 9 = 108$$
$$12 \times 8 = 96$$
$$12 \times 7 = 84$$
$$12 \times 6 = 72$$
$$12 \times 5 = 60$$
$$12 \times 4 = 48$$
$$12 \times 3 = 36$$
$$12 \times 2 = 24$$
$$12 \times 1 = 12$$
$$12 \times 0 = 0$$

Ring out false pride in place and blood! March on! March on! Lazarus, come forth! Wild bird, whose warble, liquid sweet Rings Eden through the budded quicks. Where is my Tennyson? He wrote to comfort me. 'Tis better to have loved and lost Than never to have loved at all. It was but unity of place That made me dream I ranked with him. A little flash, a mystic hint. Bright and beautiful thoughts, bright and beautiful thoughts!

There are two great Forces on Earth, one that would bind us to Earth, one that would keep us away from the things of the Earth. I walk between them and the way is narrow. I must hearken to the introspective injunction, turn my eyes inward and walk by faith alone blind to both the Sirens and the Rocks. So many worlds, so much to do. The sad mechanic exercise Like dull narcotics, numbing pain — I met with scoffs, I met with scorns — I found an angel of the night — Everyone comes to his own, none can escape from reaping what he has sown — how absolutely just is the law that governs destiny! The fame is quench'd that I foresaw. Let the dead past bury the dead. We have been banished into the Physical.

Oh, Bede, Bede, watch over my child! Oh, Christabel darling, come soon! It is four o'clock. Life is around us

always, you will soon understand — I crave your pardon, o
my friend.

> Be near me when my light is low
> > When the blood creeps, and the nerves prick
> > And tingle; and the heart is sick,
> And all the wheels of Being slow.
>
> Peace; come away: the song of woe
> > Is after all an earthly song:
> > Peace; come away: we do her wrong
> To sing so wildly: let us go.
>
> > Come; let us go: your cheeks are pale;
> > > But half my life I leave behind:
> > > Methinks my friend is richly shrined;
> > But I shall pass; my work will fail.

It is soothing to write out my favourite words and yet —

$$12 \times 13 = 156$$
$$12 \times 12 = 144$$
$$12 \times 11 = 132$$
$$12 \times 10 = 120$$
$$12 \times 9 = 108 \qquad 12 \times 8 = 96$$

I spoke splendidly about Our Duty to the Unfit once I had
masticated the ethics and the economics. Bim is one of the
Unfit but as a matter of fact the Unfit are mostly men. As long
as Men are involved in Procreation the human race will be at
a standstill, for Evolution is shackled by their genes of aggres-
sion, militarism and materialism. Every time a man fathers a
son we go back a step. It would be more natural for Woman
to procreate without their interference because Woman is the
creative force and Man the destructive. The only men fit to
be parents decline the privilege, they unerringly make the
choice of chastity. Bede, for instance, felt no need to per-
petuate his Ego by fathering a swarm of offspring and yet his
name will live forever. I don't thank my father for his legacy.

Science has made such great strides and I feel sure that this dream is not impossible to achieve.

> *Dear friend, far off, my lost desire,*
> > *So far, so near in woe and weal;*
> > *O loved the most, when most I feel*
> *There is a lower and a higher.*

> *Known and unknown; human, divine;*
> > *Sweet human hand and lips and eye;*
> > *Dear heavenly friend that canst not die,*
> *Mine, mine, for ever, ever mine.*

$12 \times 7 = 84$, $12 \times 6 = 72$, $12 \times 5 = 60$. I must beware, I cannot believe my mind is loosening. There is nothing but Good at the Source of things but even so, I must act promptly, before it is too late. I cannot rely on Tennyson and Bede indefinitely. Nature designs that food be retained in the alimentary canal only long enough to ensure proper digestion and absorption. If the residue remains longer than fourteen hours, poisonous substances are developed. I have done what I could. I shall tell Bim to call Dr Simpson. Where is she now? Oh no no, I don't want to know. I could have done without Bim and I could have done without Stan. If a girl has a gift for cooking and cleaning and tidying, let it be cultivated as the beautiful talent it is. Kate and I had more important work, a more noble vocation than Motherhood. It was our destiny to make the world safe for mothers.

When she got all those milksops together and called them the National Council of Women that was too much. That wasn't the NCW, it was a feeble shadow of our first brave body. Dead fish and baa-lambs, most of them! I left her to it, I went into the real world instead, the real council, the city council. All right, so they have realised one long-awaited goal harboured in tens of thousands of incoherent breasts, and so the way is open now for women to enter Parliament — yet none of those women has taken advantage of it, I note! If we'd got that law passed thirty years ago I'd have been in Wellington before you could say Jack Robinson.

I won't complain. She led a different army. She had her William, I had my Wilhelmina. Her charm was her armour, her smiles shot out like bullets. She stunned us all with those smiles as sweet as stone. I should have reached out when William died, that was the time. But I was too proud. She came half-way — Midway to me, she came — I should have walked the other half, walked from Cathedral Square to Midway and met her there. She was no monster, not last century, not in the century of my joy. But time turned over, the Future arrived and a hundred years of devotion sluiced away in a cold douche. 1900! I awaited the turning of the tide with joy for I knew that was the beginning of the Future, but oh what dread catastrophe it brought. She gave her tongue to the Water-Witch and split her flesh into legs for love of a man. Splitting in two is all very well for cells in the soft silken wrappings of the womb but in a grown woman it is monstrous, yes, I have to say it. There was a time we spoke with one voice and delivered the very same speech. She gave up the voice and I had to speak for both of us. Now she walks on knives, she totters — well, she was warned!

But I do have a soul, I do. I was born with a soul well-worn. They expect a lot of me. I will sit in the front row of Heaven and no one will laugh at my hat. Bim, empty the wastepaper basket!

No. Don't interfere. How dare you read my notebook! So you admit it? Again you disappoint me. I say no! Do your duty and no more. I forbid you to telephone her. She doesn't like phones, she puts them down. She understands telegram boys with caps and bicycles and epaulettes, not telephones. I could write to my love but what could I say? Tomorrow you will be with me in Paradise? Take up your bed and walk? Lazarus, come forth?

Death has come midway to meet me. I am ready but that is not enough. I must walk the other mile, it is the moment which mustn't be missed. No More War! Set Bede against Becket, bran against rotten meat, peace against the black slime of the war-mongers, truth against jingoism, a healthy death against a sickly life. March on! Blaze out! Bim, ring Dr Simpson.

Chapter 20

KATE

Hello, Jessie. I'm glad you could come. I've missed you. I see you are ready with your stenography pad.

But first I wish to clarify one little matter. I began the tale of Kate Sheppard for one reason only, to pass the time while I wait for Elizabeth to return from Parliament. I did not expect to be asked to justify my move to Westcote! That's all over and done with. What did you expect, that I give you Fourteen Reasons for the move?

Forgive me, Jessie. I know I startled Christchurch at the time, but I thought you understood. And you still regard it as a mystery? Perhaps after all I should try and explain. Why not? All right, let's have a little fun.

1. It was Economically Sound. One rich woman living in a grand house. Fifteen people living in a cottage. By combining my income with theirs we achieved a more equitable distribution of wealth and services.

2. It solved the Domestic Servant Problem. Having servants was wrong; it belonged to the Age of Privilege. I could not persuade Poppy and Derry to retire. Pensions did not tempt them and their loyalty shamed me. Yet I was not eager to learn the domestic arts in middle age! Jeannie and Win could cook and clean and still retain their dignity.

3. I wanted to claim my Monsterhood. I was utterly sickened by the way I was always singled out as an exception to the rule. Every newspaper which sang my praises as a sweet sensible womanly woman would inevitably attack the Monsters of the Female Rights movement — yet I was surely the Archmonster, the Queen of the Monsters!

4. I thought it was a way of escaping Ada. She was far too highly seasoned for everyday fare — too meaty, too pungent! It was a foolish idea, for Ada came with me to Westcote in my blood. I have feared her all my life, the Ada within me. Ada has loved me all her life and what she loves is also lodged within her. That is our nourishment and our horror.

5. Five! Will I get to fourteen?

Women are Not Made in a Factory. We claimed that a woman in Parliament, any woman, would automatically purify the atmosphere. It was a popular belief which we did not closely scrutinise.

I know two women, and one is chaste,
And cold as the snow on a winter's waste;
Stainless ever, in act and thought —
As a man born dumb in speech errs not . . .

The other woman with heart of flame,
Went mad for a love that marred her name;
And out of the grave of her murdered faith,
She rose like a soul that had passed through death . . .

Yes. We were always trying to better the lot of the 'fallen woman' as if she were something one found in the gutter. We are all fallen women; it is a meaningless term. Compassion is not enough, compassion brings its own rewards. I wanted to confront others with a truth about themselves.

6. I wanted my Share of Tolerance. Years ago I defended Ada from the jealous piety of the WCTU, when Mrs Fulton tried to make Ada swear she was an orthodox Christian! I maintain it is dangerous to sit in judgement on our fellow-women.

7. I intended my move to bring Relief to Jeannie. I could not foresee all the consequences.

8. It was a Question of Diet. I could not train Poppy to change her ways, nor could I cook my own food. I was trying to eat less meat and cakes, simple food like the Smiths.

9. William Sidney Smith hooked into my flesh like a thorn on the day I first saw him playing the cello among Mrs

157

Ballantyne's red roses, an arrogant, touchy boy of seventeen. I never managed to expel that thorn; at last I could not tell where the thorn began and my own cells ended.

10. William Sidney Smith slipped underneath my shadow. When I sat by candlelight and threw three shadows on the wall, one of them was his. That was as far as our separateness ever reached.

11. I trusted William.

12. To his children I was Just Another Aunty.

13. It was Convenient for William and me to travel to work together in the mornings.

14. I had served the women of New Zealand with all my energy for fifteen years and it was for women that I now made my move. Seize your freedom! That was not my message. Do not wait until a law is passed entitling you to live with your beloved! That was not my message.

This was the message: the Friendship of Women is mighty. Women are not the possessions of the male. Men are not the possessions of the female.

There! Are you satisfied? Good. Now I shall continue the story.

William tacked a room on to the south-east corner of the house. It was cold and dark and poky. His way of building was to slap up walls and roof and think about a floor later, so there were a few awkward steps. I made my little cubbyhole pretty with silk rugs and some good flowered linen from Beath's. In place of my walnut desk William built me a shelf in the corner, and I covered it with black oil-cloth and stuck on a little frill. On the walls I hung my favourite watercolours. I kept my photographs on a little table inlaid with ivory, and my dresses were hidden by a curtain. I liked my little room, prettied up with silver and fabrics and flowers. It had the only frills in the house; I was equally incongruous there in my fine gowns.

George very kindly stored some of my furniture in Beath's warehouse and some at home. I could not bear to part with everything at once; I know it was contradictory of me, but there you are. William erected another shed beyond the orchard and into that I crammed all my papers and many treasures. When I got it arranged to my satisfaction I was very pleased with it!

I went to tell Jeannie, who was podding peas with Win and Hilda Kate.

'It looks wonderful — come and see!'

Kitty jumped up in excitement and spilt the peas.

'We'll wash these on the way,' Jeannie said. She carried the colander out to the well and the peas were duly washed. She was in no hurry to see inside my famous shed! We picked our way past the quince tree and I opened the door with a flourish.

'Oh!' said Kitty, her eyes all big. 'It smells lovely!' She wandered through the rows of cloth samples and veils and dresses and shawls. 'It's like Aladdin's cave!' The shelves of books excited her; she greedily ran her finger along the leather bindings.

Win being Win said nothing, but she hovered over a bolt of dark blue wool gaberdine shooting meaningful looks at her mother.

'Choose something,' I urged them. 'I'd like you all to have a little gift.' I measured out the cloth. 'There's seven yards here. Is that enough for a dress, Jeannie?'

'There's no need for that. She's got three frocks. I don't believe in waste.'

'Jeannie, dear, it's not waste if it's actually used!'

Kitty asked hurriedly, 'May I borrow this book please Aunty Kate?' If I remember rightly it was a copy of *Erewhon*.

Jeannie looked rather glum. Where was my happy, funny friend?

'Perhaps a new rug for the sitting-room?' I suggested carefully.

'That's kind of you but we don't need a new rug thank you,' she said politely.

Well, I thought, this is not going quite as I hoped. When the Smith family — oh, let's start calling them the Lovell-

159

Smiths! William got tired of being confused with the other Smiths and changed his name, and his sisters followed suit. I thought that was perfectly sensible though Ada said curtly, 'Are they married to the man, for goodness' sake?'

When I moved in I did hope the sum total of love among the Lovell-Smiths might be increased. Love was the flavour of their family life, it was there in great abundance, streaming out of Jeannie to children and adults alike. She put poultices on tummy aches, she sweetened every quarrel, she made up games with the children and read them stories. I loved Jeannie far more than William did and I had more respect for her. His love for her was grudging and dutiful.

I regard the arrangement we made as my finest achievement. It required more commitment than gaining the vote for women, more time, more effort, more pain. In personal terms it was more rewarding. I don't mean everyone should do the same. The challenge is to be elastic in marriage, to reinvent it as necessary. Only one thing might have made it perfect. If only Jeannie could have shown her fury when she felt it, instead of letting it stew for twenty-four years beneath that excruciating, relentless good nature! Apart from that the arrangement has been a success. The Lovell-Smiths have cared for me and I have loved them. I have been part of the family and yet not fully absorbed. That was the intention. Our lives have been stirred together without dissolving. The first three years were the most difficult. Once I accepted it would always be difficult, the next thirty years were better.

Shall I describe a typical day? Jeannie and Win were the first to bath, followed by Lucy. Then they ran me fresh water, provided the electric pump was functioning. In winter they might add a kettle of boiling water, but it was still chilly, I assure you! One day I surprised Ada by saying,

'I've almost grown to enjoy the shock!'

She chuckled. 'It won't do you any harm.' She and Jeannie seemed to take great satisfaction in my cold baths. Naturally the Lovell-Smiths believed in cleanliness, though not quite as Ada did. She saw it as a source of self-respect and spiritual purification, water being the essence of her healing methods.

Win would serve breakfast, oatmeal with milk, a cup of tea and fresh fruit. She'd spruce William up with a clean hanky in his pocket, behaving more like a mother than a daughter. All the family members who had jobs in town would then set off down the road on foot, rain or fine. It was not just a little stroll, it was an hour's walk to Church Corner. Later on when Russley Road was macadamised we were able to cycle to the tram terminus, which was far more convenient. William and I talked all the way to town. We never ran out of talk!

Lucy had always worked for her brother's printing business, and so did most of William's children at different times. The *White Ribbon* office was in the same building, and Jeannie as business manager would join us twice a week. I would often meet Ada for lunch at the WCTU coffee rooms or the YWCA.

When we returned to Westcote at night, Win would give William and me the royal treatment — chair by the fire in the front room, warm slippers, bowl of soup. Lovely! That sitting-room became our haven. I changed nothing, apart from adding some of my books. Jeannie most of the time kept out.

At dinner we always kept the same protocol. I sat on William's right hand, Jeannie at the foot of the table with the youngest children, and any extra friends or relations sat on William's left. After dinner we'd talk in the sitting-room while the others did things in the kitchen. Before bed William would interview the children on the day's achievements and give them advice. Then Jeannie or the aunts would tuck them into bed and sing them a song. The sounds of the house would gradually die down, and we would go to bed.

I have no intention of telling you what occurred in my bedroom. However, I must assure you that William behaved with impeccable discretion. Our gentility was impenetrable. I am quite certain the aunts never had any cause for uneasiness about our relationship.

Saturdays were full of activity, as the children all had

chores like gardening, tidying, cleaning. There were choir practices and Temperance meetings and fairs and teas. The children made their own weekly newspapers and there was noisy competition over who was the best editor. It goes without saying that on Sundays they attended Riccarton Methodist Church, while I usually travelled with the Beaths into Trinity. On wet Sunday afternoons we had great sing-songs, and Jeannie showed the children the family Bible with its many illustrations. On warm days they played on the big lawn, croquet, chasing, all sorts of fun and games. The generations were rather mixed up, since there were nineteen years between the oldest and youngest Lovell-Smith children.

It wasn't easy adjusting to this big warm busy family. I had always seen my home-life as a background to my work. Now I found there was no division, because I worked with my new family all day, and then I went home with my family to my family. Yes, despite the happiness I was under a strain. The *White Ribbon* work was often irksome and thankless. I felt the WCTU slipping into apathy and smugness. The National Council of Women was a full-time load in itself, but there too we were growing old and tired. When we won the vote we thought that a Bill sweeping away all the legal handicaps of women was almost within our grasp. After ten years that goal was no closer.

One night at the dinner table my hand shook so badly that I spilled my glass of salted milk all over the cloth. Win mopped it up and brought me another, and William held the glass as I drank. I felt quite unable to eat my dinner and retired to the sitting-room.

Shortly William joined me. 'What are we going to do with you?' he asked, tucking my cashmere shawl around my shoulders. Jeannie followed him in with a cup of tea.

'Perhaps our household is too tiring for you,' Jeannie suggested. 'Why don't you stay with your sister for a while?'

'But Isabel is in England!' William looked shocked.

'I meant Marie! But yes, a sea voyage might be just the thing,' Jeannie smiled.

'You must give up *The White Ribbon*,' William proclaimed. 'It's too much!'

'If Kate resigns, I resign,' Jeannie stated. 'My children come first. Eight years as business manager is more than enough.'

It was a sensible step. Lucy agreed to shoulder both tasks, relieving the dismay caused by our resignations. Naturally I continued to help but I had no energy. Sometimes I would weep and not know why. The NCW convention left me exhausted.

'William,' I said a few weeks later, 'I must go to England. Douglas needs someone to see to his digs, and Walter hates leaving Bath.' It was true but it sounded a very lame excuse.

The cracks in his face deepened; he was terribly distressed. 'My dearest Kate, you can't, you mustn't! This is your home!'

I sighed. Jeannie's coolness was deeply troubling.

'If you leave us, Kate, my life is in ruins!'

'I am only contemplating a short journey,' I assured him. Jeannie hugged me warmly as I departed.

In England everything went wrong. Oh, I saw Douglas and Isy and Walter, but my nerves were no better. If anything, I felt more jumpy than ever. I could not sleep for thoughts of William. Blessing the speed of the steamship, I was back in Christchurch within four months.

It was Alfred Saunders who convinced me to return so promptly.

'Aren't you missing William?' he asked. We were alone in the sunroom while Sarah was resting. 'He always wanted a woman with a bit of gumption.'

'When he married Jeannie she was just the ticket!'

'Jeannie is quite somebody,' Alfred agreed.

'But all those children! He married her and ruined her.' I was shaken by the thought. 'Twenty years of babies!'

'Sex is a cruel trick,' said Alfred. 'Doomed if you do, and doomed if you don't.'

'She'd have another child tomorrow if she could, but she's fifty-six.'

'Some people call him a hypocrite. The feminist whose

163

word is law. The puritan with two wives.'

'Oh, stop it! I hate talking about him!'

'Then you must love him,' he said bluntly. 'And I should know.' He beamed like a courting lad as Sarah entered the room painfully on her two sticks, and helped to seat her in the weak sunshine. I thought, William Lovell-Smith is a mirthless tactless tyrannical tormented bundle of anomalies, life at Westcote is always going to be agonising and I can't wait to get back to him.

Chapter 21

KATE

This is a Catechism I made up at the beginning of the war. We used to chant it to boost our spirits.

Q. What did the helpless woman do?
A. She wrote a letter to the House,
   She made a speech, she made a magazine.
Q. What has the helpless woman banned?
A. The CD Act and baby farms,
   Children buying cigarettes
   And children buying liquor.
Q. What has the helpless one achieved?
A. Ten o'clock closing,
   Old age pension,
   Married Women's Property Act,
   Rights for the illegitimate child,
   Technical Schools and Juvenile Courts,
   Equal standards for divorce,
   Maternity care, minimum wage,
   The principle of equal pay.
Q. How may the helpless woman serve?
A. On city councils, hospital boards,
   In civil service, visiting gaols,
   As Doctor, Lawyer, Type-writer,
   As Teacher, Nurse, and Journalist.
Q. Where is the helpless woman barred?
A. From Parliament, from Parliament,
   From Parliament alone.

You will recognise some of Ada's special interests there. We did remarkably well, even after I let the National

Council of Women collapse. We had a celebration every year.

The ten years before the Great War were years of travel and of deaths. When Alfred was widowed again he followed Sarah quickly. George Beath died; it was like losing another father. What gaps in my world! Marie stayed in the family home with some of her children and grandchildren. Then Sir John Hall died and then — no — yes — my son Douglas.

It was a shattering of nature. It is not natural for the child to precede the parent. To my great joy Douglas had married Meta Seivwright, daughter of a dear friend, one of the most radical women on the NCW. This was in England. He never returned. I cannot speak of his death — nor of the death of my only grandchild.

Walter came out to New Zealand several times. He would stay at the Gentlemen's Club and cycle out to see me at Westcote. He wouldn't go back to town till the wind turned round! We caught up on news, fussed over each other's health, went for walks. William and Jeannie both liked the old boy. We all got on splendidly.

William and Jeannie were to take a long-planned journey in 1913. One week before their departure he and I were taking our soup in the sitting-room as usual when I noticed him looking at me strangely.

'You miss Isy, don't you?'

Surprised, I agreed. She spent most of her time in England.

'You would like to see Walter again?'

'Oh, certainly,' I said. 'I always like seeing Walter.'

'And you have business in England?'

I looked across the room at him, sitting so upright in his armchair.

'Are you feeling sorry for yourself?' I teased lightly. I was quite sad enough for us both. 'A year will fly! You'll see Ceylon, the Pyramids, Paris! How could you miss me in Paris?'

He frowned that steamy frown of his. I did as he wished and booked a passage on the same ship.

Jeannie was very delightful that last week, full of fun, quite her old self. The household had an air of elation.

'I'm so glad Jeannie and William are going to have a holiday all on their own,' confided Lucy, and I felt ill at heart. No matter how I chided William he would not tell them! I packed, I arranged my money matters almost on the sly.

On the very last evening Annie put fizzy raspberry drink on the table as a special treat.

'Raise your glasses!' she said. 'Here's a toast to William and Jeannie!'

'Father and Mother!' joined in Win and Macie and their young sisters and brothers.

'Father and Mother!' said Leonard and his wife, who was cuddling baby Brian. They were living in a cottage on the property.

'Grandfather and Grandmother!' chirped young Joan.

'Uncle One and Aunty Jeannie!'

The fizzy drink went down with great glee. Jeannie smiled all over. William could delay the announcement no longer.

'Aunty Kate is going to travel with us,' he said.

Jeannie's face crumpled. She seized some plates that were not even empty and ran out of the room. Later that night I overheard her in a rare moment of carelessness.

'That dreadful woman!' She meant me.

In Paris we learned that William's mother had passed on, Eleanor Phoebe Smith. We could not turn around and go home; William decided she would want us to carry on. He grieved terribly, and Jeannie was tormented with guilt. Had her last letter reached Eleanor Phoebe? Had she loved her enough? In reaction Jeannie made an even greater effort to be affectionate to me. I knew my Jeannie; she tortured herself. Instead of saying to my face, 'Kate Sheppard, I can't bear you in my home nor in my marriage' she would say to herself, 'I am a bad person, I should love Kate as myself, I must sacrifice my own needs for the greatest good, I mustn't be nervy, Love One Another.' Her lacerating self-sacrifice was something to behold.

I was so happy to have William with me. All of England was transformed because of that and of course my presence comforted him.

We spent time with Walter. William took great delight in borrowing a car and showing Walter the countryside! Walter was amazed to find so many pretty spots within twenty miles of his own home. We also drove with Isy all the way to Inverness and Nairn and it made me joyful that William saw the home of my youth.

But it was no time to dilly-dally in Europe. We got back to New Zealand just as war was declared.

War or no war, on September the nineteenth there was a big celebration for the majority of the female franchise. Ada and I were on the stage together holding huge white bouquets. We smiled at each other across the camellias. When I gave my speech I had rather a fright: for a few seconds I could not recall the name of the mayor!

Ada and I had arranged to meet the next day in the Botanical Gardens. She was there at the gates to greet me. We strolled arm-in-arm to a seat by the river where we could admire the daffodils on the other bank. Boats full of girls rowing rhythmically swept past.

'Aren't they beautiful, Ada?' I loved their free, vigorous movements and the determination on their young faces. 'They must be practising for a race.'

'Not nearly as beautiful as you are,' she flattered. 'You never grow any older.'

'Oh, but I do!' I told her about my slip of the memory.

She brushed it aside. 'We have more important things to think about,' she said firmly. She was the firmest woman I ever met, though soft enough on the surface. I was a little afraid of our toughness, but Ada relished it. William was the other way round, like a woman turned inside out.

People were strolling by in the spring sunshine. Some of them threw more than casual glances at us. I remember that particular morning very clearly because we shared the insults evenly. First I was hissed at by a society lady in a fancy hat. The next passer-by positively spat at Ada, 'Fool! Our boys need discipline!' Then he rushed off as if anti-conscription was a communicable disease.

'Honoured in the evening, humbled in the morning,' said Ada.

I had developed a very thick skin, well trained by Jeannie's coolness. The forest of gravestones sprung up in my life had taught me one lesson, to abandon needless guilt. It was strangely freeing and frightening.

'I heard that your Stan has joined the Navy?' I said delicately.

Ada was clearly furious. 'He is no son of mine. He's a traitor!'

'We have to expect these things, my dear. William's Colin is talking of joining up.'

'Clutched by the tentacles of war! Our own sons! Barbarians!' I sometimes felt Ada was capable of murder if she felt morally justified.

'Ada, I've been having doubts,' I said. 'I'm starting to think we've been singing a nonsense song. I've sung it, you've sung it, a chorus of spinsters is carolling away even now.'

'What on earth do you mean, Kate?'

'We have never stopped quoting this one silly reason when we ask for our rights. We say we need them in order to be fitting helpmeets for men! We, we — who are we? Why don't we ask on the grounds of fairness alone? Why is it always for the sake of Wifehood and Motherhood?'

She got the point. 'We're not exactly copybook wives and mothers, you and I!'

'And Jessie and Wilhelmina will never wed or I don't know human nature.'

'It's an ideal,' said Ada uncertainly.

'But do we want that, honestly? Is there a man on this earth whose helpmeet you would be?'

Ada burst out laughing, that rich contralto laugh that almost made the daffodils ring. Then a peculiar mood struck her and for some reason she couldn't speak. I suppose it was rather confusing.

'Ada, is it true or not? Are Wifehood and Motherhood

really so glorious — or are they a source of misery, are they even a disability?'

'Sh! This is heresy!' she whispered with enthusiasm.

'Jeannie is the perfect wife and mother,' I said irrelevantly, 'and I'm the scarlet woman.'

'Nonsense! She is Martha to your Mary,' Ada stated rather too quickly.

'We have been softening our message so the men will still love us.'

'Speak for yourself!' laughed Ada. 'I think it was their message.'

'Well, now I see plainly I shall speak plainly. Let's be what we are and say what we mean.'

'I shall always be proud while you're on my side,' said Ada. She was a loyal friend. The warmth went out of the sun and I began to shiver. Ada wrapped her coat around me and we walked to the Square together.

Of course I had replaced one ideal with another, and naturally I fell short of it for where does feminine manipulation end and masculine political manoeuvring begin? We went our different ways, Ada and I. Yes, she was a pacifist who would kill for the cause. During the Great War she made herself very unpopular, so much so that I deliberately excluded her in my last great push to get women into Parliament.

I quoted the patriotism of women in making my case. The war exploded all sorts of fossilized prejudices; it was impossible to dogmatise about 'woman's sphere' while one woman bound up the soldier's wounds and another was doing his work at home. It was the perfect time to grasp our rights with both hands. Now why am I telling you this, Jessie — you of all people? You and I and Christina Henderson were the three who revived the National Council of Women and caught Parliament on the hop! Never mind, I want to talk about it.

When was that first meeting — in 1916? We made a point of inviting the moderate women's groups, didn't we? It was very important to arouse ordinary women to their responsibilities, to have a firm base. And you held that first convention right under the nose of Parliament straight after the war. Well, no, it wasn't the first at all, it was actually the thirteenth, but after so many years in limbo it did feel like a new start. I couldn't go, I was seventy-one and my memory was playing up. No, it's never improved yet it does behave quite well when I'm talking of things long in the past. Just don't ask me what I had for breakfast. I agreed to be president, but only till the council found its feet. You read my speech for me, Jessie, and I hope you read it as boldly as I bade you! I think you'll agree I avoided all sentimental twaddle about Wifehood and Motherhood. I was sick of explaining 'Why' we should have equal rights with men; this time I said flatly, 'Why not?' I blush to recall how once I asked for the ultimate right, the right to enter Parliament, with coy disclaimers that I knew no woman who wanted to, and probably no woman ever would. This time I simply repeated that it was just, it was logical, it was fair, it was right.

And it worked! After all we had done for the nation in war, the men had no grounds for refusal.

Oh, Jessie! It was so long ago! From 1919 to 1933 we waited. Where was our Joan of Arc? Not that we were looking for a martyr. Oh, I expected to wait, perhaps even for two or three elections. But not so long! Well, no regrets. I have lived to see Elizabeth storm the bastions. I am ready to join William and Walter and Jeannie and Ada except for this one last appointment. Yes, I want to encourage her and perhaps to advise her.

My story is nearly over. Poor Walter died in 1915; because of the war I was unable to be by his side. I don't think he ever got over the loss of our son.

And yes, I must talk about our move to this house where we are chatting so pleasantly in my own sitting-room. I lived at Westcote for twenty years, you know. We all grew older, and the thirty acres got rather out-of-hand. There were heaps of rubbish all over the property and Jeannie's lovely garden was totally gobbled up by oxalis and wandering willy. I was not exactly spry myself. William used to call me

Aunt Creaky, and Jeannie's legs would scarcely carry her along. We'd go for walks on Sunday afternoon, the three of us; William and I would be talking nineteen to the dozen as usual, and every now and then we'd realise Jeannie was trailing behind. We'd stand and wait while she tottered up to us. She'd stop to pick those wild daisies by the side of the road. She wasn't short any longer, she was tiny!

When this block of land came up in Riccarton Road I urged William to buy it, using my money as a mortage. It was only a few acres and close to the church and to Marie's, midway to town, so we called it Midway. We began making plans for a house on a grand scale with cottages for the married children. Well, as you see, it's a truly splendid edifice! I know, you're very rude about the size of my wing. I deny absolutely that this sitting-room is as big as a football field. Yes, the bedroom is just as large, and why not? Perhaps I reacted rather strongly after twenty years in a cell but even so, it is nice to have room to move.

When Midway was ready we still hadn't found a buyer for Westcote. We had electric lights but the pump from the well was broken and we'd never got a telephone. When young John invited a friend to stay he jumped on the bed, and it went right through the floor! One day Clara Alley's husband came cycling past our gate. Connie called him in and persuaded him to buy the house. I was very disconcerted when he gave his word without consulting Clara. She had to leave a lovely house she'd designed herself. She got Westcote looking very pretty in the end, but what a struggle!

As for us, we moved into a rectilinear palace. The Lovell-Smiths did not embellish.

'Why did we wait so long?' I asked William.

'Is that a rhetorical question?' It was because of Jeannie, of course. To suggest that Westcote was not perfect was to threaten her very being. She only agreed to move when it was totally out of control.

I'm sad to say she didn't live to enjoy the change for long. In 1924, she and William had their golden wedding. Every year the family made a great fuss of the wedding anniversary with breakfast in bed, special editions of the children's news-paper, flowers and so forth. I went to Marie's on those days, and at Christmas and other big family events. The golden wedding was a grand parade. There were feasts and speeches and relatives turning up from all over the world. There's a photograph on the mantelpiece, Jessie — yes, that's the one. William looks utterly miserable, doesn't he? And Jeannie crumbling before our eyes but still, what a determined cheerfulness! A few months later she died. She had been my friend for forty years. We all missed her dreadfully. Although she grew bitter towards me in spite of herself, she was the heart of the family. She was always very devoted to William.

One year after her death there was a special ceremony at the church, unveiling a plaque in her honour. The memorial service was a solemn event and the church was filled to capacity. At dinner that night our mood was strange, subdued, as we wished Jeannie was with us, yet exhilarated because the whole day was a celebration of her life.

Why did I love William so? His insensitivity was at times monumental. When I was treading on eggs he would blunder in like an elephant. I think he enjoyed making those spectacular gaffes. They weren't accidents, they were punishments.

'Aunty Kate and I are getting married,' he said, deadpan.

The blank looks followed by horror and malice, oh yes, he wanted those, they were his tribute! They were his compensation for twenty-five years of tip-toeing in the dark over borer-riddled floor-boards, the culmination of our perfect Victorian conspiracy.

One month later we married at Marie's house. I wore a rather elegant tan suit and I was very tickled to find that William had obtained a pair of gloves in the exact shade. Marie had a fine little family party for us. Not surprisingly, none of William's family wanted to come. When we returned that evening to Midway, a little apprehensive about our reception, the house was absolutely quiet. No one was there! We called out, we searched the house and the octagonal library, and we found a note on the mantelpiece:

'Dear Father, We know that you and your bride will want to be alone for your honeymoon, so we have gone to Diamond Harbour for a holiday.'

That was all very well, a good joke, but what were we to eat? I could boil an egg and that was the limit of my culinary skills. We managed breakfast but for our other meals we had to visit our friends. After three days we admitted defeat. We took a taxi-cab to Diamond Harbour and pleaded with Win and Macie and Lucy and Annie and Eleanor to come home. They were our base, now; Connie had died at sea, a terrible shock to us all. Doris and Kitty were away in Dunedin at the time, but they too were essential to the household.

Now, of course, there's just me and William's daughters here at Midway, Macie, Win, Kitty and Doris. His sisters have gone to live in Papanui, and his sons are married and living in their own houses nearby. There are still great family gatherings.

Where else would I go? I have lost my only grandchild, don't let's talk about it. This is my home. To all intents and purposes I own it. Naturally the girls will have it when I go.

I waited half a lifetime for two things: those four years of marriage to William, and the election of Elizabeth McCombs. Both have brought a most astonishing relief, as if I had been bound with steel springs for a century and then released without warning. To play golf with William in Hagley Park — two old dodderers with failing eyesight — to take his arm legitimately, to wear that wedding-ring — these have quietened my heart. I long to join him soon.

Receiving Elizabeth's telegram was the second great joy. She had to become a widow before she could make her Maiden Speech. No, Jessie, that's not strange. At my age, nothing is strange. But I still have something to contribute before letting go. That's all it will take, letting go. I am not nervous about dying. The act itself will be exquisitely easy and I am not afraid to meet my Saviour.

I am eager to abandon my self. I imagine Heaven as a sea of white handkerchiefs flapping in unison, or a mountain range of white camellias, or perhaps a thousand thousand miles of white ribbons that fly and float in place of clouds. Every handkerchief is clean, no camellia is bruised, the ribbons never tangle. Any distinction of lace or petals is no more visible than a temporary surging of a single wavelet in the sea. We merge. We lose our personal voice in the great choir which wraps its tones around the earth and harmonic notes ring out though no one soul has sung them. We sing white chords and a rainbow arrives uninvited. No event can be attributed to me. I am part of the whole, I wave, I glow, I contribute my note and it is lost and I rejoice.

And yet I admit to ambivalence. Is it conceivable that William is not William any more? How is it possible for a soul of such domination to drown itself willingly? Though people swarmed over him like bees William was always visible to me as the only person. How can this change utterly?

Then there is Ada. It is years since our ways parted. When I married William she could not forgive me. So strange! I expected the marriage to restore our friendship for it made the relationship thoroughly respectable, but Ada saw it as the final insult. Since then we have never communicated in the conventional way yet she is always in my mind. Her death last year made no difference whatsoever. The past is potent. There is nobody like her. She presses strongly, rubbing her very soul against mine. So how can she now be merely a wave among other waves unknown to me? Surely she is re-organising Heaven in some grand new plan, culling out the weak, demanding perfect peace, writing the rules for good behaviour in eternity!

Well, we are told that in Heaven there is neither marriage nor divorce, no male or female, no Anglicans or Congregationalists or Plymouth Brethren. I yearn for that to be true for then I shall not be singled out, and I shall not have to work out eternity in a difficult *ménage à trois* or *quatre* or *cinq*, there will be no jealousy and no pedestal and no Kate Sheppard. Yet I restrain myself from dying, for fear that in Heaven to my eternal desolation there is neither William nor Ada.

That's all, Jessie. Nothing more. No, I've got no advice apart from — no. This is the end of my story and my name. You're the journalist. If you want to make sense of it all, that's up to you. I've said enough.

PART TWO

My Famous Mother

by Bim Wells

Chapter 22

Cooee! How's that? Press this thingumajig. Oh! That's not hard, nothing hard about it. I've got the hang of it. Here goes, I'll start with what happened this morning.

This morning I put my head down and got cracking with the writing. *My Famous Mother* I'm going to call it. I was doing all right but I got a pain in my arm. Just about decided to give it away when guess what big idiot came knocking at the door! I stuffed it under the cushion.

'Can't you keep away,' I said to him.

'I've brought you a tape recorder,' he said. 'To help you do that book about your mother.'

'Get away!' I told him. 'I'm not writing any darn book!'

He barged inside and plonked it on the kitchen table and tried to show me how it worked.

'I don't want that thing in my house!' I yelled at him. 'I'll get electrocuted!'

He dumped a heap of tape things on the table. 'Just play around with it, Bim,' he said. 'It won't hurt you!' Then he was off. Rude! Didn't even stay for a cup of tea.

I fiddled with it just to spite him. Serve him right if I bust it! Clem down the road came in when I was poking at the buttons.

'What've you got that for?' he asked. So I told him. He reckoned the tapes were duds and he took a couple to swap for proper ones.

'What are you here for anyway?' I asked. Everyone's bothering me this week.

'Saw you were having a bit of trouble with your drive,' he said. 'I could fix it if you like.'

'I do like!' I said. Clem's a big beefy man, not pale and skinny like you know who. He's not a builder but he knows what he's doing. He's going to order the concrete blocks and everything.

So here I am. Feel a bit silly talking to myself. Hope nobody comes knocking at my door tonight, they'll think I'm a loony! Don't usually do anything at night except listen to the wireless. I'm a bit tired after all the gardening and feeding the chooks and the cats. Any day now those eggs'll hatch and that'll be more work.

But I've got the hang of this thingumajig now and I'm going on with the story. I think I was up to Mother going teaching.

She loved her teaching! She loved poetry and Latin and music, and she had high ideals. Everybody said so. But she had to help Gran at home a lot, especially when her sister Connie — well! Her name was never mentioned. I only found out about her when I was about nine years old. I overheard my Aunties saying Connie had been gone ten years. They were topping and tailing gooseberries on the back porch and I was in the garden playing with worms. So I popped up from behind a bush and I said,

'Who's Connie?'

Well! The look on their faces! They didn't know what to say!

'We don't talk about Connie,' said Auntie Nell.

'Who's Connie?' Oh, I was a cheeky brat! Rude!

'Ask no questions and you'll be told no lies,' said Aunty Blanche.

'But I want to know, I want to know, I want to know!'

Aunty Nell gave in. 'Connie used to be your aunty but now she's gone.'

'Gone where? Is she dead?'

'She might as well be dead. And if you don't mind your manners the same thing will happen to you!'

I was impressed. Gone! Just like that! I thought Mother only had four sisters: Blanche, Nell, Kate (not Kate Sheppard!) and Edith, and the baby who died. That's how well they blanked my Aunt Connie out of the family. They crossed her name out of the family Bible as if she had never been born. I wondered what awful thing she had done. It must have been awful. The Pikes were very strict because they were Plymouth Rocks. Later on, when I had my own trouble, I found out what she did.

Now why did my mother go and get married? She should have stayed single like me! But then you get called an old maid and that's supposed to be a fate worse than death. Well, not as bad as being crossed out of the Bible. But close. Sometimes I think I was the lucky one! Nobody tried to make me get married. Except for Ken Smith, that is. Some of the other fellows asked me later on but they were just after my money. I was a born old maid, anyone could see that.

Anyway Mother married Henry Wells. He wasn't a healthy person. He was a chronic asthmatic. They had a short honeymoon at Diamond Harbour. That was a good holiday place, still is, over the Port Hills and round the edge of Lyttelton Harbour and there you are. Nice hills, nice water, not like Christchurch. But a nice place doesn't make a nice honeymoon.

When they came back she went to visit Gran at Office Road. Gran was out the back in the kitchen garden. Office Road was a great big house and it had a lovely garden. Big magnolia trees and real primroses out the front. A good big vegie garden out the back and a paddock for the animals.

'Well, Ada!' said Granma. 'So what do you think of married life?'

You know what Mother said? 'If that's what it's all about I don't think much of it!' And she pulled off her wedding ring and looked over the fence at Gran's horse. 'Here! You can have this! I don't want it.' And she chucked that wedding ring at the horse and it fell into a heap of manure. It wasn't a very good start.

Gran was a lovely person, always the one they called when there was any trouble. One time I asked her, 'Granma, why did Mother and Father get married?'

She was posting a sheet through the wringer and I was winding the handle for all I was worth.

'Goodness me, child — what a question!'

'For love?' I wondered. Mother was always talking about love. 'Love beats at the heart of things,' she'd say. What did she mean? I didn't know then and I still don't know. I thought I'd get the hang of it when I got older. Now I'm eighty-eight I think it was just a fairy tale. Except that's wrong, I do know about love because she loved Chris, my eldest sister. When Mother was sick and Chris came visiting, her face would light up — oh it was amazing to see! And she would say 'Bliss!' Yes, she loved her emotions, getting angry and loving people and all that. But I'm different.

Now where was I? Gran was catching the sheets and twisting them into the washing basket.

'Was that why you married Granpa?' I asked her. 'Love?'

'Careful, Bim!' she said. 'Granpa had kind eyes, that's why I married him.'

'Even though he was a Plymouth Rock?' I asked.

'Hush!' said Gran, as if Granpa could hear us.

'But why did Mother and Father get married?' I nagged. Once I got started I couldn't stop. The sheet got tangled up in the rollers and Gran took over. 'Father hasn't got kind eyes.'

'Men and women get married and that's that,' she said firmly. 'Now hush with your questions and keep your mind on the job.'

I tried my Aunty Nell. I was starting to feel funny about boys.

'Miss Fine and Fancy Ada thought she was too good to be a home-help so she upped and offed. Personally I thought it was very selfish of her.'

'And personally I think you were jealous,' I piped back. Oh, I was a pig of a kid!

'Jealous? I was only five years old!'

I tried again with Gran. 'Were you cross when Mother got married?'

'Love-a-duck, no!' said Gran.

'Then why was Aunty Nell cross?'

'Oh, she adored Ada!' said Gran. 'I suppose she missed her when she got married.' Didn't make sense.

Mother had babies one two three and I was number three. She should never have had me, it was too soon. I was nothing but a darn nuisance. She had a lot of trouble having me — I nearly wasn't born at all!

I wasn't wanted. One of my Aunties said Mother tried to get rid of me. But I don't believe it, she wouldn't do a thing like that. That was an awful thing to say!

I suppose Mother wasn't very pleased about having me because Father never gave her any housekeeping money and there was no law that said he had to, either. I don't know what he did with his salary.

Anyway, I was born on the nineteenth of September, 1887. That's one date I know for sure! And do you know what she wanted to call me? Guinevere Alice Cecile! What a mouthful! That was Mother — she always had big ideas. She should have called me something like Jane. I would have suited Jane. She told my father to go and register the birth. He must have been drunk or something, he got the name completely wrong. He didn't care. Fancy wanting to call me Guinevere! I was always called Bim.

I didn't find out till I was in my forties. That's when I went to Australia and I had to get a passport. So I got a copy of my birth certificate and there it was: A-lice, Ce-lice. Chris thought it was so funny! She hooted when I told her! What a name!

Mother got a job and we were looked after in the daytime by Elsie the cook. Elsie was good to me. She was with us most of the time for seven years. Sometimes she had a holiday and then there were others who looked after us. They weren't so good, not all of them. One of them was a bit of a thief. She stole my Faith, Hope and Charity that someone had given me — those nice little trinkets. But Elsie was good. I spent a lot of time with her. She was a decent sort of cook! Just as well, because Mother didn't like cooking.

Mother was a great admirer of John Stuart Mill. He could read and write in Latin when he was four years old. So Mother thought if he could, why not us? On Saturday afternoons we had to sit and learn our words. I hated it!

'What's that, Bim? Come on, you know it!' I stared and stared at the copy book. The squiggles didn't make any sense to me. I was more interested in the outside world. I looked out the window and I saw Father unhitching our horse Dolly from the trap.

Bam! A belt on the head with the ABC book. Mother was trying to bang it into my head. Cos was snickering; I could just about hear her thinking how stupid I was. Chris put her head down deeper into her own book and copied out another word.

'Come on now, Bim, I've told you this again and again. You can't be that stupid, you're just doing it to provoke me.'

Her finger pointed at the squiggle, a fat circle and a line.

'I don't know and I don't care!' I squeaked. Oh, I was a devil!

'You will care!' threatened Mother. Chris and Cos were both popping their eyes. Mother dragged me by the ear and pushed me into the cupboard under the stairs. I didn't care! I wanted to go outside and feed the horse.

'I'm only four years old and I'm too young to learn the ABC!' I bellowed. 'I don't want to grow up!'

I was a brat, I was a little horror! But I didn't care about being shut in the cupboard. There was a slit in the wall and a bit of light came through. I just stayed there and played. I pulled down all the coats and made a soft bed. I rolled around in the coats for a while. Then I got one of the brooms and played horsey. It was better than learning the ABC.

Later on Mrs Fletcher came to see Mother, and after a while she asked, 'Where's Bim?'

Mother came and opened the cupboard and the two ladies stared in at me. Mrs Fletcher had her hair pulled back tight with a little fringe.

'She was naughty so I pushed her in there,' said Mother.

I just shoved past them and ran outside. I wasn't a bit upset.

We lived in Mays Road. It had dark panelling inside, too dark for me. I liked being outside better. Mother pulled down the heavy curtains to let in the light.

We were lucky, we had a paddock next door. Dolly was a nice placid horse, and we had a cow, Buttercup, and some pigs. Father used to milk the cow but he never really took to it. He was too impatient. Buttercup was always nice and warm to touch. I was the one who weeded the path and fed the chooks. I didn't mind, I liked it. Better than doing the ABC!

Mays Road was a bit out of town, and the drains were just ditches along the side of the roads. People had cesspools behind their houses for all the household slops. Not from the dunnies, the nightcart came for that. We had pigs to eat up our scraps. Mother said cesspools brought disease, and by Jove she was right!

She never liked flies. I remember a tremendous argument with the butcher. She told him off for letting flies in his shop.

'They spread disease,' she said. 'You must get your boy to swat them, every one. And you must keep the door of your shop shut.'

The butcher roared with laughter. 'You hear that, people! Mrs Wells says that flies spread disease! I don't know where she gets her information from.' We didn't eat much meat.

Henry didn't help much with bringing us up. He used to get up at night and walk the streets for hours, he couldn't sleep. I don't think that would have helped the asthma much — Christchurch was on a swamp! On cold nights all that water used to rise up in a fog. That's what I like about New Brighton. The sea breeze blows away all the muck in the air. But in Christchurch with all those coal fires going sometimes the air was slimy like an old dishcloth. Don't tell me that's good for asthma!

But what could he do? He didn't have the patience to just lie in bed, he didn't have the patience full stop! And that didn't help the asthma either. In the middle of the night I'd wake up and hear him shouting, and Mother shouting back and then some awful noises, and then the door would slam, he was gone into the night.

He had to have his tea at six o'clock sharp. And us kids, we kids had to be upstairs and pushed out of the way. We had to play quietly and not make a noise. He couldn't stand to see us around. We'd have a musical hour, you know, with combs and whistles and things. Chris and Cos were very clever, very musical. But sometimes we got a bit noisy and Henry would come upstairs with his slipper. He had a flaky sort of skin that went red and patchy when he got mad. He would lash out at anyone who wasn't in bed. You had to be quick. I was shrewd, I used to hop into bed with all my clothes on. He hated kids that cried. Half the time he couldn't even aim straight.

I can't stand kids that cry. Wah wah wah! They make me so mad!

It was music music all the week for Father, that was his job. On Sunday afternoons he had time off, and three men would come to the house and we had to go upstairs while he played the violin in this quartet. One time Chris and Cos were reading as quiet as mice but I got restless. I hated staying still at the best of times. I started bouncing on the bed in time to the music. Thump thump thump! Then the music stopped and I heard that squeaky stair halfway up. Quick as a flash I crawled under the bed and pulled the covers down the side, and Chris and Cos got the slipper! I was a devil! Most kids are little horrors and I was the worst of the lot.

Chapter 23

I wish I was more like Mother. I get so mad! Stan came round to see how I was getting on and I told him straight.

'What's the point? I haven't got the brain!'

He doesn't waste time telling me any different, even he's not that stupid.

'Are you having trouble with the tape recorder?' he says.

'It goes bung,' I tell him. 'I did about Chris and Cos being born and it all fell off or something.'

So he labels all the tapes Monday, Tuesday, Wednesday, and so on.

'That'll stop you using them twice,' he says.

'I don't want them in the house! They're full of electricity.'

So he takes the ones I've done and puts them in his pocket. Butting in like that! Who's doing this story, me or him?

Lots of times Mother woke us up very early and she'd say, 'Come on, girls, we're going to Gran's for a little holiday.'

A quick wash of the face and off we'd go. No sign of Father. Granma would meet us at the door with a set look on her little face, and give us all a hug. She would add some water to the porridge in the big pot and all the aunties and uncles would gather round and stare at us in a special way. Aunty Edith was only three years older than me.

'So, here you are again,' said Aunty Nell one time. 'As if Maria hasn't got enough mouths to feed!' They all called Gran Maria, I don't know why. But that was a strange thing to say because Aunty Blanche had left Christchurch and the baby was dead. There was plenty of room. I think Aunty Nell was just jealous.

I liked being at Granma's. She was so kind to me. We ate

a lot of potatoes at Gran's and there were always plenty of dumplings in the stew. And she always had pumpkins. That might be where I got my taste for them. People laugh when they come here because I've always got my pumpkins sitting round the house, my own little suns, shining out in every room. They grow in the sand and they keep well as long as they're in the dry.

This running back and forwards to Gran's went on for years before I found out what the actual reason was. And it's not very nice so I won't talk about it.

I should say why Aunty Blanche left home. She was the second oldest, after Mother. She was very upset that Mother had left the family church. They used to argue hammer and tongs. They woke me up one night when I was little. I heard Mother at the top of her voice: 'So you believe the Devil rules the world?'

She loved a good argument. But she didn't convince Aunty Blanche, oh no. There was a Miss Wildman visiting Christchurch at the time, and she was a strict Plymouth Rock. She used to scare us half to death with her talk of Hell. Aunty Blanche went off to Sydney with her and they ran a girls' boarding school. They never went out after dark, they wore old-fashioned clothes and they never cut their hair, not even an inch.

Father was back at St Michael's. There was a new young vicar, Averill, and he made Father furious. Averill wanted easy music that the congregation could sing. Simple things like 'All Things Bright and Beautiful'. Can't see anything wrong with that myself, hymns with a bit of oomph. But Father kept training up the choir to do oratorios. Spohr's 'Last Judgement' was a favourite one of his — terrible stuff I call it!

Father used to say if Averill wanted sing-songs he should join the Salvation Army. When the vicar was taking a quiet little communion service, Henry would have a choir practice in the schoolroom next door.

'Louder!' he'd shout at the top of his voice. 'God's in his heaven, he's not listening outside the door!' He had a knack of hitting a climax just as the vicar was blessing the bread and wine.

The vestry was always calling Father in for a telling off. The church was hard up, they wanted popular music so their income would go up. Half the time Father didn't even turn up for practices. The choir would be waiting in the schoolroom — no choir master! Sometimes he took a snitch against the hymns. The vicar would say 'Hymn 166' and Father would pop up out of his little cubby hole and announce, 'Hymn 166 is not suitable. We shall sing Hymn 160.' And away he'd go — 'Holy Holy Holy!' Oh, he had some battles at St Michael's all right. But with his Motette he could do what he liked, they could sing 'The Last Judgement' to their hearts' content.

Well, when Mother was teaching at Main School, Father's Motette put on a concert and I went. I was about four. Rows and rows of long benches. Every few feet there was a round hole with an inkwell in it. I put my finger in the ink and wiped it on the desk and Cos smacked my hand. The coal stove was going and there was an awful draught. The concert was mostly classical but there were a few good tunes. It was a sort of graduation for the ones who passed the Third Standard. Mother was in her best grey dress with the big lumpy sleeves.

That was the only time I ever saw her at St Albans School. By the time I was five Mother didn't work there any more.

The school committee was very pleased with their headmaster but Mr Speight had a down on Mother for her modern ideas. Jealous — he was jealous of her! She was all for Votes for Women and he didn't like that. One of the men on the committee was always trying to stir up trouble, telling on her for this so-called excessive flogging of his sons. But if she flogged them then they deserved it! I reckon their father put them up to mischief on purpose.

Mother got up a petition that summer asking for a longer holiday. She was so tired and the nor'westers got on her nerves. A lot of people say the same. They've bothered me except when I was trying to bike across town in the wrong direction. Anyway, St Albans had to have just the five weeks, same as other schools and when school went back Mother stayed home with us. The last two years she'd been flat out. She had enough to do what with earning a living and running the household and singing in the choir but every spare minute she was on the go doing Votes for Women. They didn't get it that year but Mother wasn't put off.

'The voice in the wilderness!' Chris and Cos nodded wisely. I bet they didn't know what it meant either. 'Our time will come.'

At Christmas she seemed to sort of collapse a bit. I did everything she told me, all the dusting and carpet-sweeping, but sometimes I wanted to go and play with my mates and I did. I was an awful kid. We had one of those chairs that the back goes down if you fiddle with it — a Morris chair. When Miss Bain or Mrs Edmond came to call I'd slip round behind them and pull out the rod and they'd go flat on their backs. They looked so funny! I couldn't help it! I saw Mrs Ballantyne's bloomers! I was a trial to Mother, and that was probably why she collapsed, but I didn't do that trick after Mrs Fletcher injured her back.

Mother got leave of absence from the Board of Education on account of ill health. But one of the teachers happened to know what sort of ill health. He told the committee and they were horrified! She was expecting! I didn't understand all the fuss. Mother believed in telling children the facts of life and she probably thought she told us but I only remember hearing about the grand old oak tree and the dear fluffy little chick, not about babies. I probably wasn't listening properly.

The school committee were just dying to get rid of her. It wasn't just the flogging, she upset them more with her radical opinions. They hated her writing to the newspaper. She was the best teacher they had but they didn't like her extra-curricular activities! Anyway here was their chance. They told her to resign. They sent a deputation to Mr Henry Wells! Couldn't have done anything stupider if they'd tried. It was none of Father's business!

In the end Mother did resign, she didn't give in, she just

changed her mind. Well, thank goodness the next baby was a boy. Mother didn't care, but Father did. I just thought, you little beggar, you're the youngest now, they'll have someone else to pick on.

Father was beside himself — a boy after three girls! All puffed up as if it was the first boy in the world. When the musicians came round on a Sunday, Father showed them the baby and told them to play quietly! Play quietly! I ask you! He was in a good temper for weeks. He said Mother should stay home and look after the baby, he would pay for the groceries. Well, she didn't go back to her teaching, but she didn't exactly stay home and look after the baby, either.

Where was I? Oh, that's right. Mother collected a heck of a lot of signatures for that first petition. It was seventy yards long, but it wasn't enough, Parliament wasn't impressed!

So Mother carried on regardless. They had their meetings at our place or at Gran's. Talk talk talk! They couldn't wait to say their piece. Mother's voice was the strongest and could she use it! You wanted to agree like mad or else wriggle away, you couldn't just take it or leave it. When she laughed, she really laughed, she would roar! Mrs Sheppard's voice was lighter, a fluty voice, very pretty. She wore the most wonderful dresses with silver brooches and furs, and the softest leather gloves. I know because the ladies left their outdoor things in the hall and sometimes I used to fiddle with them when I came home from school.

I wanted to be like them but I wasn't and I never would be. It took me years to get the message.

Mother loved singing but Father wasn't nice to her. In fact he was a bit of a bully. Once he gave her a solo part in a piece of Handel. She practised and practised. Then a week before the performance he stopped the rehearsal.

'Can anyone tell me the source of that caterwauling? Oh, it was you, was it Mrs Wells? I thought someone must be torturing a cat. Mrs Gough, you take over Mrs Wells's part.'

Mrs Gough didn't even know it! But Father wouldn't change his mind, Mother had to go back into the chorus.

Oh, he wasn't kind to her at all. He was always picking

on her at Motette practices. One time Mother had a new hat. It was quite something! She hardly ever had new clothes but she liked to look respectable. Well, if Father didn't give her what for over that hat, he couldn't stand it! The first time she wore it he stopped the singing with a loud chord.

'Mrs Wells,' he said. 'Why are you sitting in the front row?'

'Why shouldn't I?' says she.

'I suppose you want to show off. Stand up and give everyone a good look!'

'That's not what we're here for, Henry. Get on with the practice,' says Mother. The choir sat like mice.

'Oh, I thought it was a sideshow. Stand up, Mrs Wells! Show us your tea-tray! Go on!'

What could she do? There were over a hundred people waiting to get on with the rehearsal. So Mother stood up and paraded in front of choir. She smiled and turned her head to every angle. They laughed, they enjoyed it! She turned it into a victory.

I just had to stop in the middle of the story. They came round with my copy of *Plain Truth*. I always give them my tithe in cash.

Now, that was the hat. So. Father was pleased when the second petition failed. That was mean, after Mother had worked so hard!

'Perhaps I'll come home and find tea ready tomorrow. That'll make a nice change,' he said.

Mother tipped her head on one side. 'You won't starve to death while Elsie's here.'

Two days later Mother was taking the new petition forms into the shops and up and down the street. People didn't rag her half so much now. They were getting used to the idea of Votes for Women.

Mother started taking the forms to Motette. More than half the choir was women, she got them signing right under Father's nose! The first time he went red in the face.

'This is a choir practice, not a cackle club. Put those tracts back in your bag.'

'Oh, but this is our tea-break,' said Mother. 'We can do what we like.'

Everybody hushed when Father and Mother had a spat. They didn't want to miss anything!

'Oh, sign your silly bits of paper then! It won't come to anything.' The scaly bits on his forehead used to go blotchy when he got cross. 'Only freaks want the vote. Real women are perfectly satisfied to wash their husband's socks as God intended.'

Mother smiled and turned to the women near her. 'You see? We shouldn't be here. We should all be home washing socks!'

'Quite so!' crowed Father.

'Then who's going to sing in your choir, Henry?' Mother said sweetly. 'If we women all stay home?'

'One male voice is worth a dozen female! You're all wobble and no body, you women.' Talk about the pot calling the kettle black! He would bark like a dog when he was ticking you off.

Anyway that didn't go down very well. She got a lot of new signatures that night. She wasn't against the 'woman's sphere'. As a matter of fact she did a lot of tapestries and she was keen on Home Science, but more in theory than practice.

Now I was going to school like Chris and Cos. I stayed in the baby class for quite a long time. I could have gone faster, course I could but — oh, look here, I wasn't in a hurry to move up to the next class with Cos. She was a teacher's pet. I used to pretend to have a tummy ache so I could stay home with Elsie.

One day the teacher gave me a note asking Mother to come after school. It was a jolly nuisance but Mother went because it was about my education. I had to clean the blackboard even though I wasn't a monitor. I had sharp ears.

'Mrs Wells, I'm concerned about Bim,' said the teacher quietly.

Mother laughed. 'You can't make a silk purse out of a sow's ear!'

'Chris and Cos were a joy to teach.'

'Bim is not like other children. She is odd.'

I wasn't odd! There were plenty of kids like me. The dust went up my nose and made me sneeze.

'Scuse me, miss, I'll go and bang the duster outside,' I said.

'Bim!' Mother was shocked. 'Miss Elmsley, if you please.'

'The other kids call her Miss,' I said.

'A lady would never say that,' she said firmly. 'And don't say kids!'

She held my hand till we were out of sight of the school and then she shook it off.

'Oh dear, oh dear! What are we going to do with you?' Her beautiful eyes met mine full on. They were like two moons shining into your soul when she looked at you like that. She was telling me I was a lost cause. But I didn't believe her.

Writing wasn't hard for Mother. She wrote many, many letters. Not because she had to. She wanted to! There was a pile of letters on the hall table every morning. I would look at those envelopes and know that every one was full of words that she thought up out of her own head. Not copied words! Little parcels of ideas. I could never do that. I didn't have anything in my head.

Well, she didn't give up on me easily, but she began letting me off early from our Saturday afternoon classes. One day she announced to Chris and Cos,

'I'm afraid that Bim is not scholastic.' She sent me out to weed the paths instead.

I didn't mind being called the silly one. I didn't want to study study study all the time. I loved the animals! I took scraps out to the pigs and I brought in the eggs. I didn't mind weeding. I used to cheat a bit, ripped the tops off the dandelions and they came up bigger than ever. I was a brat!

It must have been hard on Mother knowing I wasn't scholastic. She said every woman must reach the highest possible standard of education and now it looked as if I wouldn't even get to Standard One! Poor Mother! It was lucky she had something to take her mind off me.

I'll never forget the day I turned six years old. Elsie prepared a special tea for us with treacle pudding and lots of cream. There was a roast of mutton and Elsie promised me the knuckle bone with the lovely chewy bits. But Mother was late. I wanted my birthday tea but Elsie kept saying wait for Mother. The table was set in the dining room with nice clean damask table napkins, even one for me instead of my usual bib. I wasn't a tidy eater! Father was in his study waiting till it was over. He wouldn't eat with the children, not even on a birthday. I was worried, it was nearly six o'clock, time for Father's tea.

Then Mother walked in with a pink glow on her face. She looked younger than she had for months. She paused at the door to make sure we were all listening.

'The Governor has signed!' she announced in triumph.

'Hurray! Hurray!' Chris and Cos and I started dancing round the table. Mother went out to the kitchen and called Elsie in.

'Elsie, you have been given the right to vote!'

'Arise, Sir Elsie!' I screamed at the top of my voice.

Elsie's big face went purple and she burst into tears.

'Excuse me, Mrs Wells — I'm just so happy for you!' she sobbed through her apron.

'And I'm happy for you, Elsie. It's about time you got some credit for all your domestic skills.'

'You're so clever!'

'Oh, but you signed the petition, Elsie! You did it too!'

I couldn't stop screaming so Chris gave me a bit of a shake.

'Mr Seddon sent Mrs Sheppard such an obsequious telegram.' We all had a good laugh at that even though we didn't know what obsequious meant. 'He knows he'll have to watch his step from now on!'

Elsie burst into giggles. She made two of Mother!

There was a crash behind us and we all turned to look. Father had come into the room. He'd pulled one of his paintings off the wall and smashed it on the floor.

'Henry!' Mother said sharply.

'I never liked that one,' Father said quite calmly and he stamped on it. His foot went right through the canvas. 'And that's a womanish sort of thing.' And he pulled down Mother's favourite water-colour, one of the Port Hills.

'Don't be silly,' she said but he stamped it out of the frame and threw it on the fire. 'Henry, please!'

He was wrecking Mother's nice room! She didn't say a word, just took us out the back where Elsie gave us our nice hot tea on the kitchen table, using the kitchen silver just like an ordinary day.

Mother looked surprised when Elsie carved the roast and served me first with the knuckle.

'Birthday girl,' said Elsie, and Mother remembered.

'Well, Bim, you've got the best birthday present you'll ever have in your life. Even you will be able to vote when you're old enough.' Wasn't that a wonderful present? And she gave me a new pinny too, with a green frill around the edge. In the background the crashing went on and on as Father went through every room in the house.

Mother couldn't say a thing. The paintings were Father's property. He'd painted them all and he owned everything in the house, even things that Mother had bought with her own teaching money. That was the law, you see.

Chapter 24

This morning it was drizzling. I like swimming in the rain. The mist was blowing away by the time I got home. Brushed my hair inside in front of the heater. That old wooden hairbrush seems to get heavier as it gets older. I didn't do a good job of pinning up the hair — missed a bit. It makes such a difference if you can get the sunshine on it! It thickens up so the pins can get a grip.

Knock knock knock.

'Come in, come in, don't stand on ceremony,' I called out. I thought it was Clem from up the road but it was you know who along with his awful kids.

'I don't want those kids inside!' I told him. 'They'll frighten the chickens!' My eggs have hatched in the hot water cupboard, cheep cheep cheep all day long.

'We can't stop,' he said — as if I cared! 'I'm taking them for a picnic. Here's some more tapes.' He put the used ones in his bag. He counted them once and he counted them twice.

'What's the matter?' I said. 'Lost something?'

'Never mind,' he said.

'I'll give you picnics!' I flicked my tea towel at the little horrors.

'Goodbye, Bim,' said the boy. 'I hope you're feeling better.' He's quite tall now. I don't like them in the house. I had Mac staying with me last year, that chap whose wife left him high and dry, and he said those kids stole money from his drawer and that's why he was always behind with his board. I never caught them at it — they're sly all right! Well, I helped set him up in his own flat so he's gone now. But my word I watch those kids like a hawk!

Can't tell Stan that though. He won't listen. He thinks the

197

sun shines out of those two brats. They hang around him like he was Father Christmas. It makes me sick!

Maybe I shouldn't have said that stuff about Mother expecting, she mightn't like that. But she's dead, what can she do? But I haven't said why she got married. That's a secret. What would people say? They might feel sorry for her. Oh, she'd hate that!

I opened the hot water cupboard to feed the chicks. They ate up their mash like anything. I put one on the table and it pecked up the crumbs. What a racket! Like a little pea shooter. It reminded me of the time I took some acorns to Sunday School and threw them at Mrs Hoare's black grosgrain bottom when she bent down. She wouldn't let me go back again. I didn't mind!

Well now. I suppose I was over-excited because of my birthday and getting the vote. I never could keep my feelings under control. When I woke up and heard the noises in the night I did something different. Got out of bed. Chris and Cos were sound asleep. I still had my socks on.

The noise was coming from Mother's and Father's bedroom, and I tip-toed along the hall to the door. It was open a crack and I pushed it a weeny bit more. I wished I hadn't.

Mother was right down the floor squeezed tight into the corner as if she was trying to get down a mousehole. That was the strangest thing. She was always saying 'Stand up straight, Bim, stand up proudly!' And although she was short in the body, she always seemed to be tall. Now she was all crumpled up like a dirty sheet ready for the copper.

Father was on the far side of the bed. He had a bit of wood in his hand all spattered with blobs of paint. He biffed it across the room and it only just missed her. My heart went stop start. Then he clambered over the bed and he was on top of her with his hands round her throat, squeezing his thumbs in and banging her head against the wall — her beautiful throat full of words, her beautiful head full of brains! I couldn't bear it! I felt sick, I felt awful! As if I'd known all along that this was what happened in the night and I'd just let it happen. But I didn't! I definitely did not.

'Father!' My voice sort of gobbled and his head spun round. He let go Mother's throat but when he saw it was only me he said viciously,

'She asked for it!' And he stood up and started kicking. She got it in the back and even on her bosom, no matter what way she turned he found somewhere to kick. I rushed straight at him trying to pinch some part that wasn't thrashing around.

'Stop it stop it stop it!' I tried to yell, but my voice went funny again. His musical fingers peeled my hands away and I chomped his leg with my teeth. I had a mouthful of horrible-feeling tweed, I felt like being sick but I wasn't, I bit right through like a dog, then I heard Mother whispering.

'Sh! You'll wake Chris and Cos!'

I was so amazed! What would she say a thing like that for? My bite went loose and Father shook me off. He gave me a darn good shove with his foot and went down the stairs two at a time and out the door, slamming it behind him.

For a moment I didn't move, I just couldn't. Then I started crawling towards Mother. I didn't want to stand up and be taller than her.

'Mother! Stand up!' I was so mad at her for just lying there! My throat was burning, it tasted like sick. The heap of clothes shifted and I could see her face. I put my head in her skirt so she wouldn't see how mad I was, but she pushed me away.

'Hush, child! Do you want to wake your sisters?'

'Yes I do! Chris can help me get you into bed!'

'She'll do no such thing,' said Mother briskly. 'Chris isn't strong, you know.'

She always seemed perfectly strong to me but I suppose Mother knew best. Mother sucked her mouth in and I got scared. She was pale and sweating, it was awful. I wanted to get her into bed but I was too small. She couldn't even talk! I tucked a blanket round her.

'I'll get Elsie,' I decided. Mother's eyes were shut tight and I thought I saw a squint of water. I tried to wipe it up. Couldn't have that! She knocked my hand off and I ran downstairs. Elsie slept out the back of the kitchen under a patchwork quilt. I shook her and pinched her till she woke up.

'Come and help Mother!' She put on a dressing gown and slippers and followed me up. She frowned and tut-tutted when she saw Mother.

'He'll get his come-uppance one of these days, that man,' she muttered. She tidied the bottom sheet and we got Mother on to the bed and lying down properly. I did help a bit I think.

Elsie told me to go downstairs, put some kindling in the range and heat the kettle for a cuppa. I did all that and then I made the tea, I knew how to do it, I'd watched Elsie hundreds of times. I took it carefully carefully up the stairs, a big cup with milk and no sugar. Mother loved her tea. She used to say, ' I know it's poison but I love it.' I got it exactly right but Elsie sent me down for some sugar. Elsie held the cup while Mother drank it. Her face was so white!

Elsie told me to get my clothes on, wrap up warm. Then she said carefully.

'Bim, I want you to run and fetch your Gran.'

'No!' I said like a shot. It was dark, it was the middle of the night! And it was cold and Gran's was a long way away, oh, at least a mile. Elsie sat on the bed and took me on her knee.

'Your mother is very ill. She needs your Gran right now. And who will go if you don't?'

'You go,' I said. 'I'll look after Mother.' Did you ever hear such cheek from a kid? Mother had another pain and her face scrunched up.

'No, Bim, Mrs Wells needs me here till your Gran comes.'

'I'll wake up Chris, she can go!' I told her. Chris was nine! 'Or we could go together.'

Mother opened her eyes. And she looked at me, oh dear oh dear did she look at me!

'Bim! Must you always let me down?' I ran downstairs, put on my coat and gumboots and went into the dark night.

There were streetlamps, it wasn't really pitch black. But

they were a long way apart. Fog kept swirling up and blotting out the houses and the lights. Things gloomed up out of nowhere. Scary. My hands were frozen before I got to the first corner. The fog caught in my throat and made me choke. But I ran and walked, walked and ran on my tough legs along the streets. I went the short way through the rough part of Papanui, past the public house that was full of rowdy men and shrieking women. A drunk man staggered out the door and shouted into the night.

'Curse on the women! Curse on the women!'

Then he was sick all over. I crossed over the road and there were two dirty men sitting in a doorway and they reached out their hands to me! I ran and ran!

It seemed so much further than usual to Office Road, but I got there. I opened the door and shut it quickly behind me, shutting out the cold swirly dark and the drunk men. My heart was banging like a mad thing, my breath was burning holes in my chest.

Gran came down in her nightie. She wrapped her warm arms around me and I burst into tears. I was a horrible crier, I made a horrible narky noise like a chook. I never cry now, it was just when I was a kid. I could feel myself shaking all over. At the same time I was thinking, oh, why do I have to cry! What a drippy kid I was! Gran made nice noises into my wet hair and patted me on the back.

When I told her about Mother she said nothing at all except 'Hmm.' She rubbed my head with a towel and then she got dressed and we walked back together as fast as we could. It was much nicer holding her hand.

The rest of the night was terrible. They made me go back to bed! I wanted to help, I could have but they wouldn't let me. Elsie gave me a nice hot cup of milk in the kitchen and then she put me into her own bed so I wouldn't wake up Chris and Cos. It was lumpy but it was warm. I did go to sleep and when I woke up I felt awful.

I crept up the stairs to see what was going on. It was still dark and Chris and Cos were still asleep. Elsie hurried down holding the baby's bath covered with a towel. She didn't even talk to me! I suppose she was tired, she must have been up all night. I hung around the door of Mother's room, not wanting to barge in. They thought I was a rowdy kid but I could be quiet when I wanted! It was dead quiet in there. Mother just lying in bed with a poultice on her forehead, Gran holding her hand with her back to the door. Down by my foot I saw something horrible, a cloth covered in blood! Mother must be dying!

Then Mother said, 'What was it? Could you tell?'

And Gran said quietly, 'Ada, it was a boy.'

Mother gave a sort of choking laugh. 'Serve him right!' she said.

'Now don't say that, Ada. Don't say anything at all.'

'There's nothing to say. There's just a whole lot of things to do. Laws to change.'

'Shush now! You rest.'

'But why oh why —' Mother stopped in the middle of her sentence and that was funny, she was very hot on grammar, we all had to finish our sentences.

'Please don't say it. You know I blame myself.' Dear Gran, she always tried to take on other people's troubles. Then a terrible thing happened or nearly happened. I thought Mother was going to start crying. I tip-toed away. She wouldn't want me to see her crying. I picked up the horrible cloth and took it down to Elsie.

She kept us away from Mother all that day. But in the evening Mother was starting to feel better because I heard her say in her old voice, 'Chris darling! Come and give me a kiss!'

And Chris went running in and I heard Mother say, 'Mmmm — bliss! My lovely clever Christabel!'

Father came back that very day. He had nowhere else to go.

A long time later, I was over forty, I met someone who used to be in the Motette and she said, 'It must have been hard on you children, having a father who drank.'

You could have knocked me down with a feather! For a moment I believed her, see. Then I got my wits about me.

'He did not drink!' I told her. 'Where on earth did you get that idea?' I gave her what for, believe me.

I would have known if he was a drinker! I did use to wonder what he did with his money because Mother never saw a penny of it. But it must have been something else because he wasn't a drinker. I'm sure he wasn't! He just had a nasty temper. It was the artistic temperament. Not drink!

Actually there was an enormous pile of bottles hidden in the bushes in our garden. I used to play with them. I found them when I was little and I took one in to Elsie.

'What does it say?' I asked.

'It's a vinegar bottle,' she said.

'There's hundreds of them!' I said. She must have used a lot of vinegar over the years, with the pickling and so forth. When I was older I said to her,

'But it says WINE, see?' She explained that meant the vinegar was made out of wine. Father wasn't a drinker at all.

There was a grand party the following week for all the women who had worked for the Franchise and the men too. It was called a Meeting of Thanksgiving and Enrolment. Mother rested during the afternoon. Then she got out of bed and dressed in her best, including the famous hat. We were allowed to go too! She said we were women, Chris and Cos and me — even me! She said we were witnessing the dawn of democracy!

What a party! Ribbons flying all over the hall, green and violet and white. White camellias in bunches big as bushes. So pretty! There was a lot of singing but for once Father wasn't involved. He didn't even go to the party.

Best of all I remember the anthem sung by the Smith family. William Sidney Smith composed it, and his wife and his sisters and daughters and sons all stood up and sang together. I liked it so much I learned it off by heart for my recitation that year. Mother liked it too, but she said Lord Tennyson's poetry was better.

The Smith family were all of them wonderful singers.

They sang in harmony and it was lovely. Ken was still a soprano, he was about ten I suppose. Look, I'll recite it now.

A SONG OF NEW ZEALAND

From the lone Pacific Ocean,
Where the waves, with restless roar,
Rear their heads in wild commotion,
Ere they dash upon the shore:

From the hills and vales of Zealand,
From those lovely sisters three;
Which (combined to make our free land)
Stand engirdled by the sea:

Lo, there comes a shout of gladness,
Wafted far across the sea,
Banishing all fear and sadness —
'Tis the voice of people free!

Gone the ancient days of evil,
When the women — oh, the shame! —
Treated like the driven cattle,
Bore men's burden and men's blame.

Now, those wrongful times are ended:
Women here are women free;
And the children, face upbended,
Listen at the mother's knee

To the story oft-repeated,
How Truth, like a swelling tide,
Made the yoke to be uplifted,
Placed the woman by man's side.

By W. Sidney Smith.

I always say the name at the end so people will know who wrote it. I might have left some out.

Oh, what a nice song that was! 'Those lovely sisters three' — I thought that meant me and Cos and Chris.

It was interesting to see the men. Mr Smith was the most

dashing! He wore knickerbockers and he had a beard with a lovely shape and flashing eyes. Mrs Sheppard mentioned Mother in her speech and Mother got a good clap. And when Sir John Hall talked about Mrs Sheppard everyone stood up and shouted and threw their flowers in the air. She looked very embarrassed and so she should. It wasn't just her who won the battle! Her hair was frothing out round her face, a bit too curly for my liking.

Then it was suppertime. I said to Mother, 'You stay here, Mother, I'll bring you a dish of raspberry ice.' She was sitting with all her friends. I loved raspberry ices! We used to have them on the School Treats. I got one but I couldn't get through the crowd so I ate it myself. What a pig of a kid I was!

The people thinned out and I saw that Mother had some anyway. Somebody else must have brought it. I got some little sandwiches instead but Mother said, 'No thank you, Bim.' So I gave them to Mrs Sheppard. She was wearing a velvet dress in a beautiful lavender shade, with a big bunch of lace round the neck all caught up in a silver brooch. She said thank you for the sandwiches and I went all hot. When she started talking to the ladies again I took a handful of that velvet, I couldn't resist. I'd never felt anything so soft! I was overexcited and I rubbed my face in it. She turned around to see what was happening.

'Do you like my dress, Bim?' she asked. I was so embarassed I ran away and hid behind a curtain and I heard Mrs Sheppard laugh her fluty laugh and Mother apologising.

That was the last bit of fun for ages. The elections were coming up and every woman had to enrol. It was like organising an army! Mother went to all the election meetings. She made those men wriggle! They didn't know what had hit them! She just about wore herself out but the results put the roses back in her cheeks. The women turned out in their thousands!

Chapter 25

After my swim I washed my hair in the basin. My arms get tired doing that, I get so shaky with it. I wish I was young again! Mother always said cleanliness was next to godliness and I always keep neat and tidy, at least when I go to the shops. She loved baths, she had one every day of her life. I like the sea better. Sometimes I hose myself down in my bathing costume. Always dry my hair in the sun, it kills the germs. I must look a sight with my long grey hair crackling in the sunshine. But I have to come inside to do the story because of the electricity.

When they started the *White Ribbon*, Mother was a proper journalist. She wrote the Home Page! She could put down whatever she liked. I've got those articles right here.

'Most of us have erred and strayed from the path of Nature in our diet, and therefore the sooner we betake ourselves to a simple and natural mode of living the better for our bodies.' She was all for the simple life because she hated housework. Oh, she was so clever! She told people how to treat typhoid and croup and scarlet fever and how to make oatmeal jelly. She learned all that from Gran, of course, Granma was a great one for that sort of thing.

When she was writing her Home Page we had to keep very quiet. That was never my specialty. But if we made a noise she didn't spank us, if anything she spoiled us.

She loved her Home Page and she loved her CWI, the Canterbury Women's Institute. They were a busy lot and no mistake. They all agreed with Mother, every time, even over the Minnie Dean affair. Minnie Dean got caught out murdering a couple of illegitimate tots, buried them in the flower bed. First woman in the country to be hanged. Everyone in New Zealand was screaming out for the death sentence, every man woman and child, except for Mother.

'The state has no right to commit murder,' she said. I heard the women jabbering, I listened outside the door. Mother's voice was the loudest. 'Hypocrisy!' she said. 'Were they sinless, the grandmothers who paid ten pounds to get these unfortunate infants off their hands? We're all guilty, we're cowards all of us. Mrs Dean was simply doing our dirty work. I blame society for holding these little ones cheap.' And so on and so on. In the end the women did exactly what she said, they petitioned the Government to let her off, repeal the death sentence. Mrs Sheppard couldn't stop them because she was overseas. It made Mother very unpopular but she said she didn't mind that, she said she was right and she was. Of course Minnie Dean got hanged all the same, they didn't listen. That hurt Mother, that upset her a lot.

The National Council of Women was another big thing. Mother arranged it practically all by herself. And once again, Mrs Sheppard got back from England just in time to get all the honour and glory. People said it was all her own idea, but it wasn't! It was Mother's! This is exactly the sort of thing that makes me so mad.

Mother was big-hearted. She didn't mind being secretary, not a bit — she loved it! Of course she was a lot younger than most of those women.

Those women wanted the horrible CD Act out the door. Nobody knows about the CD Act any more. CD was short for Communicable Disease. Nowadays they call it VD. They thought that prostitutes spread it all by themselves with no help from the gentlemen. Poisoning poor innocent boys, ha ha. Under this CD law the police could arrest any girl over the age of twelve and make a doctor examine her. You know, in her private parts! Then they could force her to have 'treatment' and a fat lot of good that did. Mercury, that was the so-called treatment. It was an awful law because nobody ever arrested the men! They went home and gave it to their wives and nobody said a word. But any young girl could have her reputation ruined, just like that. For nothing! Just because some man got a snitch against her!

Lots and lots and lots of men had a CD. That is something I know for a fact.

But this is a sad thing. That's enough about sad things, I'm going to talk about Gran instead.

When they had that first convention, Mother was out every day and every night for a whole week. Except one afternoon we all went with her in the horse and trap to a garden party at Professor Bickerton's. What a place! I ran wild over the sandhills and I pushed another girl in the lagoon when she teased me. I loved the sea-side, still do.

The rest of the week we all stayed at Gran's. I disremember whether I talked already about Gran's treatment. I don't think so.

After Granpa died she made ends meet with washing and lodgers. She was always helping someone or other. If they were sick, Granma would rub them and give them hot and cold packs. She got fevers down when the doctors could do nothing. I don't know where she learned it, maybe out of pamphlets. But she was a natural, she had the healing touch. Very nice.

One day the mayor's brother Dr Thacker came to visit Granma with two other doctors. A deputation! They wanted her to start doing massage and water-treatment for their patients. They would send her clients and Granma would get paid for doing what she'd always done. So Gran set up one big room with a bath and basins and a massage table, and olive oil and acetic acid, and lots of towels and blankets and a big tub, and she wore a special white smock.

I started helping!

When Mother was at the women's convention, Gran had a patient with influenza. He had to have steaming hot blankets wrapped round his legs every hour or so, and Granma asked me to wet the blankets with hot water, hot as I could stand. When it was time to change the fomentation I helped her wring out the water and wrap it round his legs. He had thin white legs with dark hairs on them, you could see the blue veins through the white skin. Then I put the other blanket in the copper.

Gran rinsed a white towel in cold water and packed it round the man's head. He looked like an Indian in a turban! That was to bring the fever down and the fomentation was to make sure he didn't get a chill. Every now and then Gran would take his temperature. Once it was up a point and then there was a flurry! I had to run for more cold towels and Gran packed them round his tummy. She was always asking, 'Is that comfortable?' It didn't look very comfortable to me but he said yes, he felt better.

That week I could hardly bear to go to school. The first day I rushed home and into Gran's treatment room and asked her, 'Is he better?'

She always had a funny cock-eyed smile for me. The man was better and his wife had taken him home. Gran told me never to barge into the treatment room again, not running like that and I never did. She had screens she put round the bed or the bath to keep the draughts off and make it more private.

Anyway she gave me a piece of bread and treacle. Then she gave me some more jobs, rinsing towels and hanging them over the stove on the big wooden clothes-bar. I had to hoist the clothes-bar up to the ceiling.

'You're not too tired, are you, Bim?' Granma asked at bedtime.

'Not a bit!' I said. I was tired but I wasn't going to say so. 'I'm strong!' I was too.

So the next day after school she let me stay while she rubbed Miss Aken's legs. One of them was weak and wasting. Gran rubbed on some warm olive oil, gently, not too hard. Her little dry crinkly hands went whisking over the skin, she pressed and she squeezed and she rubbed. Miss Aken looked happy enough on the table. When Gran was finished she pulled the blanket over so she didn't get chilled.

'You need rest after rubbing,' Gran explained. 'Rest is part of the remedy.'

'What's it feel like?' I asked Gran. She put her bird-head on one side and thought a bit.

'I'll have to give you a rub and then you'll know,' she said.

'Chris gets rubs and Cos gets rubs,' I pointed out. They were delicate. 'But I've never been sick.'

Gran gave me one of her small hugs, so quick you hardly knew it. 'Clever girl!' I was so embarrassed.

Miss Aken got out of bed and I brought her hat and coat. When she'd gone I said to Gran, 'Pretend I've got infantile paralysis like Aunty Edith.' Mother used to nag my Aunty Edith all the time about dragging her foot. She didn't understand it was infantile paralysis.

'Take off your shoes, dear,' said Gran and she popped me up on the massage bed. 'Have you got poor sore legs?'

'It's just pretend, Gran!' I lay back and Granma covered most of me with a blanket. Then she started rubbing my legs. Well! If that wasn't the nicest feeling! Soothing all my pains away. I didn't even know I had any pains till she smoothed them all away. It was a little bit exciting too. I never wanted her to stop.

She did stop in the end. Pulled a blanket over me. Next thing I knew it was tea-time. I'd gone right off to sleep!

I went off to Gran's so often that Mother got quite used to me not being home. I don't think she minded as long as I did the dusting first and the sweeping and my other jobs. She had a lot of meetings to go to. I always fed the animals properly but I learned how to skimp the cleaning. There were some places I did properly like the hall table and the piano and some she never looked at that I just did once in a blue moon. It wasn't a bad house to keep clean. Mother liked things simple, a few flowers and no clutter. She didn't let me touch her desk with all the papers and stuff. The books were the worst.

Chris and Cos studied hard, they didn't do any housework, they didn't have time. Mother gave them extra lessons in literature, history, Latin and German. Then there were piano and singing lessons, and Chris was learning the violin. Music music music! Mostly I didn't like the classical. I learned some good tunes from the kids at school, unfortunately some of the words were rude. But I had one lesson a week on the piano as well. Mother still belonged to the

Motette, and when Chris and Cos turned twelve, Father let them go in the chorus. I think he was quite proud of them underneath.

I played with my brother Stan quite a bit. We got up to some good tricks. We used to steal rides on the trams, had it down to a fine art. The conductor had to go up one side of the tram and down the other so we'd hop on the opposite side and ride till it stopped, then when he was about to change sides, we hopped off again! It was easy. Sometimes we'd go all the way to New Brighton and back like that! Stan was allowed to play with his friends most of the time. It wasn't so important for him to have an education, being a boy.

Mother got the idea in her head that Chris and Cos would go to the School of Music in Leipzig. It was going to cost a lot of money. Father gave them a bit because it was for their music education. Chris started giving concerts and earning money like that. She played the violin at garden parties and weddings, then she'd come home and tell us all about it!

I was in the Main School now. We had to work too hard. My friend Biddy was still in the same class as me and that was the only thing that made it all right. She didn't go very fast through the standards either, mind you, nobody expected her to, being a Donahue. We weren't allowed to sit together in school, but at lunch-time we'd have a spot of fun playing tag and so forth. Biddy was often away though, I don't suppose she was at school more than half the time. I had to go every day, it wasn't fair.

Sometimes Biddy came to play. Mother didn't mind as long as we stayed out of doors or in the kitchen. Elsie would give her some bread and treacle and did she love that! One day Mother came in to the kitchen when we were helping Elsie bake.

'Dear me, Biddy, what's that on your arm?' asked Mother.

Biddy started rolling down her sleeve. Her hands were covered in dough and she got her blouse all sticky.

'Don't do that!' said Mother sharply, and she pulled the sleeve up again. She was a bit heavy-handed sometimes. 'You poor little mite, you're black and blue. I won't let anyone bully you!'

'Her arm's hurting, let go!' I told her.

Mother didn't realise! She gave Biddy my old navy blue knitted jacket. It had been darned a lot but it was comfy.

'You can keep this, Biddy,' she said kindly. 'Bim won't mind.'

'No, I don't mind,' I said.

Biddy sniffled. 'Now what'll happen?'

Mother patted her hand. 'I must do something to help your poor mother. Things can't be worse than they are now.' She was wonderful like that, always very keen to help the woman. 'I'm going to speak to Sister Torlesse about Biddy,' she said. That's how I knew Biddy was a neglected child.

Biddy was worried she might be boarded out or sent to the Lyttelton Orphanage. Mother thought she should have a technical training like horticulture. Biddy thought 'orticulture sounded 'orrible. She wanted to be a milliner. So did most girls!

Now I've got to say some more about Father. People can't appreciate what Mother did unless they know what she had to put up with.

After that awful night we got the vote, things were never the same. I couldn't pretend it hadn't happened, but I wasn't allowed to talk about it, not even to Chris and Cos. Mother made me promise not to tell! She didn't want to spoil things for them, specially their music. Even Elsie shushed me if I tried to talk about it. It was like a dirty stain inside where no one could see, it was always there, I couldn't forget.

I knew it must have happened before so naturally I kept expecting it to happen again. Every morning when I woke up I felt worried till I saw that Mother was all right. But how could I tell if she had been kicked in the night? I'd never noticed anything wrong before! So I tried to stay awake. I would wake up with a jump at the slightest noise.

One moonlit night, I suppose a few weeks after, I woke up suddenly and I heard the noises. There was no mistaking them. A thump thump thump, then a silence and another thump. I made myself get up and creep along to Mother's bedroom. I pushed the door open and there was Father in his rage. I wanted Mother to scream but she just stayed there with her lips white and her hands over her head.

Just like last time I rushed in like a dog and I grabbed his leg. 'Stop it!' I screamed, and he grabbed me by the neck and put his other hand over my mouth. 'Always under my feet! She should be sent away!' His breath got stuck, he couldn't talk and I was glad. He threw me away and charged out of the house.

'Mother!' What did she want me to do? I couldn't tell! She stood up and painfully straightened her nightdress. 'Can I get you a cup of tea?' I asked. It was the only thing I could think of.

She looked at me oddly. 'Yes, Bim, that's a good idea. But be very quiet! Don't wake anyone up.'

The next day we went to Gran's again. Now I understood. If we got there fast enough Gran could fix up her bruises, put cold packs on and smooth the blood out of them. Granma could make anyone feel better. We stayed about three weeks that time.

That was almost the last time I saw it happen. You know what Father did? He put a lock on the bedroom door! The next time I heard the noises I went along to stop him but the door was locked! I banged on the door and yelled, 'You stop that, do you hear?' And Mother answered! 'Quiet, Bim!'

'No! No! I'll make a big noise and make him stop!' I screamed. Father growled through the door. I suddenly knew if I made a racket it would be worse for Mother. I don't know how I knew, I just knew. I sat on the floor. He'd got me. I had to stay outside while that thump, thump went on and on I don't know how long. Just when I thought Mother must surely be dead, Father unlocked the door and ran out. I think he only ever stopped because of the asthma. He went so far and then he ran out of breath, he had to stop.

Well there, I've talked about that and I certainly hope I don't have to again. But I still have to say about the public meeting. Father never hit Mother where you could see the

213

bruises, it was always on places under her clothes or her hair. He was shrewd. But the night before the big meeting about neglected children he forgot to lock the bedroom door. I suppose he just got carried away.

Anyway, I tried the door and it opened. Father was talking in a soft puffy voice. 'Gorilla! Fanatic! Can't leave well alone!' I made a noise and Father lost his concentration and he hit Mother right over the eye!

When he saw me he tried to get his breath back and he pulled on his trousers and coat over the top of his nightshirt. 'Cretin! Cuckoo!' He cursed me too and I was glad. Then he was gone into the night.

Mother's eye was swelling up already. She told me to get a piece of meat from the safe. I cut the right size with a sharp knife. When I went upstairs she was lying down and she put it over the eye. I was glad I was awake! She needed someone to help and I was the only one who could. I was the only one who knew what had happened!

I stayed up till morning. Every now and then I bathed her eye with a cold wet towel, then I'd put the meat back on. I tried to talk to Mother just to cheer her up but she didn't talk to me, hardly. She was worried about the eye. 'You silly girl, why did you have to walk in like that?' she said.

Well! I couldn't answer. I couldn't say anything. I just stood there in an awful knot. Then she patted my hand.

'I'm sorry, Bim. I know you were only trying to help. But sometimes it only makes matters worse.'

I nearly felt like crying but I stopped myself. I just put a cork in it.

Mother let me stay away from school that day. I slept all morning but when I got up I saw she had a terrible eye, all swollen up, she could hardly see out of it. I must have put the steak on the wrong place.

'Can I go to the meeting tonight?' I asked.

'Silly billy, it's not for children!' she said.

'Yes it is,' I said.

She laughed at herself. 'If you want to come you shall. But you must stay as quiet as a mouse and it will be very dull.'

Chris and Cos thought I was dotty, and Mother would never have let me go except she felt sorry for growling at me. I wanted to look after her, that's why I wanted to go.

I was ten, I wasn't too young. I was tall for my age. I sat in the front row. There was no other kids so I didn't whisper, I mean there were no other kids, children. The St John's Hall was full, I mean — oh, never mind the grammar! Mother was on the stage. She wore her hat with a veil pulled down over her eyes. There were a lot of speeches about bad parents and young criminals running round the streets. Mother stood up as proud as Punch. After she got going I don't think anybody really noticed her eye, she gave such a grand speech. She said that kids were taken away from their awful parents by the state and sent off to homes that were even worse!

'Every child is a child of God,' she said. 'Every child has talents that must be cultivated.' Something like that.

And that's how the Children's Aid Society got going. It's got a different name now, Society for the Protection of — something. Mother went on the committee of course, black eye or no black eye. When it was time to go home she took me by the hand to pull me through the crowds, and one lady asked about her eye even though you're not supposed to make personal remarks.

'I was very foolish I'm afraid. I didn't look where I was going,' she said with a smile. Afterwards I said to her, 'Mother, you told a fib.'

'I did no such thing,' she said.

Chapter 26

Yesterday the concrete blocks were delivered. What a shambles, all over the front lawn! But today I had to laugh. Along comes you know who to mow my lawns and did he goggle!

'Something bothering you?' I asked.

'That's far too many blocks, Bim,' he said. 'Don't pay the bill whatever you do, not till the job's been done. I'll take the other ones back.'

'Fuss fuss fuss!' I said.

He made his usual finickity job of the back lawn and said he'd leave the front one till he'd done my wall. He swapped the tapes for clean ones and took my shopping list. 'See you on Saturday,' he said.

He's in for a big surprise! Because, good as his word, Clem came today and started the job. All day I've heard that concrete mixer roaring. He knows what he's doing, he's started on the big steps up to the house and he'll do the wall next week. I can't wait to see Stan's face!

I don't know why I start talking about me on this tape machine. I must get back to Mother's story. This is the story of my mother.

Granma was amazed at Mother. Everybody was! Such energy! Meetings and articles and speeches and she still had time to read, not only Hansards but poetry, and oh yes, Mother was so busy! Children's Aid, National Council, CWI, secretary, president, always for women. There were some men she liked but they were mostly dead. St Bede was her favourite, she adored him!

I went to Gran's a lot. One Saturday she was flat out and she put me in charge of old Mrs Sweet who had lumbago.

'Take that bran poultice off Mrs Sweet's back, Bim dear,'

she said. 'Rub in the oil when you take off the poultice. Not too hard, now! And don't press on the spine whatever you do.'

Well! I didn't know how to rub! But I knew what it felt like on my own legs. I used to say I had pains in my legs, Gran said growing pains but actually I made them up. Her rubs felt like — oh, I don't know! All sorts. A kitten rolling on you or a pumpkin. You could feel your bones when she rubbed. That was her way of teaching me. So that's what I tried to do with Mrs Sweet.

'Are you ready for rub-a-dub-dub?' I said. Mrs Sweet was flat on her tum. I sloshed a bit of nice warm olive oil on my hands. I rubbed away, keeping it flowing like Gran did. I found a little lump of muscle and looked after that bit. Went over and over the back and did some nice little twirls. Then I thought I should do her bottom because lumbago hurts right down to the you know what. It was a bit pimply. I kneaded it like a lump of dough. It was fun! When I finished I wrapped her up warm in two layers of flannel under the blankets, then I went off to get another bran poultice.

Granma said, 'Goodness, Bim, what have you been doing all this time?'

'Rubbing Mrs Sweet!' I said.

'Oh, Bim! I didn't mean a proper rub,' said Gran. 'I just meant a quick do with the olive oil.'

'Well, I enjoyed it,' I told her, 'and I think Mrs Sweet did too.'

Sure enough, Mrs Sweet told Gran I had given her a lovely rub. Was I proud!

'What are you going to do when you grow up, Bim?' Gran asked me. It was something that worried Mother. I couldn't be a clerk or even a shop-girl because I wasn't scholastic. Mother didn't want me to work in a factory and neither did I! Locked up inside doing the same thing day after day! I always thought I'd like to work with animals but when Gran asked me I answered quick as a shot, 'This of course!' I was as surprised as her. She just said, 'Good idea. I'll train you up. You're a good little worker.'

When I got home I told Mother straight away. 'I'm going to work with Gran when I leave school!'

'And what does Granma say about that?' asked Mother.

'She's happy!' I said, and so was I.

After that whenever Chris or Cos teased me I had an answer.

'You can't do this! You can't do that!' they used to say. 'You can't do sums! You can't do German! You can't do Latin! You can't play the violin! You can't read the paper!' I hated that. I used to run away and hide. I could do a lot of things but they called them servants' jobs. Now I could answer back.

'You can't do massage!' I would crow, and dance around and yell. 'You can't do fomentations!' They couldn't pretend that was nothing, because that was Gran's work. Everybody knew her work was important.

Mother used to do some rubbing. She had her own patients. Gran never taught her. Mother did it just by intuition, she called it spiritual healing. But it wasn't, it was something you had to learn and it took a long time too.

Father's big quarrel with St Michael's came to a head and he went to Durham Street Methodist. He persuaded them to buy a nice new organ and then he had to sell the old one. One of the people who came to see the old one was Mr Ferguson. He'd come a long way to see it, all the way from Oamaru. Oamaru sounds like Timaru but it's much further south, it's nearly as far as Dunedin. I didn't know it then but I found out later. Anyway, Mr Ferguson was choirmaster at a church in Oamaru, and Father and he got on famously.

A nice house went with the job, in Chester Street right in the middle of town. But I wasn't very pleased because there was no paddock for the animals and also it was further away from Gran's house. Sometimes I caught the tram. One time I ran all the way — I must have been strong! I had to change schools and I didn't have any friends.

When Chris was eighteen she went to Germany. I think some of the relations helped a bit. Mother made Chris three new day dresses, two of wool crêpe and one georgette. They were all navy blue with short skirts, well above the ground. Mother hated long skirts. She said they were unhealthy, dragging in the mud and slowing us down. I liked running! But I can't do that any more.

Chris had a new collar and cuffs on her old top-coat, and a good stout pair of shoes. She also had a new white muslin dress with a lot of lace and frills around the shoulders. That wasn't a luxury, she needed that for performing. I wasn't jealous. Imagine me in white muslin, people would fall about laughing! Her things were packed up in a trunk with her violin. Mother had her own coat relined and got some new white collars for her old frocks. We all drove to Lyttelton in the Ormerod's trap to see them on to the ship.

'Look after Mother,' I said to Chris.

'You funny monkey!' Mother said.

When we said goodbye she nearly kissed me, she gave me a hug and rubbed her cheek on mine. It was so smooth. She looked very beautiful in her new collar. Her cheeks were pink after the long ride, and her eyes were flashing, sharp as anything.

To tell the truth, I didn't mind them going because it was the start of a lovely time for me. I was allowed to leave school and go and stay with Gran! It was the start of my real job, giving the treatments.

Gran's was a great big draughty house. I had to share a room with Aunty Edith because most of the house was for patients. Gran gave me a white pinny so I would look professional. The first morning I woke up I couldn't think for a moment where I was. The sun shone through the cracks in the blind. Then I remembered, and I felt the sun shining right into my mouth.

No more school! My chest felt like it was full of wriggly kittens, I mean as if. I jumped out of bed and splashed my face in the cold basin of water. No more chalk dust and no more sore hands! Gran would never give me the stick for getting my homework wrong. I dressed quickly and I tied on my lovely white pinny.

Aunty Edith was still asleep. She used to get very tired

because of her poor foot. She had a mirror on the wardrobe door and I saw my hair was all untidy so I brushed it a hundred times and pinned it neatly back the way Gran liked. I looked nearly grown up! I had little breasts, not big ones like Chris and Mother. But they were all right. I liked them bouncing when I danced around.

Then I ran downstairs and called out, 'Gran! I'm ready!'

I found her helping one of the patients to sit up for breakfast.

'Early bird!' said Granma. 'It's only six o'clock.'

The man in the bed had twinkly eyes. 'If you ever wake me up in the morning, young lady, I'll want my money back.'

I said, 'You should be wide awake to get your money's worth!'

Gran had a good laugh at that one. 'Mr Elwyn comes here once a month just to get a good sleep,' she chuckled.

'You're Bim, are you?' asked Mr Elwyn. 'Your grandmother has certainly got the magic touch. Have you?'

I blushed red hot and Gran told me to run along and get some breakfast. Later on she told me how to treat insomnia and I wished I could have done it to Father. Last thing at night she used to massage Mr Elwyn's head with warm soapy water, then she rinsed out the soap and dried his head with a warm towel, then he got into bed and she brought him a big cup of hot milk and honey. When he lay down she put a cold bandage round his head. Well! He slept like a lamb.

It's funny, when Gran rubbed you, you could feel it all over. If she rubbed your head the tingling went right down your arms, up and down your back and all the way to your feet.

Well, it was hard work all right and no mistake. The blankets were heavy as anything when they were wet, and there was a lot of fast walking back and forwards. No running or you might get burnt. There was bed-making and lifting people and emptying commodes and chamber pots. There was a lot of washing but at least I only had one lot of monthly rags to do, Cos and Chris could darn well do their own! Some of the patients were crotchety but I loved it. There was always something new to learn. They came to us with all sorts! Pleurisy, indigestion, skin trouble, all kinds of fever, influenza, ulcers, poisoned wounds, constipation, bronchitis, sciatica, inflammation of the bowels, burns, bladder problems, toothache, earache, headache — they all came to Granma. Mostly their doctors sent them. I learned how to do sitz baths and enemas and take temperatures, special drinks from oranges and lemons, special diets, sulphur baths, pyretic baths and Turkish baths, hot packs and cold packs and of course lots of rubbing.

Gran didn't mind if I had a joke with the patients. We had a bit of fun!

There was just one kind of fun she didn't approve of. If she caught me at it she would send me out of the room. I didn't want to upset her but I couldn't help it, I was sexy. I was the only sexy one in the family, I couldn't help it! It wasn't only my fault either, there were some men who couldn't keep their hands to themselves. A bit of slap and tickle cheered them up.

The first time it happened I thought I was imagining things. I was turning a gentleman over on the massage table when he leaned against my bosom. I thought, 'Oh, that's nice! He doesn't know how nice.' Next time he did it again and I thought maybe he did know. I didn't mind! I gave him an extra nice rub over the kidneys.

The same chap, I won't say the name, came back a couple of months later and when Gran went out of the room to get the vinegar he put his hand on my bosom. It was lovely, I pushed right back, I didn't see the harm! Well, Gran must have known something was going on, she gave me such a funny look when she came back into the room. So I was more careful after that. I just thought, well, I'll see what else these men get up to.

I had a few adventures while Mother was away. On my half-day off I was supposed to go home and see Father and Cos and Stan. That first Saturday afternoon I set off walking. I was fifteen, old enough to walk round town on my own. It was a nice day. The cherry-plums were in blossom.

I took a slightly different way for once. Well, who should I bump into but Biddy Donahue with a red feather in her hat! I hadn't seen her since we moved to Chester Street.

'I've got my own room,' she said with a giggle. 'Want to see it?'

Of course I did! It was right next door to a hotel. She had a bed and one chair and a rag rug and she worked at the sewing factory.

'Have you ever been to the Opera House?' she asked. Of course I hadn't! Mother said vaudeville was frivolous. 'Come to the matinée!' And she dragged me down the stairs and off across town to the Opera House. It was such fun! Best of all I liked Ferry the Human Frog, he had long muscly legs and I liked Cleopatra and her Snakes, live snakes they were, squirming all over her body. I didn't think much of the ventriloquist — I could see his lips moving. The theatre had a beautiful ceiling, even nicer than the cathedral. So many people, all having a good time! My eyes were opened, my word. There were a couple of chaps beside us and we got on like a house on fire. After the show they asked me to the hotel but I wouldn't go. Who wants to go to a hotel, not me! Horrible places. I was just about to walk off when the chap called Dick says to me, 'Hey, Bim, are you coming next week?'

'Maybe I will, maybe I won't,' I said and ran away down the street. When I turned round for another squiz they were walking arm in arm with Biddy in the middle. Well! I thought. She knows how to have a good time!

All next week I thought about this fellow Dick. Saturday I hurried along to the Opera House. I couldn't get there quick enough. Dick was there on his own. He was a bit rough-looking but a good sort.

'Coming in?' he said. 'I'll pay if you like.'

It was a lovely sunny day. 'I'd rather go to the sea-side,' I said all of a sudden. He didn't blink an eye, just took me by the arm and walked me to Cathedral Square. We got on the tram and went all the way to New Brighton.

I felt so excited when I saw the water! The sunshine glittered so bright I could hardly look at it. 'It's so big!' I said.

Dick snickered and I didn't know why, I was as green as grass. Well, we had a lovely time! I took off my shoes and stockings and hitched up my dress and went paddling. It was cold but I loved the waves coming at me. Dick went paddling too and we larked around a bit, but when I started making a sandcastle he got impatient.

'Come on, let's go for a walk,' he said.

'Not yet,' I said. But he looked so sulky I went with him into the sand-hills. I didn't want to spoil a lovely afternoon.

I certainly found out a lot that day. We were all on our own. Dick got all lovey-dovey and we went rolling down the slopes together. Then he showed me a very peculiar part of his body, it was all red and standing up like a pump handle! I laughed and laughed!

I said, 'Come on, show me, how do I make the water come out?' And I pumped it up and down.

'Just carry on like that,' said Dick. He squeezed me close and started fiddling and tickling and — oh, you know! I thought, I'll do that any time!

Mother was away four months and did I have fun! I had a small wage from Gran every week, just two shillings to start off with. I should have saved it all to help Mother with the housekeeping but I didn't want to. I wanted to spend some on myself, even if it was just a tram fare. On Saturday afternoons Gran thought I went straight home but I had a bit of fun on the way.

Dick was all right but he used to get the sulks. Lots of times I just went riding on the tram and had fun with the conductor or some of the passengers, or I'd go by myself to New Brighton and go walking on the sand. I might go to a nice coffee shop and meet up with some man there or some girls I knew. The older men liked to have a chat too, they said I sparked them up.

I needed someone to flirt with, I was just a young girl. But Gran was right, you shouldn't flirt with the patients. I mostly had women patients. Most of the men were all right. It was my fault. I was odd. I was a weird bird when I was young. Mother always used to say I was odd.

Well, Mother came back of course and I couldn't fool her, I didn't even try. I had to move back to Chester Street and get the tram to Gran's every day.

Mother had great stories about Germany! On the voyage over there she and Chris sat at the captain's table, a Captain Mead, on the Norddeutscher Line. She settled Chris in at a 'pension', that means a boarding house. There was a very nice elderly woman who always waited for Mother to go in to dinner. And Mother would say, 'No, you go first, you're older.'

And she said, 'But you're married, my dear,' Mother had more prestige because she was married. She was very fond of this nice woman.

She couldn't afford to stay long so back she came. We were all together again, except for Chris.

Father got a bad kick on the leg from the horse, right down to the bone. Gran treated it and it healed up right as rain but it upset his nerves. He was quite fond of Stan but everyone else got on his nerves. Then he had a quarrel with the Durham Street Church. They wouldn't do something or other he wanted and he just resigned. We moved back into Granma's place, so that was good.

Mother loved getting letters from Chris in Germany. She was so proud! Chris did so well in her music. Of course Mother always thought that Chris and Cos were wonderful, she thought the world of them.

Sometimes we went on picnics. I loved that. And we had holidays, too. People were very good to us. We went to Conical Hill, Hanmer, Oxford, Diamond Harbour, lots of places. Sometimes the Skellerups or the Ormerods would lend us their house in the country. We'd set off in a horse and cart, about six or seven of us, friends and relations. Not Biddy though. Mother and Miss Bain and some of the Smiths or the Fletchers, we'd just get together a group and off we'd go.

Usually Ken Smith would be driving the horse. He hung on to me for seven years. I said I'm not going to be Mrs Smith! He used to shake hands like a piece of fish. I wanted a grip! I wanted a man who would take me by the hair and say, 'Come on, woman!' I never found one, they were all so soft, too wishy-washy, all of them. I think Mother wanted me to marry Ken Smith. I liked his father better! William Sidney Smith, now he was a real man. Very stiff and upright but he had sexy eyes. A few years later he started calling himself Lovell-Smith. Good for him, I say!

When I was seventeen Mother took Cos over to Germany and I kicked up my heels a bit, I ran amuck! To tell the truth I got sick of all the fuss. Cos kept preening over her new clothes, she had the same as Chris, three new dresses, et cetera. She needled me.

'You're not going to Germany. You can't play the piano, you can't sing,' she said whenever Mother wasn't listening. I could so play! I loved the piano but I only used to play it when they were out. 'You're odd, you're the silly one.' I was glad to see her go and I didn't mind how long Mother stayed away. That's the sort of girl I was! I was better off with Gran, Gran didn't tell me what I couldn't do, she said I was good at the rubbing.

And I wasn't so pleased about Chris coming home either. Chris was always Mother's favourite. Mother thought Cos was wonderful but Chris was even better. And Chris had done so well over there! She didn't tease me, mind you, she was a good sister. When she came back she was different, more grown up. She and Mother read the same books. They were all in German. I couldn't understand them even in English! Too hard! Mumbo jumbo!

Chapter 27

Saturday's over and it's my peace-and-quiet time now. It's always a different sort of a day. On Friday Clem didn't turn up. He left the place in a terrible mess but that's how it is with a proper builder.

Stan came round with that darn boy of his.

'What's he here for?' I said.

'He's my helper, aren't you, son?' says the big boob.

I took them round the back of the house. 'Look at that!' I said. 'Now that's what I call steps!'

That took the wind out of his sails. 'Who did this? Was it that man down the road?'

'He's a proper handyman,' I said, proud as Punch.

'But he'll charge you,' said Stan. 'I would have done it for free!'

'Don't you like them?'

'You didn't need steps, Bim. And they're so clumsy-looking!'

He made me mad, criticising like that! That's all I've ever got in life! You can't do this and you can't do that!

'I'm eighty-eight years old and I can do what I bally well like!' I told him. He didn't hang around. Dropped off the shopping and took his trailer of tools and his jolly kid and that was that.

Oh, listen to me going on about myself again! I did that yesterday too. Blow it. People want to hear about Ada Wells, not her terrible daughter Bim. Still it doesn't hurt to show what Mother had to put up with! Poor Mother, I didn't make life easy for her. She was battling on as always. We didn't see Father for months on end.

That winter we had terrible frosts. Gran was getting feeble. I'd been helping her for three years and in that time she'd gone to pieces and no mistake. Little mite looked as if the wind would blow her away, you could see right through her skin. In September Gran got pleurisy. I'd seen a lot of people get better from pleurisy, even though it was a nasty do. Oh, I did everything right, I did, but she was so little and weak I could only do the treatments twice a day.

I got a shock the first time I packed her chest and spine with cold towels. She was like a poor bird without feathers. Every day her bones got sharper and her eyes got bigger. She used to tell me, 'You're a good girl, Bim.'

It wasn't true but she said it anyway. Gran didn't talk much now, she just lay there in her white bed watching me.

Mother tried to rouse her interest in the orphanage doings. 'That poor little Percy Whittle! The matron gave him a terrible beating last week and just because he was running around in his nightshirt.'

Gran gave just a little frown, she hardly moved.

'He shouldn't be beaten when he's got TB,' said Mother. She wanted Granma to chip in. Gran knew all about children with TB, and Percy Whittle only had one leg. I could see Mother was bursting to talk but she looked at Gran and just stopped. She gave a her a little kiss and went off to do something else.

Granma didn't like doctors except for Dr Thacker. He was her greatest admirer. He came to visit but he couldn't do anything, he said so. On the eighteenth of September her little peaky face was all shadows. So tiny in the bed I could put her in my pocket. I said to her, 'Granma, hurry up and get better. It's my birthday tomorrow, I'll be eighteen!' I felt so mad at her! She always made a fuss of my birthday.

When Mother got home from her meeting she came straight in to Gran as usual. She stroked her hand and said in her usual voice, 'Maria, there's a big celebration tomorrow. Twelve years since we got the vote! You must get better so we can tell you all about it.'

And Gran just lay there. Oh, I was so annoyed at her! She wasn't even trying.

Late that night I was sponging her forehead with warm

vinegar and she was sliding away. I said to her, 'Granma, don't you dare go and die on my birthday! It's mean — you mean old woman!' So she didn't wait another minute, she died right then and there! I started bellowing and screaming! 'Granma! Come back!'

I made a terrible racket and Mother came running. She told me not to scream but she was upset herself, I could tell. I just kept crying and staring at Granma's yellow face and I was shaking all over. I shouldn't have said what I did, I made her die!

Mrs Ormerod came and Mrs Ballantyne and Miss Sherrif Bain and I don't know who else. Mrs Ormerod wrapped me up in a blanket and took me to her place and gave me a lovely hot bath. She tucked me into bed like a kid and I said to her, 'Mrs Ormerod, Granma won't go to Hell will she?'

'Dear child, Maria Pike was the kindest woman in the whole world. If there's a Hell there's a Heaven, and Maria's with the angels.'

'It's not fair! What'll happen to me?'

Mrs Ormerod told me not to worry and turned off the light.

It was an awful time. But when the lawyer read out the will, what a surprise. Gran had left Mother the big Office Road house. Wasn't that wonderful? I knew Gran wanted me to carry on with the massage. But I couldn't cope on my own, I couldn't! It was far too much work. Too much responsibility. I wasn't very mature.

And do you know what Mother did? She decided to take up the treatment herself! She'd picked it up from Gran. She took over the practice because of me. Chris and Cos could earn good money with their music lessons but I couldn't manage on my own. She was so good to me!

Aunty Edith didn't know whether to stay on in the house now that Gran was gone. She was a great admirer of her big sister, but Mother used to criticise her.

'Stop dragging your foot, Edith!'

'She can't help it,' I'd say.

'I'll take charge,' said Mother. 'I'll rub it till it's better.' But after the rubbing Aunty Edith felt worse.

'You have to make an effort,' Mother said. 'The flesh is only the casing of the soul. The whole person has to want to be healed.'

After a couple of weeks Aunty Edith said she was going to live with Aunty Nell.

Now about the orphanage business. Things went from bad to worse. Mother was up in arms, I can tell you! This was the Waltham Orphanage, and if that was how the state treated its neglected kids — well! The inquiry was in the paper every morning. Mother told us all about it. She was all excited. She loved a good fight and the more public the better.

'What about Mrs Carpenter?' Chris asked.

'Oh dear, I said several times that I did not wish to attack her,' Mother said. 'The sad thing is, I'm sure she could learn new ways if only the secretary was on my side.'

'What about those horrible green frocks she made for the Catholics?' Chris said.

'Oh, she has her faults,' Mother agreed. 'If you could have seen the filth in the kitchen! But the real problem is those men. They just don't care about the children! They do not care.'

'Well why are they on the board?' I asked.

'They just want those children out of sight,' she stormed. 'They see it as rubbish disposal. And not just the children, either.'

We knew what she meant. She was talking about those horrible refuges for fallen women. They were filthy ugly places, vicious, too. If you went in you might never come out! The board didn't care about fallen women! They would rather you starved to death, but not on the streets, thank you.

Chris went to the inquiry with Mother every day, and one day I went too. I couldn't stand it! They were all telling lies! They said the orphans didn't mind having bread while the matron ate roast meat in front of them.

I've got all the newspaper cuttings here. Mr Friedlander

was so sarcastic and John T. Smith was even worse. I was horrified. He was Ken Smith's grandfather. Next time I saw Ken I gave him what for.

Anyway, the commissioner says to Mr John T. Smith, 'Were there any progressive ladies on the board in your time?' He said Mother was a fine intelligent lady but she was aggressive! Here: 'Mrs Wells has ideals, which she is anxious to reach. Some of us are not so fortunate as to have ideals beyond our reach; we are satisfied with the commonplace. But I have no fault to find with the ladies on the board. I think they are very useful.' Oh! I could have bopped him one! I'll never forget that smirky look on Mr Smith's face but I was stuck in the middle of a row, I couldn't get out.

'Mrs Carpenter was never severe with her punishment,' said this awful young woman. 'I never saw her give more than twelve strokes of the strap.'

'Did you hold them down while she strapped them or whipped them?' asked the magistrate.

'No,' said she. 'I guarded them, in case they should struggle and get the strap on the face.' I'll bet you did, I thought!

'Did the children scream and get depressed after punishment?'

'She only beat them on a Sunday. She was only there on a Sunday,' says she. 'Sunday was a fairly lively day. Mrs Carpenter liked to see things moving.' Well I know kids are little horrors, but it doesn't seem right to spend your Sundays beating them. Mother never hit us, she spoiled us.

'The majority must rule, and the majority has decided that we are right and Mrs Wells is wrong,' said the chairman. Mother raised her eyebrows. She'd heard that one before.

On the last day she came home rather excited.

'It was a Pyrrhic victory!'

'Hooray!' I crowed.

'Silly old Bim,' Chris giggled. I'd said the wrong thing again.

'The court blames the board, but the board blames the matron,' she said. 'They can't see that they've done the slightest thing wrong — after all that! They get off scot-free!'

'Poor Mother!' Chris said. 'Is it worth it?'

Of course it was.

What Mother wanted was cottage homes, small places with just a few children. More like a real home, you know.

'Why don't they do as you say, Mother?' asked Chris.

'I'm afraid in the end it all comes down to money, dear,' said Mother with a sigh. 'The more children they have in the Home, the more money flows into the coffers. They tell me I don't understand about finance, but my word, I understand only too well.'

As usual, Mother was right. Instead of getting smaller, the orphanage got bigger and bigger. And that made it harder to control the bad things. Still, she'd done the best she could.

'Give to the world the best you have, and the best will come back to you.' That was one of Mother's sayings.

The very next year both Chris and Cos got married. Chris married Roy, a lawyer, he was pretty slick, I liked Roy. He used to climb mountains and act in the amateur theatre. Mother was very broad-minded about his theatricals. He was in *Lady Windermere's Fan*, I remember that. Oh, he was quite something! And Cos married Reyn, he ran the Kaiapoi Woollen Mills. She went to live in a huge big house and got rich. They both started having children, so that was the end of the Wells School of Music, it only lasted one year.

You'll never believe what Father did. He upped and offed, went to a farm called Edendale way down south. A farm! He didn't know the first thing about farming! Farming and music are absolute opposites. I don't know what put that into his head. I think someone at Durham Street Methodist asked him to manage it. Stupid! People rooked him left right and centre. So he was gone, miles away, right out of Christchurch.

Chris and Cos were far too busy to help Mother at home. They were married women! It was just her and me in the big Office Road house, working away at our treatments.

I didn't want to get married. I had more men friends than Chris and Cos put together and multiplied by ten, but I didn't want to get married. They were all so weak! I was looking for a real man. Ken Smith kept after me for seven years, he wouldn't take no. He always thought I would marry him in the end. I was terrible to him! He used to come courting and we'd sit in the front room and he wouldn't have anything to say, so he'd go 'Ffff' like that, and I'd look at him and I'd go 'Fffff'. Oh, I was a weird bird when I was young, I was awful!

Sometimes I'd bike out to see him in Riccarton. It was quite a long bike ride, they were right out in the country. That house! I never saw anything like it! Ken boarded in town but he always went out to Westcote in the weekends. Mr William Sidney Lovell-Smith didn't care about appearances as long as there was room for everyone and fresh air and fresh fruit and vegies. When they changed their name to Lovell-Smith, Ken said, 'Won't you marry me now?' We were wandering round the orchard at Westcote, picking up windfall apples. They were all a bit wormy, those apple trees needed a prune. 'You wouldn't be Mrs Smith, you'd be Mrs Lovell-Smith.'

'Only if I can be Mrs William Sidney Lovell-Smith,' I said. Ken was horrified! What a terrible thing to say! I was only joking of course. Ken's father never looked twice at me, not to mention the fact that he was married. But he was a proper man if ever I saw one.

'I don't think Mother would like that much,' said wishy-washy Ken.

'I think I'll get divorced, Bim,' Mother said to me one day at breakfast time. 'What do you think?' There was only me to talk to.

I said, 'What for?'

'We went to all that trouble to make it easier for women. I should set an example.'

'Aren't we all right like this?' Father didn't bother us. He was floundering around on that farm in Southland.

'Legally we are still man and wife. It's ridiculous!'

Well, she talked to Chris and Chris talked to Roy, and he came round with some thick pieces of paper. They sat in the front room for ages and ages. I took them in some afternoon tea and there was Mother staring at these papers.

'Have you signed it yet?' I asked her.

'It's a lost cause, Bim.' Roy winked at me. 'She's too soft, that's her trouble.'

Mother pushed the papers away from her and sighed. 'Take them away, Roy. I just haven't got the heart.' Roy used to like seed cake I remember. Elsie was gone by then, gone to live with her sister in Dunedin but she wasn't the only one who could make a decent seed cake.

My brother Stan went off about this time to be an apprentice engineer somewhere in the country. He was just a kid of fourteen, he always led his own life and he was ready to go. He stayed with Father off and on. I don't think Mother minded him leaving. He didn't always fit in with Mother and Chris and Cos. Even I fitted in better than Stan. He needed a man's world I suppose. Sometimes men came to Office Road. I used to entertain my mates in the kitchen. Yes, I liked a yarn with the chap who delivered the coal, and Fred the milk man.

Mother's meetings started to take a different turn. No More War! She was against Joe Ward's Defence Act, she couldn't bear it! And it wasn't only her either. There were big meetings in Victoria Square, everyone yelling their heads off. Christchurch blew its lid. We were much more excitable than the rest of the country. Oh, there was no peace in our house after the Defence Act, she read it right through, she had the headpiece! She was right, war is a terrible thing. It says here in this *Plain Truth* — well, never mind. The MPs hopped from foot to foot but they wouldn't repeal the Act. A boy of twelve could be hanged as a traitor! It didn't happen, but what a law! What a law! No wonder Mother was mad.

It was hard on Mother only having me at home to talk to.

She would read bits out of the paper. It was like a play!

'Listen to this, Bim: "Long years of peace are sapping the virility of the race." Well I never!'

'What does it mean?' I asked.

'This ninny thinks our men are turning soft, so they need a war.'

'Poor old Ken!' I said. 'It wouldn't make any difference to him.'

She would write her letter to the paper, then I'd shoot off to the office of the *Lyttelton Times* on my bike. Other women signed themselves 'Mrs' this or that, or 'Another Englishwoman', but Mother was always A. Wells, none of your Mrs, thank you!

There were still a few laughs. At one meeting Mr Ell stood up and said to Mother, 'Come now, Mrs Wells, you are the kindest-hearted soul in this community. I wager if you saw a great big Turk beating a poor little Armenian girl about the head, you wouldn't just stand back and watch! You'd pick up the biggest stick you could find and lam him over the head.' Mother just laughed. He had her there.

One time a lot of women got together to tackle the Minister of Defence, and I tagged along. Mother spoke first, she was the leader really. She told him off good and proper! 'It would be better for these young boys to be taken off and shot!' she said. She was a marvellous speaker.

And you know what the Minister said? 'Yes, yes, I quite grasp the position but I have a train to catch at two o'clock and I would like five minutes for my lunch.'

Did those women get mad! He was lucky to get away with his shirt. The others all gave their speeches and too bad about his lunch. Finally he had his say. 'You seem to think that military training will take away your influence on your sons,' he says, sarcastic as anything. 'Quite the reverse is true!'

'Rot!' one woman yelled out. Well, he made a big fuss about her bad language — bad language! I bet he used a lot worse than that. That woman's boy was in jail and she said her piece, like it or lump it. Then he ran off to catch his train. Good riddance to bad rubbish.

Mother was really in her element. She read me out bits from the paper next day. 'The editor thinks we should apologise to the Minister,' she said.

'That'll be the day!' I always stuck up for her.

'He thinks Mrs Wells should have known better.' She enjoyed that bit! 'Hysterical, incoherent, indiscreet and vulgar.' Mother gave a mock sigh. 'I do wish these men could think of some new insults. They said that twenty years ago, almost word for word. They didn't stop us then and they won't stop us now.'

But it was a fact that when Mother got on to the subject of war she seemed to forget she was a lady. Many a time I saw her screaming abuse at the soldiers marching by, she was beside herself, I thought she'd have a fit. She was always on the side of the bottomdog, she didn't mind as long as they won in the end. She was always right and women got the vote, we got pensions and unions and technical training and milk in bottles and Lord knows what else. But this one! Why couldn't they see?

'I can't bear it, girls,' she would say to us. 'This militarism is against the spirit of the age. The whole tide of history is against it. Herding our boys into the mouth of the cannon!'

I think that's what upset her the most: she felt as if the world had started spinning backwards. Still, sooner or later she'd talk herself back into optimism.

I pitied anyone who came to be massaged without knowing Mother's views. We had all sorts of patients now. Mother thought she could cure anything at all. The Seventh Day Adventists used electricity but we never did, Mother said it wasn't natural. One day some poor muggins came along with kidney trouble. I gave him the sitz bath and passed him on to Mother for a rubbing. When he was lying flat on his tum she asked him, 'And what do you think of Mr Myers' latest speech?'

'Rousing stuff,' said the man. 'If I were younger I'd enlist at once.'

'Oh yes?' said Mother. 'And how would you like a bayonet stuck in your back — like this?'

The poor chap gave a puff and a groan and his face went grey. I said to her later, I couldn't help it, 'Mother, that's wrong, you shouldn't hurt people!'

It could have been because of the Defence Act that Ken Smith went to Sydney. No, I think he was just fed up with me. He'd been at me to marry him for so long and he was sick of it. Or maybe he was sick of his father. It wasn't easy having a father like William Lovell-Smith. He was hard on the boys, they had to toe the line or else. Ken didn't want to go to jail and he didn't want to go in the army so he went to Sydney. He expected me to beg him to stay. After a few weeks I got a letter. 'I've met this nice little widow,' he wrote.

'Well, carry on! Marry her!' I wrote back. 'It's nothing to do with me!' And blow me down, he did.

So that was what happened to Ken Smith. Plenty of other chaps asked me to marry them but nobody else tried that hard.

Mother had another go at getting divorced. She went along to Roy's office and when she came home I asked her, 'Did you do it?'

She looked ashamed. 'I'm sorry to say I didn't.'

'Mother!' I said. 'Aren't you being weak and vacillating?' She hated people who were weak and vacillating.

'It would hurt his pride if I divorced him,' she said firmly, and that was the end of the matter for a few more years.

Soon after that we got the news that Father had gone bankrupt. Poor Father down there with the animals! I would have liked living on a farm, I would have managed a lot better than him. Father didn't have the first idea. The farm just went from bad to worse in the time he had had it. Roy sorted it out so we didn't have to pay Father's bills, thank goodness.

Mother helped him in other ways though. He got sick and he came to our place as one of the patients.

'Home is good enough for you when you're sick, I notice,' she said, but she helped him just the same. He had a pigeon chest and he was quite thin now, and his hair was scruffy.

Soon he was right again and he got a job as organist in a small church in Ashburton. It was a far cry from the cathedral! If only he hadn't quarrelled with everyone.

Whenever Father came back into our life I wondered why Mother never stood up to him. I'd seen people cheer her and jeer her and nothing ever fazed her.

'Why did you let Father hit you, Mother?' I said. What a nerve I had!

'You don't answer violence with violence,' she said.

Another time she got cross. 'Use your head, Bim. He was bigger than me!'

Mother was thrilled to bits when Chris had a little girl, Celia. It was only a baby! She and Chris talked about how Celia would be an academic genius.

'With your musical brilliance and Roy's analytical gifts, she'll have everything!' said Mother. She got the name I should have had, Celice doesn't mean anything, it's a cross between Celia and Alice. If Father had got my name right I might have turned out different, more like Chris.

Then war was declared. How I found out was like this. I couldn't find Mother anywhere. I looked all over. It was time for lunch, which was a nice vegetable pie.

Then I knocked on her bedroom door. There was no answer but I heard a bit of a noise in there. So I pushed the door open and I saw Mother flat out on her bed with her head down. I hurried over and put my hand on her shoulder. 'Mother!' I said, and she shook it off. 'Mother! What's the matter?'

'Go away! You stupid stupid girl, let me grieve in peace!'

I couldn't go away, not with Mother like that. I tried to stroke her pretty hair and she put the pillow over her head. In that moment I saw she had red eyes.

'Now now, Mother, things aren't that bad,' I said. 'Can I give you a rub?'

Then she threw off her pillow and screamed at me. 'We're at war, you great baby! How are you going to rub that one away?' She jumped off the bed and pushed me out the door and slammed it shut. Anyone would think it was my fault!

Chapter 28

Now I've got up to the war. I'm doing all right! Once war was declared things got hot, people with Mother's opinions were even more unpopular than before. When she gave her speeches on street corners, people would hiss. They called her pro-German and that was supposed to be the worst insult there was. More soldiers, more war-talk, more conshies in prison — it was awful.

The war was the worst thing in Mother's life. Only a few days after it started we got a telegram. My brother Stan had gone and enlisted! He went straight into the Navy as an Engineer Lieutenant. She never got over that. It was a real slap in the face. He was no good.

Mother went the opposite way and joined the Prisongate Mission. They started up to visit women in jail. My friend Biddy got in a spot of bother once and she said it was men men men all the way, police, magistrates, warders and all. Biddy had a way with men but she didn't like that. She wasn't in for long, and that was due to a Prisongate woman. Not that Biddy thanked her! Some of them were a bit bossy I dare say.

But Mother wasn't visiting women, she was visiting the conshies. Took them soap and socks and so on, and Robinson's Biscuits, big cartwheels full of bran and malt. One day she took Celia along. She was only two! Paparua Prison was miles away.

'We saw Robin Page,' said Mother when they got back home. 'He's a brave man, isn't he Celia?'

'Nice man,' said Celia.

'He said whenever the other prisoners find a cockroach or a maggot they drop it into his porridge.'

'Mother, that's frightful!' said Chris.

'Don't worry, I told the Governor,' Mother said tartly. Even the Governor was a bit scared of Mother, I bet.

Church, I mustn't forget to say what happened in church. Mother was a Theosophical but it didn't stop her going to church. When she was dying she wrote to me, 'Stick to Labour, Bim, but read the Bible.' She knew her Bible inside out because when she was a kid they had to read it all day Sunday or else. She said it was great literature. We used to go to St Mary's Merivale. It wasn't draughty like the cathedral. One Sunday off we went and sat up the front as usual. Well the first hymn was, 'Oh hear us when we cry to thee/For those in peril on the sea.'

I was singing like billyo, thinking about Stan on his ship. He'd been torpedoed, but he was picked up and now he was back in action again. Then I hear Mother muttering away. 'Why should He listen? He's the King of Peace.'

Then in the Benedicite when we got to 'O ye Wells, bless ye the Lord' somebody snickered. What a morning! 'Onward Christian Soldiers' was the last straw.

'The church is glorifying war!' Mother called out over the top. After the hymn the vicar said, 'If Mrs Wells will graciously permit me, I am ready to deliver my sermon.' He preached about how God would part the goats from the sheep.

'He can't tell a sheep from a shaving brush,' hissed Mother. Afterwards the vicar took us into the vestry and told Mother she was banned from church till the end of the war.

Going to the pictures with Mother was pretty hot too. Chris used to play her fiddle at the Pathé pictures, she earned quite a good crust like that. In the Great Exhibition she was the leader of the Exhibition Orchestra! She didn't need the money but Mother said, 'You must use your great talent, don't hide it under a bushel!'

Yes, she gave Chris little lectures about economic independence.

'Coming to the pictures, Bim?' Mother would say, usually when she was half-way out the door.

'Not tonight,' I'd say. I'd rather go with my own friends

because Mother did the same in the pictures as she did in church. When the shorts of the war came on she'd mutter and carry on and there was no stopping her.

'Quiet there!'

'We paid good money for this!'

'No respect for the King!' they'd say, and all those other horrible things. Oh, her opinions were very unpopular!

What else did she do in the War? Oh yes, she started up the Housewives' Union with Mrs Taylor and Mrs McCombs and Mrs Cunnington, all the usual people. They were on about the big profit made by the clothing factories. It upset Mother to see shop-girls spending all their money on frippery. Some of it just fell to pieces. I like good strong stockings and a skirt with plenty of stuff in it, I don't care what colour but I always try and look neat, at least when I go to town.

Mother liked to look nice but she never had any money. That didn't matter because she would have looked beautiful in an old potato sack. She tried to put a bit of lace on me once but I only looked ridiculous. I wanted to wear trousers when they came in for women and I did get one pair. Mother couldn't get used to them and to tell the truth nor could I. You can stride out in a skirt, they're better than trousers as long as they're not too long. They don't cut you round the crutch and you can tuck them into your knickers if you want to climb over something. No, I'm quite happy with my skirts.

Bother! There I go again, talking about myself! Anyway, Mother was busy. As a matter of fact she was so busy with the No More War that she didn't notice I was up to my old tricks with the fellows. Ken used to keep me on the straight and narrow, and when he left I didn't miss him exactly but I had to find something to do in my spare time.

I had quite a few little affairs. I had some fun with the mayor, but then I gave him the shove. Then there was Roy. There was a fine old fuss when Mother and Chris and Cos came back from a picnic and found us in bed together. Chris was rather cool to me after that. I always had a soft spot for Roy. No need to talk about the others.

Well, one day I noticed my bosom was getting big. I

wasn't half pleased! Twenty-eight and growing a decent bosom at last! I left the men alone after that because it was sore. They all want to nuzzle but I couldn't stand that any more. I thought it was growing pains and they would pass. Then my monthlies stopped. Naturally I didn't mention that to Mother. I was glad! But then my stomach started getting fatter. Couldn't do up my skirt. I thought something was wrong so I told Mother.

'Mother,' I said, just after Sunday lunch. 'My stomach's getting fat.'

Well! The look that came over her face! I knew I'd said something terrible. Now I really got frightened.

There was just Mother and me and Chris at home that day. Sally the cook was out and Chris was there for lunch. Mother was so kind! She took me by the arm into the room where we had the massage table. 'Let's have a look at you, Bim,' she said. 'Take off your dress and we'll have a jolly good look.'

There was a fire in the room, it wasn't cold, so I took off my dress and petticoat. Mother put a sheet on the table and I climbed on to it. She started to poke around my tummy with her fingers, harder and harder. This way and that way, from the top, sides, and down below.

Then she turned me over and poked around from the back. 'Get down, Bim,' she said finally. 'And let's have a chat.'

Chris brought a cup of tea and the three of us sat in three chairs in front of the fire for a chat. I don't know when we'd done that together! I felt like one of them, as good as Chris or nearly.

'What's wrong with her?' asked Chris.

Mother patted my hand. I could tell it was going to be bad news. 'Bim has a growth in her abdomen.'

I panicked. 'No!' I'd seen people with tumours, it was one of the worst things you could get. 'I'm too young! I can't have!'

Mother smiled, so serene. Her hair looked lovely that day. 'Calm down, Bim, control yourself. Your body is strong, and

Chris and I will reinforce your spirit. We'll start the treatment right away. The sooner we break it down the better.'

She sent Chris off for a bowl of olive oil to warm by the fire.

'Mother!' I said, too scared to say anything else.

'Don't be afraid, dear. The I is Lord over the physical body, you know. We all have a kernel of the true and good within our inner beings.'

Mother kept soothing and encouraging me, till I felt there might be some good in me. All the same, I got the message that the tumour was somehow a result of my badness. Because if the true and good flowers within you, there's no room there for other sorts of growth, you're too full. I think that's what she was trying to say.

She talked to me for ages by the fire, patting my hand. Half an hour at least, I would say. And even though I had failed her again I began to feel better. Mother would heal me. Then I could start again.

I got undressed again and on to the table. Mother rubbed the warm olive oil over my tummy and then she started the treatment.

'Ow!' I yelped. I couldn't help it!

'Be brave, Bim,' said Mother firmly. 'We have to break up the lump.' I thought her fingers would go right through the skin! It was murder! I roared, I couldn't help it. When she got tired Chris took over. Her hands weren't so strong but I was so bruised — oh! Finally I couldn't take any more so Mother had another feel, then she wrapped me up in a blanket and sat me by the fire. I could hardly move!

They gave me an egg for tea but I couldn't eat it. She forced me to drink a cup of tea but I brought it up again.

'That's a good sign, Bim,' she said. 'The body is starting to get rid of the rubbish.'

The next day Mother said I should exercise. She made me bike round and round the house. But when I fell off I couldn't get back on again. She didn't get in a flap. People used to say in later years that she was a tower of strength in illness and she was.

Then she gave me another treatment. Oh, it was awful! I wished Gran was there. She always said it was wrong to bruise people. I think I must have fainted.

Mother went on trying for two more days. I could tell she was getting a bit worried. I couldn't eat a thing.

'I can't break up the lump,' she finally admitted. 'If only you'd told me sooner! It's grown too big.'

'I didn't realise!' I wailed.

'You'll have to go to the doctor,' she said.

Well, I couldn't go that day, I could hardly move. She said I could wait till the bruises faded and that was about a week. Then she sent me off on my bike to Dr Simpson. It was the seventh of April, 1916. A terrible day.

I was scared. I thought I was going to die. I shivered and shook while he examined me and I kept my eyes shut tight. I didn't want to see his face when he found that tumour.

He didn't say anything till I was dressed again and the nurse went out of the room. He twiddled his watch chain and looked at me with sorrow. He was a nice man, a friend of Mother's. He was trying to work up his courage. Finally he got it out. 'Bim Wells, you are going to have a baby.'

'No I'm not,' I said. 'I hate babies!'

He coughed and looked out the window. 'I'm afraid you have no choice in the matter,' he said. 'Nature has ordained. You're going to be a mother in August.'

The shock! I felt like dying! It was such a shock!

After the doctor sent me out of his office I sat there, just staring, in the waiting room for ages. I couldn't get used to it. I was still there when the last patient left. The nurse shooed me outside like a stray cat. She didn't seem to like me any more.

Mother wasn't there when I got home, she was at a meeting. I went in to Sally and sat down at the kitchen table. My legs would hardly hold me up. She gave me a cup of tea with lots of sugar.

'I'm going to have a baby, Sally,' I said. I was nearly howling. She went tut-tut. 'Why am I? I don't want one!'

'You should have thought about that before you started

fooling around with the men!' said Sally. She was a good cook but a bit sharpish.

'What's that got to do with it?' I asked her. She looked at me hard.

'Bim, you're twenty-eight years old! Don't tell me you don't know where babies come from?'

It was like a nightmare! She had to tell me why I was having a baby. I was horrified, I felt sick. I didn't even know until she told me! If only I'd known! I sort of knew but then again I didn't. I remembered the time Mother talked to us about beans in their snug little nests, the offspring of the bean flower and so forth. But she never said anything about the father bean!

Mother took the news quite calmly. She wasn't hard on me. What she wanted to know was, who was the father? I didn't know! Who did I fool round with last November? How could I remember!

'You have a good think, my girl,' said Mother when I went up to bed that night. 'Because — well, because.' What a peculiar thing to say!

Sure enough I did a lot of thinking and in the end I worked out who it was. I won't say the name. He was a big burly man with black hair, he worked in the tram yards mending the trams. He was a bit rough on me so I only went with him for a few weeks. His wife's sister was a friend of Mother's.

'So he can't marry you,' she said. 'I suppose that's just as well.'

I didn't want to marry him! I hadn't seen him for ages and I didn't want to.

Mother was wonderful. She said I would have to go out of Christchurch to have the baby. Mother would be a laughing-stock if I stayed in town. Every day she was dealing with fallen women! I know she really did feel sorry for me but even so she pulled no punches.

'Bim,' she said, 'you have brought disgrace on the whole family. When I think of your grandmother! How sad she would be if she knew.'

'But she's dead!' I said.

'She is watching you,' said Mother sadly, and looked me in the eye.

Oh! I felt awful! I knew she was right because sometimes Mother and I went to the Spiritualist Church and Granma sent us messages. Just little things like 'It's so beautiful here, so simple, if only I could tell you!' and sometimes 'You're a good girl Bim.' Just enough for us to know she wasn't in Hell thank goodness.

I started to carry on like mad. 'Oh! Oh! Oh! I'm terrible, I'm wicked! I don't want to go to Hell!'

Mother pulled me up smartly. 'It's not too late,' she said. 'You can start right now to make amends and to lead a better life.'

'I can't! I can't!'

'You can and you will,' she said strongly. 'You will shoulder your burden manfully. You are only reaping what you have sown.'

'But it's terrible!' I yelled. I couldn't see any way out. She calmed me down and reminded me this wasn't my only chance at life, I would be reincarnated one day and have another chance. She didn't believe in Hell.

Mother did another good thing for me, at least she tried to. She went to see the man at the tramway yards. Told him straight that I was going to have a baby and he was the father. He was a tough nut to crack! She wanted money for me and the baby, it was his duty after all. But he said he couldn't, not without his wife finding out. Mother got cold feet. She started feeling sorry for his wife and two little daughters.

'Ignorance is bliss,' I said. Mother usually jumped down my throat when I said that.

'For once the aphorism is apt,' she admitted. 'Telling his wife would only compound the problem.' This went right against her principles. The man should pay!

Mother went through a chest in her bedroom and made up a bundle of clothes for this darn baby. I didn't want them but she made me take them.

Before I left I had to say goodbye to Aunty Nell. 'I'll be

back in no time!' I said. 'I'm just going for a little holiday in Dunedin.' That's what Mother had told me to say.

'What for?' she asked, but I think she really knew.

'I'm in disgrace,' I said. 'I've been a naughty girl. I'm going to have a baby.' I couldn't help giggling, it was such a queer idea.

She looked funny. I just waited and finally she spat it out. 'Like mother, like daughter,' she said. 'Maria had to make Henry marry Ada. She was having a baby too. But don't say I said so.'

That took the wind out of my sails! I didn't know what to say.

'I just thought I'd tell you,' Aunty Nell went on. 'You're not the only girl in the world to get in the family way.'

I just got on my bike and rode off. She should never have told me that!

I went into exile on the railway train. I didn't feel happy about it. The lady from the Refuge came to meet the train in Dunedin. Mother had arranged it all. It was a scary place, that railway station, I didn't know which way to turn. This lady came up to me and said, 'Are you Bim? Come along with me.' She carried my bag.

There were usually about twenty girls at the Refuge but they kept changing, they'd have their babies and then clear out, so I never made any friends. We all had one thing in common but some of them were not very lady-like.

They didn't like us going round the town. We went to a little church on Sundays but most of the time we worked in the Refuge, did the cleaning and laundry and washing-up or else we did sewing for these blankety-blank babies. They had a piano, not a very good one. I played Beethoven duets with one woman. We slept four to a room on hard beds.

Those women talked a lot about where their babies would go. Baby farms were against the law, Mother had seen to that, but some of those foster homes were not so hot either, your baby might die and the people there would go on taking your money! I wouldn't mind if my one died, I thought. That wasn't a very nice way to think.

I remember Mother chuckling over something Mrs Sheppard wrote in the *White Ribbon* once. She said we spend more time and effort raising healthy sheep than we do rearing our children. They were both in favour of the new scientific methods and the Plunket nurses. But later on, Mother said that Dr Truby King was just trying to fatten up baby soldiers! In the end she had mixed feelings about the Plunket way.

Anyway, I didn't want to raise it myself! I couldn't think of anything worse.

The 'Adoption' column in the newspaper was a good place to look. 'Couple would like to adopt healthy child 1–2 years old.' You never knew if they just wanted their own little slave. Or you could advertise your own kid. But mostly people didn't want brand-new babies.

Then there were orphanages. Mother had done her best but you could never be sure what went on in those places.

I tried not to think about it too much. I thought, Mother will know what to do. She came down early and started hunting. And after a week she said, 'We're in luck! I've found a nice couple who want to adopt your baby.'

'When?' I asked her. I couldn't take it in.

'As soon as the baby is born. Isn't that wonderful?'

Roy recommended a lawyer in Dunedin who drew up the adoption papers. I signed them and the couple signed them, everything was hunky-dory. That was a weight off my mind! Now I just had to wait and it would be out of my life forever.

Of course it cost money for me to stay in this place in Dunedin. And who do you think paid for it? Mother, of course! It was so good of her. I didn't have any money. Mother thought the state should look after fallen women. I wasn't a fallen woman, not really of course. It was more of just an accident in my case but I still needed somewhere to go, same as if I was. It was a good deal of money, I might add.

I hated thinking about the baby. I wished it would never come. When it did come it was horrible. Horrible! It hurt like billyo and the midwife wasn't very nice to me either.

The couple had chosen the name for the birth certificate, Peter Stanley Robin. I had to keep the baby for two weeks before the couple took it away. Well, every day I was feeding it six times, and by the time the two weeks were up I felt different. The kid was red and it bawled a lot, but I didn't want them to take it away. So I said no, they didn't have the right. There was a great kerfuffle. Everyone was mad at me.

'Bim, you're making a terrible mistake,' Mother said.

'It's not fair, it's my baby,' I said. I wouldn't budge! I can be just as stubborn as her when I know what I want.

'We'll have to make the best of it then, won't we?'

'Can I bring it back to Office Road?' I asked. She gave me a queer look.

'Who's going to look after this child? That's the question!'

She stayed with me in Dunedin for a few more weeks and she tried to teach me how to look after it. But I wanted to be out and about. All those dirty nappies and the drying was even harder than the washing. It was no good in a boarding house.

I came back from town one day and Mother was rocking the cradle. We had a fine old ding-dong.

'Now look here, Bim. If I thought you would look after this boy I would be quite prepared to have you both at Office Road. But my destiny is not to be a mother to my grandson!'

I yelled at her. 'It's only a darn kid, it's no big problem looking after a darn kid!' On and on we went. I didn't want to lose the kid but I didn't want to look after it either.

'Raising a child is a sacred duty,' Mother said.

'It is not, it's smelly bottoms!' Oh, I was all mixed up. In the end Mother worked out a compromise. The kid would go into a foster home and I would go and see him now and then. She found a place that seemed all right. So we left the kid there and Mother went back to Christchurch.

Of course this cost money! From now on I was on my own. Ten bob a week for fifteen years I paid for that boy. So I had to be out and working. I was supposed to stay in Dunedin close to the kid. I got one job after another, I couldn't settle. Mostly as a kitchenmaid or a cleaner. I missed my massage!

Sooner or later I always had a row with the boss. They all had their mean little ways, all out to exploit the workers. After a few months I went back to Office Road.

For the next year or so I was always going backwards and forwards. I kept going back to Christchurch to stay with Mother, and she kept saying, go back and do your duty. She'd let me stay a few months and send me off again. But I'd just stay a few weeks and then come back as soon as I had the fare. The truth is I didn't go and see the kid, only once.

It was too depressing. One look at him and all those awful feelings came back — how I had disgraced the family and Granma being disappointed and the horrible pain when he was born and trying to get things dry in the boarding house. I didn't want to look at him. All the kids were bawling and my one had a runny nose and a poo in his nappie. That horrible smell! He didn't even know who I was. What was the point of going to visit a baby? I thought all right, I'll go and see him later when he can talk. I'll send the money by postal note.

Chapter 29

Now I'm going to talk about the city council. It's funny Clem hasn't come back though. Sometimes I forget those steps aren't finished and I nearly go for a six. He said he'd be back on Friday and that's a long time ago.

Stan tried to give me a fruit cake today.

I said, 'I don't want that. Where'd you get it from?'

'Someone gave it to me,' he said, 'but I don't eat fruit cake.'

'Then you shouldn't take it!' I said. 'You should just say you don't like it!' He's got no manners!

'I think it's more courteous to accept a gift,' he said.

It's not right, taking a cake when you know you're not going to eat it.

'When's this man going to finish your steps?' he asked. Just needling me! 'He shouldn't leave it like that. You could break your neck.'

'He's a busy man, you leave him alone,' I said.

He spent half an hour shifting concrete blocks and bits of wood around the place. I let him have his bit of fun.

'There!' he said. 'Now at least you won't fall down the gap.' He made the tea for me. I'm just a bit shaky this week.

'Are you sure it's not too much for you, telling the story of your mother?'

What a fool! It's not tiring. Just talking to myself! He might call that hard work but I don't! He poked his nose into everything. Gave the cats some milk and swished out the bath. Then he went to his van and brought back a sort of little chicken coop. He reckoned the chicks were big enough to be outside now. I told him to mind his own beeswax, they stay in the cupboard.

What am I saying, I must get back to Mother. While she

was with me down in Dunedin she was itching to get back home because 1917 was election year for the city council. One day she got a letter that sent her over the moon.

'Oh joy! Joy!' she raved. 'There's going to be a Labour ticket, and can you imagine what their slogan is? We Do Not Believe in War!'

'I thought you didn't approve of party politics,' I reminded her.

'Not when men toady to a single leader,' said she. 'Not when they all baa together like lambs. But this is the party that wins my heart!'

So off she went to Christchurch, and blow me down if she didn't decide to stand for the council herself!

It was a wonder she got any votes at all. The Reverend Mr Fitzgerald at Avonside Church had a snitch on her. The Sunday before the election he gave a blistering sermon against the Labour men and specially Mother. Said they wanted us to lose the war. It was all grist to her mill.

They'd just brought in that thing, proportional something. I think they only used it that one time. And they got Mother! Yes, she was a winner! I went back home, I couldn't miss that. People kept calling to congratulate her and I would give them a little something like fig-meat on wholemeal bread. Mother was the first woman in Christchurch to get on the council! You'd think it happened every day of the week, to read the papers. Still, she didn't mind.

'My work is just beginning,' she said.

She used to be excited before and after the meetings. The Labour people were always in the minority. She could have her say but it was hard to get things moving. For instance, she brought up the town milk supply as soon as she was elected, but two years later nothing had changed, the milkmen were still driving their horses and ladling out the milk with the same old dirty hands. No good!

We had so many visitors! Mostly they came on No More War but there was lots of council business too. That meant I carried most of the load in the rubbing. They came all the more to be massaged by the famous Ada Wells and if she wasn't there, too bad, they got rubbed by me.

When I was down in Dunedin waiting for the kid to be born they brought in registration for masseurs. I was in exile so I missed out! Anyone who wasn't on the register had to go to the School of Massage. My cousin Vincent got his ticket but it was like university, it was far too hard for me. I missed out! Ever since then I've been only allowed to give people rubs. Rubs or massage, it was exactly the same thing. But I was lumped in with all the no-good quacks and crackpots because of having the kid! That would have upset Granma and it upset me. Never mind, everyone knew I could do it and I've had patients stick with me for years and years and years.

In 1918 our brother Stan came back from the war. He'd been away four years and been torpedoed twice. He couldn't get out of Christchurch quick enough. Mother was pained to see him but she was glad he wasn't dead.

Father came with us to meet the ship. He looked dreadful, he could hardly walk. He grizzled and grumbled and no wonder. He was staying with Chris and Roy and a few weeks later he died. Poor old thing. He didn't belong anywhere and he didn't have any friends. He stayed with us sometimes but never for long. Mother said we should be kind to him but they always quarrelled and off he'd go. This time he was gone for good. Mother said it was tragic that he didn't live to see the end of the war.

Straight after the war came the big flu epidemic. People were weakened because of no oranges. We were busy at Office Road, every bed full and then some. We got people who should have been in hospital because the hospital was full. I didn't like doing those early rounds! We shunted the patients through as fast as possible. What a spring that was! I used to get over-excited and then I would just go outside and stand in the garden for a bit by the spindleberry trees. That calmed me down.

I had an awful feeling all the fun in life was over. All the best young men had been locked up in jail, so Mother said. But a lot of good blokes were killed in the war and a lot of them came back different, funny. Not so ready for a bit of fun.

When the flu epidemic died down Mother said, 'It's time you went to see the boy again. This time I'll come too.'

Dear oh dear! We reached Dunedin on a Friday and went out to the foster home first thing in the morning. We didn't give the woman any warning. Mother marched in, took one look at the place and that was that. 'Mrs Ellis, I have come to relieve you of the responsibility of caring for my grandson.'

'Oh, my little darling Johnny — you're not taking Johnny away from me!' Mrs Ellis grabbed a kid and kissed him all over the face. Johnny, I thought? Sure enough, this 'Johnny' was what she called my kid, she gave them all new names, you see.

As we rode away in the bus Mother gave me what for. 'Bim! How could you! Why didn't you tell me? The grease on the bench! Those mangy cats!' On and on. 'The poor child! He's two and a half but he's just like a baby! Why doesn't he talk? He can hardly hold up his head!'

She cuddled the boy and rocked him. I didn't like the look of him. He was horribly thin and his eyes had a funny faraway look. At least he didn't cry. He didn't wriggle either. He ducked his head, he never looked you in the eye.

'This child is scared out of his wits!' declared Mother. She peeled back his thin vest and found a row of sores. 'Oh no, no, I can't bear it! Oh, that wicked woman!'

We had to nurse him back to health again. Then Mother found another foster couple. They had three children of their own and a boarder. She was sure the kid would be all right this time. They called him Cedric Ross. He stayed with them till he was six years old.

We went back home to our normal run of patients. People came to Mother for everything under the sun. Susan Grigg came because her mother thought she was too fat. Too fat! I didn't think you could rub fat away but Mother did.

Mary Tooney had curvature of the spine. Her parents sent her to live in Christchurch specially so she could be massaged by the famous Ada Wells. She was only thirteen and she came to us twice a week before school. Poor little shrimp! In the end her doctor decided the treatment was doing more harm than good.

We could have had the place full of TB patients if we'd let them. Sometimes we got men with miner's psthisis and we coddled them a bit. Couldn't stop them dying, everyone knew that. Even Mother wasn't so jolly with the miners.

I remember one awful day they brought in a man on a stretcher, he'd been knocked over by a horse and his leg was all twisted funny. Mother had him put on the massage table and sent me for hot packs.

'He's got a broken leg!' I said. 'Better get the doctor.'

'Have mercy on the poor man,' said Mother. 'Let a little love into that hard heart of yours.'

Well! You could have knocked me down with a feather! When I came back with the packs the man had passed out cold. That was a terrible day. I went for the doctor off my own bat. Mother bound it up quite well but she shouldn't have tried to rub it.

She didn't go on the council again, and I suppose that must have been because of me.

I remember another thing happened that year, 1919 it was. There was a knock knock knock on the front door and when I opened it, there was the telegram boy in his nifty little peaked cap.

'Two telegrams for Mrs Wells,' he said. Well, telegrams were a pound a penny in our house so I thought nothing of it. But when Mother read the first one she screwed it up and threw it right across the room.

'What's the matter?' I asked.

'Oh read it yourself — and then burn it!' she said in a mood.

So I flattened it out and it said, 'Married this morning. Please send one hundred pounds. Stan.' I popped it into the fire and it went up in flames.

'How dare he!' she said. 'My own son! What sort of a woman is he marrying that he does it behind my back?' She was fuming! He really knew how to hit the sore spot, that brother of mine.

'You haven't read the other one,' I said. It was about the Bill letting women into Parliament. It was passed! That cheered her up no end.

'Mother,' I said, 'are you going to stand for Parliament?'

She wouldn't say yes and she wouldn't say no. But in the end she never did. That must have been because of me. I was too much trouble. The others were all married, but she still had me to look after.

She wasn't getting any younger and she led a very full life. So she decided to sell the big house and do the massage on a smaller scale. She bought a lovely little flat right in the middle of town, on the corner of Hereford and Manchester, just down the road from the Congregational Church. The building was brick, it was the tallest building in town apart from the cathedral. Her flat was on the top floor and if you couldn't manage the stairs that was all right, there was a lift.

I was sorry to say goodbye to Gran's house. Still, it was far too big, only two of us to run it, and Mother with her responsibilities. Somebody bought it and made it into flats, luckily he didn't chop down the magnolia trees.

Sometimes I lived with her up there and sometimes I didn't. She didn't mind being on her own. I always got on her nerves from the day I was born, and in the flat everywhere she turned, there I was! So now and then she'd send me packing. That was all right. I'd go and get a job in some place like Ashburton. Sooner or later I'd be back with Mother. I had to come back or my own patients would be left high and dry.

Mother had a different sort of client now. Business people used to pop in during their lunch hour or after work. It was very convenient. She would give them advice on diet and hygiene and do hot and cold packs and massage. But no more Turkish baths and fomentations. If that's what people needed she sent them off to Tom and Amy Pike in Bealey Avenue. Tom got a lot of clients from his Aunt Ada.

I went out to my patients on the bike. Put the oil and

vinegar and cloths into the basket and off I biked all over Christchurch. I got out and about, I even went into the country.

The flat was handy for the Theosophicals too. Chris and Cos and Mother all belonged. Christianity was too simple for Mother, she needed something harder.

I remember her upsetting cousin Edna terribly.

'The crucifixion was quite unnecessary,' Mother announced. She never took communion.

Edna started trembling. She was about fourteen and very sensitive. I can see her now with her pretty little face bright red. She said to Mother, 'But Christ's death was God's most wonderful gift to Man!' I thought that was brave of her, whether she was right or wrong.

'Wonderful? A man with nails through his hands and feet hanging on a cross in the hot sun, dripping with blood and sweat and dying of suffocation? You call that wonderful? I'm disappointed in you, Edna.'

'He gave His life for us!' whispered Edna. She looked heartbroken but Mother went right on with the lesson.

'It was quite unnecessary,' she said. 'And then to tell us to eat his flesh and drink his blood — that is downright disgusting!'

Edna burst into tears and ran out of the room. I heard her sobbing as she ran down the stairs. Mother said she was old enough to be told a few hard truths.

The Theosophical Society used to meet in the parlour every second Thursday. Before they started Mother would say, 'I'm not at home to anyone tonight, Bim. And don't come in.'

They started up when we were still in Office Road. I used to put my ear to the door. Mumbo jumbo! One night a lady arrived late and I opened the door of the parlour to show her in. Mother and Chris and Cos and all the others were standing in a circle with their arms held up high and their eyes shut chanting their thingamybob. Oh, they were really getting carried away!

> *O cosmic rays*
> *enter our sentient souls*
> *and subdue the needs of the physical body!*
> *O cosmic rays*
> *penetrate our intellectual souls*
> *fill us with the universal life force!*

They shut the door and I was on the outside again. Well! 'Our Father' made a lot more sense to me. But Mother wasn't going to be satisfied with just her daily bread and forgive us our sins, she wanted to be right up there with the angels or cosmic rays or whatever, full of divine wisdom. That night in bed I said to myself for a bit of a joke:

> *O cosmic rays*
> *penetrate my stomach soul*
> *unite me with a universal rice pudding*
> *and make my mother love me.*

They weren't only women in the Theosophicals, by the way, but nobody was the boss. Theosophy, Rosicrucians, Anthroposophy, they're all just big words to me. But they meant a lot to Mother, they went deep. I thought it was funny her being on the council and also getting right into the Theosophicals, it seemed like two opposite things to me. But as far as she was concerned the two things went together.

'All things secular are sacred,' she told me, 'including the city council. The spiritual skin expands continually with advancing human evolution.'

'Like a caterpillar.'

'After death we go on learning and changing. We're not stuck!' She liked that idea. She couldn't bear to think she might have to stop working after death.

'Then where do we go?' I asked, just to humour her.

'To Spiritland!' said Mother. 'The archetypes there communicate with chimes, melodies, harmonies, rhythms.'

'Ding, dong!' I said.

'There are seven regions of Spiritland . . .' I switched off.

You never got to the end of it. It was a like a terrible dark tunnel with seven little tunnels off the sides and every tunnel dividing into seven other tunnels.

'Oh, it's no use talking to you!' I heard Mother say sharply. 'You haven't the intellectual energy.'

Chapter 30

In 1922 there was another upset with the boy. The Rosses said they couldn't keep him any more, their own family was growing and they needed the space. Nuisance, nuisance! But Mother sorted it out again.

She always had this vision of the perfect cottage home for neglected children. I don't mean my kid was neglected but he did need a home. She went searching and my word she thought she'd found it. It was near Temuka. She came home happy as a lark.

'I've enrolled the boy at the Bramwell Booth Boys' Home, Bim,' she said. 'It's perfectly wonderful! This will make up for all his bad experiences in the past.' Oh, wasn't she proud of herself! 'They've got seventy boys, but I persuaded them they could take just one more. They won't throw him out, they'll keep him till he can make his way in the world.'

'How much is it going to cost me?' I asked.

'Ten shillings a week, the same as the foster home,' she said. 'And there's simply no comparison!'

'Why?'

'Wait till you see it! The house is full of lovely things. The gardens are just lovely! There's a conservatory and an orchard and a rose garden, and a river with a water wheel. And needless to say they grow all their own produce!' Oh, she was over the moon. If she was happy, so was I.

So then I had to go down and get the kid from Dunedin and take him to Temuka. He was properly fed now but I still didn't like the look of him. Where did he get that ginger hair from? Father had a gingery look, I suppose, but still. The kid was mighty careful what he said to me, he was just as cagey as me.

When we got to Temuka railway station the Sallies came

to meet us in their blood-red Model T Ford. The boy didn't like their uniforms. Big tears came into those watery pale blue eyes! What a sissy! We went up a huge big drive and I saw a lovely home.

'Is that it?' I asked.

'That's just the gate house,' said the Commandant and we kept on going. I saw the lily pond with big trees around it. I suppose that's where he got his silly ideas about landscape gardening from.

'What's that building?' I asked.

'That's the generator house,' they told me. At last we saw the Home itself and was it swanky!

'You're a lucky boy,' I said to the kid. 'It's a lot more grand than where I live!'

We arrived just on tea-time. A bell rang and the boys all lined up. The big ones were barefoot but the little ones had shoes on, no socks, mind you, they were toughening them up. I thought that's just what this kid needs, he's such a sissy.

The Commandant put him at a table with about ten other kids. They all had one slice of bread with dripping on it, and one slice with plum jam. The kid looked so miserable I gave his ear a tweak. 'Cheer up,' I said. 'Aren't you hungry?' Then the Commandant took me up to the officers' table. First he read a bit from the Bible about Heaven and Hell, then the boys sang grace and we all sat down to eat. I had quite a jolly time chatting with the officers. There was fresh cream and jam to go on the scones and they said it all came off the farm. Every now and then some of the boys would start talking and the Commandant told them to be quiet. They were well disciplined.

After tea they showed me where the kid would sleep. It looked all right to me.

'Now, Peter,' said the Commandant, 'it's time to say goodbye to your mother.'

He looked blank and no wonder. Nobody had ever called him Peter before! 'My name's Cedric Ross,' he said.

'It's no such thing, it's Peter Stanley Robin Wells,' said the officer. The kid frowned, he didn't like that. He wouldn't answer to it. Brat! Later on the Commandant's daughter asked him if he'd rather be Stanley or Robin. She was the schoolteacher and she was soft on him. He said if he couldn't be Cedric he didn't mind Stan too much, so that's what they called him. The same as my brother! I didn't like that, I just went on calling him kid.

I said goodbye and told him to be good. He didn't say anything, he looked so sorry for himself!

'Cheer up, kid, it's your birthday!' It was too, he was six years old that very day. I was glad to get back to Christchurch.

Three times I went to see him. I must admit the Home got a bit rundown over the next few years. The Sallies didn't have the money for the upkeep, they spent it all on evangelising. The conservatory went to pot, the electricity went bung, the whole place went downhill. I used to take the kid out for the day. Ken Lovell-Smith had a car and he did the honours. I kept the kid at arm's length and vice versa. At the end of the day it was always the same, he would stand by the gate and cry.

'I don't want to go back!' he would say. Wah wah wah!

'Don't be such a sook!' I'd say. 'What's the big problem?'

'I'm always cold and hungry and they don't let us play!' he would say or some such story. I used to tell Ken to just drive off.

Ken was just as soft as ever. He felt sorry for the kid. He used to invite him for holidays at Midway. I'd go and visit him there and we'd have a sing-song or play tennis or croquet.

When he was ten Mother decided I should give him a Christmas holiday. She was grateful to the Lovell-Smiths but she thought it was my rightful duty not theirs, so she paid the rent for a cottage in Oamaru. I collected the kid from the station at Temuka and off we went. He was happy even riding on the train! Mother was right, it was only fair to give him a holiday.

Well, the very next morning we were looking round the garden and who should we see over the fence but Mr and Mrs Ferguson! They gave us a great old welcome. Mr Ferguson was a friend of Father's from way back so they asked us to tea and for the next two weeks we were great mates.

Mr Ferguson took a shine to the kid. He decided to teach him the piano and by the end of the fortnight they were playing duets together. We went on picnics and walks in the country and up and down the sea front. The boy kept saying it was like going from Hell into Heaven! It was all Mother's doing, because the holiday was courtesy of her. Anyhow, after the holiday I got a letter from Mr Ferguson. He and Mrs F. wanted to have the boy in their own home. I thought, I might as well give the ten bob a week to them as to the Salvation Army, so I said yes.

The kid was as happy as happy could be. He'd had his heart set on being in a private home again. They were old, the Fergusons, old and set in their ways, but he liked it better. He went from a palace to a cottage. So that was that. He was a fool, really. I went to see him there a couple of times. The second time I grabbed the broom and started sweeping the place out. I thought Mrs Ferguson would have a fit!

'This place is dirty,' I told her. 'We can't have that!' She told me to leave and never come back.

'Never come back!' she said. So I didn't. I just got cracking with my own life.

It riled me that I couldn't call myself a masseuse. I thought I would train as a psychiatric nurse instead. Anyone could do it, you didn't need a brain, they were glad to get anyone at all. They called us nurses but really we were slushies. I remember we had to boil the blankets. I had a sort of wooden swish thing to poke them with. We had to boil them till they went hard and felty, because if they were soft the patients might tear them up and hang themselves.

Mother hated Sunnyside. She said it was built like a prison, great big thick stone walls and high fences to stop the loonies getting out. Cold as you know what. Big clanging iron gates with enormous locks. That first day I wondered if I'd ever get out again when they locked the gate behind me.

'Surely they're not that desperate for nurses,' I said to the sister who was showing me the layout of the place.

The patients were dressed in smock things and did they look queer! Banging their heads, dribbling, showing their bums and saying loony things in loony voices. Woopsie, Mother said you mustn't say loony. There were the mental defectives, and the old ones just sitting staring. Some got that way from the flu and some were shell shocked. One started yelling when we came in and that set off all the others. They weren't half as scared as me.

'Quieten down, I won't bite you,' I said, trying to keep my pecker up. The sister didn't know what to make of me.

After the grand tour she set me to work in the women's ward. There were some with milk-fever and some with the DTs and some with nobody at home. It was bath-day. What a way to start! All those nude bodies! The sub-matron came to inspect halfway through the morning. We got a snitch on each other right away.

I stayed at Sunnyside for two years. The buildings were all right once you got used to them. The patients started to seem more and more normal and the sub-matron more and more mad. I got fond of the old biddies. The silly ones gave us a laugh a day, and Mrs Milner, she didn't seem mad at all, I couldn't figure out what she was there for. On Saturdays I played my old ragtimes in the social room and some of them would dance. I liked a good old go at the piano without anyone criticising my fingering.

> *Just Molly and me,*
> *And baby makes three,*
> *We're happy in our*
> *Blue Heaven.*

That was one of my favourites. They'd all sing along.

I'm not saying it was all fun! One time I was helping old Mother Mackay on with her britches and Mary Ellen Gormby came up behind me with a hunk of wood. Wham! She bopped me one! I saw lightning and I woke up in the nurses' home with a terrible lump on my head. I didn't know where I was. That was awful. I couldn't go back for three days.

That sub-matron was an old battle-axe. I didn't like her and I didn't like the things she did. I played a few good tricks on her though. One day I went to the gardener and said, 'I've got a friend who's going fishing. Could you get me some worms?'

Yes he could, and I put the worms in her lily-white bed and smoothed it out so you'd never know the difference. When I told Mother she said, 'You'd better get out while you've got the choice. You're going as crazy as the patients!'

I didn't like the sound of that!

A few weeks later I saw the sub-matron whacking old Mother Mackay with a broom handle. 'You stop wetting your bed or you'll be out on the streets!' she said. 'Dirty old cow, you've had more men than lice!' Vicious! I ran off and got the key to the padded cell.

'Excuse me, Matron,' I said, 'there's something wrong with the strait-jacket.'

So she followed me along into the padded cell. I got her looking at the tie-things on the strait-jacket, then I nipped out and shut the door and locked her in! I went straight to my bike and rode off flat stick and I threw the key down a grating in the road! I didn't care if she stayed in that cell till Kingdom Come. And that was the end of my career at Sunnyside.

The next few years were all right. The boy was with the Fergusons and doing all right. Then the Depression came along. I remember in 1929 I couldn't afford the fare to go on a summer holiday and neither could my mates. So three of us decided to go on a biking holiday. We went to the West Coast, right over Arthur's Pass on our old bikes! A hundred and fifty miles there and a hundred and fifty miles back! Had to push the bikes up the hills of course. We were strong! I was forty-two. Any time we saw a woman hanging clothes on the line I'd call out, 'Have you got the kettle on? How about a cup of tea?'

Nine times out of ten we'd get a cuppa and a slice of bread.

No sense in holding back. I wasn't shy! Marge and Effie couldn't do it but I'd ask anyone.

When the kid was fourteen Mr Ferguson lost his job. The church couldn't afford an organist any more. Suddenly the Fergusons were hard-up. After a few months they wrote to ask if I could manage a bit more. They wanted fifteen bob a week. I said no! Letters went back and forward and the weeks went by and the kid turned fifteen.

I asked Mother what to do. 'I'm sick and tired of paying that ten bob a week,' I said, 'and now they say they can't afford to keep him at school.'

'It would be a crime if he didn't finish his education,' said Mother.

'He's not scholastic and he's not musical,' I told her. 'He's a ninny, he should be sent to work!'

As usual Mother had the answer. 'We must find out what his aptitudes are. I'll get in touch with Professor Shelley.'

Shelley was professor of education at the university. He made an appointment for two weeks' time and Mother wrote to Waitaki Boys' and the kid came up on the train. Professor Shelley gave him all sorts of tests. Putting blocks together, general knowledge, arithmetic, physical exercises and I don't know what else. It took all day!

He didn't tell me the results, he told Mother, and I took the kid up to her flat. It was the first time she'd actually seen him since he was two and a half. He was all bashful. She shook hands with him as if he was a real man.

'So you want to be a gardener,' said Mother.

'Yes, ma'am,' he muttered.

'Speak up!' I said.

'A gardener in a park. Or to work in a nursery.'

'Why's that?' Mother asked.

'I like to make things look beautiful,' he said. 'I like houses to have gardens that look nice. I think there should be gardens in the city. Trees.' He was unusually talkative!

'Professor Shelley thinks your back isn't strong enough for you to work in a garden,' said Mother. 'What do you say to that?'

He looked as if the sky had fallen. 'I still want to work in a garden,' he said. He was very tall and gangly and his back was weak. He was a horrible looking kid.

Mother sighed and put the letter from Professor Shelley aside.

'We'll see if we can find you a suitable job. I'm afraid there isn't enough money for you to stay at school any longer. Times are hard for everyone but we'll do the best we can.'

He looked as if he was going to start howling, I was so ashamed. 'Say thank you to Mrs Wells!' I yelled at him. 'Where's your manners?'

'Thank you,' he whispered. She patted him on the shoulder and we went downstairs again.

I looked and looked for a job that would suit. Then at last I heard of a chap in Turakina up near Wanganui who needed a help on his orchard. I thought, the kid likes trees, that'll do him. Fifteen was old enough. No more ten bob a week from me, I thought.

So he went sure enough, but blow me down, he didn't like it! Nothing was good enough for that boy! You'd think he was the king of England! He reckoned they made him work too hard, and the boss was 'bush-mad'. How would he know? Four months later he was back in Oamaru with the Fergusons. He ran away!

Oh, I was furious! Not even Mother could calm me down.

Then the Fergusons found him a job milking cows and topping pine trees on a farm nearby. You know how long he lasted there? Two weeks! All over the country grown men were out of work and Mr High and Mighty couldn't stick to a job for two weeks.

Well, the Fergusons wanted me to go back to paying that ten bob a week — just when I thought I was rid of him!

I was so mad!

'I can't stand it!' I said to Mother. 'What did I do to deserve this?'

Mother gave me that sad smiley look. 'Oh Bim! When will you learn? Each and every soul meets just those experiences which —'

. '— Infinite Love wills are best for him,' I recited. I'd heard that one before!

Mother never gave up, I'll say that for her. 'Your trials are right for you,' she said. 'Use them! You can grow!'

Could I just! Mother was quite upset.

'Love beats at the heart of things,' she said to me. She really believed that but she was wrong. 'Can't you feel it, Bim? Are you quite impervious? Can't you feel any love in your heart?'

'No I can't,' I said. 'I just feel wild, that's all.'

'But think of the Prodigal Son,' Mother said. 'You must!'

I knew what she was getting at but I didn't want to be in my Father's house, I wanted to be rid of that kid, I went to Roy and I said, 'I don't want to be that boy's mother any more! Cut him off! Cut him off!'

'He's only fifteen,' said Roy. 'Someone has to be responsible for him.'

'Not me!' I yelled. 'I've had enough! I want a divorce!'

Roy said you couldn't divorce your children.

'He's not my child! Not any more!' I screamed at him.

He finally got the message. 'Do you mean you'd let someone adopt him now?' he asked.

'Yes yes yes yes yes,' I said a thousand times.

There were a lot more letters to the Fergusons. They weren't very keen on their precious foster kid any more. Mr F. had turned right around because he'd lost his job and the boy wasn't a musical prodigy after all. So much for the kid's idea of Heaven! Even so they would have adopted him but it was too late. They should have said! You could only adopt a child of fourteen or less. Roy drew up the papers and he became the Fergusons' ward and that made them his next of kin. Otherwise he would have been made a ward of the state.

What a relief it was! That kid had been a burden from the day I found out he was there inside me. He was a curse, he ruined my life. And now he was gone! Oh, I could have flown right into the sky with relief! After all those years I got rid of my son.

Chapter 31

I haven't done anything on my Mother's story for three days now or is it more. I've just had an awful shock. On Sunday morning I'd just got back from my swim when I heard Clem turn up and get that concrete mixer roaring. Good, I thought, about time too.

All day long he was at it and yesterday and most of today as well. Although sometimes I thought, this is a far cry from my bit of corrugated iron and two sticks! Still, bigger is better I thought, it won't fall down in a hurry.

When he stopped for lunch I said to him, 'I don't need those extra steps up the back of the section. That bit's never given me any trouble in all the twenty-eight years I've been here.' I moved here in 1947. My own house! That was thanks to the Labour Government and some money from Reyn.

'Then you've been lucky,' he said. 'That bank was due to go at any minute.'

He went off for another trailer load of concrete blocks. The garden's starting to look like the tomb of Tutankhamun. My cats don't like it. I haven't seen Ugly for two days and Walter and Norman are acting strange. As for the garden, well! There'll be no pumpkins this year.

I'm not myself, I've got an awful pain in my chest. The worst thing of all was his bill! When the job was finished he packed up his tools and came inside without even knocking.

'Here's the damage,' he said and he plonked it down on the table.

Well! I couldn't believe my eyes! Triple time for working on a Sunday, so many hours and so much overtime, the cement and the blocks and Lord knows what else. It's all down in black and white, I can't argue with him. I don't know how I'm going to pay it. I can't cut down on my tithe for the Worldwide Churches of God, that's fixed. I can't cut down on the electricity or the rates or the milk for the cats. I can't even think about it!

I'll go on with Mother's story, that'll keep my mind off the bill.

She left the flat after ten years, she retired to Webb Street. She didn't want to be in the thick of things any more. She could put up with me there, we had half a house. She was sixty-nine. Strangely enough that seemed old to me and look at me now! I'm eighty-eight and living on my own. But I've lived long enough. I hate old age.

I was back to the rubbing, I'd left Sunnyside of course. One morning I had an appointment in Sydenham, I was in a bit of a hurry. I wanted to go to the WC but Mother was in there. I washed the breakfast things and when I went back she was still in there.

'Mother,' I said. 'Hurry up, I'm busting!'

She made a little noise in her throat, she didn't like being interrupted. When she came out I said, 'What's the matter, are you constipated?'

'Nothing much,' she said.

I thought about that as I biked over to Mrs Densem's. We always had plenty of fresh vegies, and Mother always had prunes and brown bread. She believed in lots of roughage.

People often came to us with constipation. It was *the* Christchurch ailment when I was a girl, and I know why! White bread and potatoes and mutton and cake. Most people had a terrible diet! Our friend Norman Bell tried to put them right but people just thought he was a crank.

'Exercise, Mother!' I said when I got home. 'You should get out on your bike.'

'Don't boss me, Bim,' said Mother. 'I don't feel up to it. I'll walk around the garden.' That's not what I call exercise, a little totter round the japonica. She hated walking unless there was a purpose! No, she just sat there doing her tapestry and talking to her mates, or else writing away in that book. I gave her an enema.

'Have you been this morning?' I asked her next day.

'Oh, mind your own business!' she said.

But one day she put her hands on her tummy and said to Chris, 'I'm getting quite stout down here. I must exercise, Bim is right.'

I got her some pills from the chemist and she flushed them down the WC.

'It's only senna pods, Mother,' I said. 'Perfectly natural!'

'Not natural enough for me I'm afraid,' she said.

Of course I was rubbing her abdomen every night. I could feel the lumps under my fingers. I couldn't break them down. If anything, they were getting larger so Mother asked Chris to help. 'She's got sensitive fingertips,' she said. The two of them managed to break down the biggest lump but Mother was exhausted, she didn't feel better, she felt worse. Next week she found another lump.

'Shall I get Chris to come and break it up?' I asked.

Mother shook her head. 'I don't have the strength for any more struggle,' she said. There was something terribly wrong. But she wasn't despondent, she didn't believe in despondency, she said it was bad for the health.

Chris didn't have time to help me with Mother. She had three children and they needed a lot of supervision, and Cos had a great big enormous house so she couldn't help either. It had to be me and I was glad.

Mother got weaker and weaker. She couldn't relieve herself at all, she was all clogged up. She went to bed and stayed there. Oh, it was awful to see her staying in bed! But she wasn't a bit sad.

I sponged her and rubbed her and did everything I knew how. I made all the little snacks she liked best, Sanitarium Granosa and shredded wheat, bottled grapejuice, nuts and fruit, even a little bit of chocolate. But in the end it all came back as a horrible black slime and choked her. Nothing would go down her gullet and stay down except for water or tea.

'It's poison but I love it!' I could hear her say that in my mind every time I took her in a cuppa. She didn't say it though. Her tongue shrivelled up into a little tiny black thing like a parrot's tongue. She couldn't talk at all! What a terrible thing! She couldn't even clear her throat. That was agony for her. She wrote down everything she needed to say.

'Get Dr Simpson to come,' she wrote. So I sent a message off to Dr Simpson. He was an old friend of hers. I felt uncomfortable whenever I saw him.

I showed him into Mother's room. It was looking pretty, with the massage things hidden behind the blue screen and Mother's tapestries on the wall and some chrysanthemums on the dressing table. The bed had a new white eiderdown that I got from Beath's when she first went to bed.

I stayed in the room while Dr Simpson examined her. She didn't want me there but I wouldn't leave. He looked sadder and sadder. 'Mrs Wells,' he began, but he couldn't go on.

Mother wrote something down and I came close so I could read it. 'Speak up. I am not afraid,' she wrote. 'You may simply confirm what I assume to be the case. That I have cancer, and am too deeply smitten to recover.'

He bowed his head. 'I'm afraid that is true. There are tumours in your bowel and liver and throat.'

I made a sort of noise and Mother wrote, 'Don't look as if you are overjoyed!'

I wasn't! Dr Simpson looked very puzzled. 'You must be in the most appalling pain!' he said.

Mother wrote, 'There is no pain.'

He couldn't believe that but it was perfectly true, I never saw any sign of pain. But then Mother had tremendous self-control. She wouldn't tell a lie. Why would she tell a lie about a thing like that?

'I've never seen anything like it in all my life!' said Dr Simpson.

'Mother is wonderful,' I told him.

'What about the mental anguish? At least let me prescribe something for that,' and he took out his pad.

Mother scribbled furiously, 'Drugs would be terrible for me! I have had no drugs in my whole life!'

'Good for you,' said the doctor. Mother was writing fast now.

271

'I have an argument with the medical profession. You should study the healthy body and not the sick. The sick body is the deviation.'

'I never see any healthy people in my surgery. That is, except for the — hmm.' He remembered about my business and gave me a look.

'I am not an Invalid!' wrote Mother. 'I have never worked harder in my whole life.'

'Then what can I do for you?' asked Dr Simpson. He didn't know what she wanted.

'My body is finished,' wrote Mother. 'I would like you to help me leave it behind. We must throw off the useless and the dead!'

'Mother!' I said. 'You don't mean that!'

'I always said that is what I would do.'

The doctor went on his guard. He sent me out of the room and they had a long 'talk'.

When he came out he didn't say anything to me but when I asked Mother she wrote down, 'He said he would do the same thing for his own mother.'

I went all trembly and I ran away to think about it. It wasn't such a shocking idea in those days. All her life Mother believed in euthanasia. The literary societies had debates on it. There was even a euthanasia society, not that she ever joined it.

But really doing it, really and truly! My own mother! That took a lot of getting used to. But once I did get used to the idea I kept smiling and laughing because I was proud to be in on the secret. And specially because I thought she was so brave.

That was over forty years ago and when I think about it now I can see it took a lot of gumption. I'm old now myself and I don't like that but then again I don't want to die soon, not at all, certainly not. It's muddly in my mind. I'm amazed how easily Mother arranged it. My doctor wouldn't do it. He wouldn't take me seriously for a minute, and if I kept on about it he'd pop me into Sunnyside or an old fogeys' home. Any doctor would do the same.

But Mother had the personality, she had the know-how. She was clever the way she didn't dilly-dally. If she'd waited a few more weeks the cancer might have got to her brain. Then she couldn't have persuaded Dr Simpson to help her out! She might have lingered for ages in a terrible state. Yes, she knew just when to do it, not too soon and not too late. She would know the hour of her death. She had the head-piece. Dr Simpson was going to keep in touch. Mother would let him know when she was ready.

She was nearly ready even then. She hated wasting time, she wanted to get it organised and be done with it. For years she'd been talking about Spiritland. It sounded like a sort of university or like finally getting into Parliament, only you talked in music instead of words. Right up her alley! Now it was her turn to go she could hardly wait.

The next day all the carry-on started. It was a big project, dying. Mother wanted it to be just right.

First I had to get Chris and Cos so Mother could tell them. Chris began weeping and wailing fit to burst. She made Mother cry. Finally they left, thank goodness.

'They've upset you!' I said to her when I was changing the cold pack on her forehead. I was mad at Chris.

She leaned over and wrote, 'I don't weep for myself, I weep for Chris. I don't want her to grieve. I want her to be happy.'

I couldn't make head nor tail of it. Once I overheard her say to someone that I didn't have normal feelings like other people. 'I'm not hard-hearted, I'm only happy you're going to heaven! You should be pleased I'm happy instead of crying like Chris!' Chris was a great boob but I couldn't say that to Mother.

'Promise me you will give Chris a rub once a week on her neck and back and shoulders and stomach.'

I felt a bit put out. Chris Chris Chris!

'She needs it,' Mother wrote. 'Will you?' I don't like making promises. 'She will pay you.'

'I don't want to!' I blurted out. Mother shut her eyes for a moment.

273

'Again you fail me,' she wrote. I couldn't help it! Then she crossed that out and wrote instead, 'I'll ask Cos. Cos is splendid. She uses her fingertips.'

Cos hardly did any rubbing, and I'd been doing it for thirty years!

She wrote down a list of her good friends. She wanted to see them all and say goodbye.

'Why isn't Mrs Sheppard on the list?' I asked her. She pretended she was asleep. All right, I thought, be like that.

I had the job of telling them. They started coming, every day four or five different ones. I made sure they didn't stay too long. I kept all her notes, I wouldn't let them burn those! But it was funny about that book she was writing in. I used to peep when she was sleeping. I wonder where it went?

After Lesley came I found a Latin lesson on the pad, 'Moneo adesse hostem.' Mother had a good argument with Archdeacon Haggitt, she enjoyed his visit although she wasn't orthodox. Then the Theosophical ladies were still asking her to straighten out their ideas. 'Plant is Etheric moving out of Stone. Animal Astral Moves and Feels . . .' Mumbo jumbo!

It was very strange reading the bits of paper without knowing what the other person said. 'She is too wandering. Critical Faculty not awakened.' She might have meant me because I did move a lot and also Mother used to say I didn't have any ideas of my own, I just copied. She said a lot of things about me over the years. But I don't know if she was always right. Except she must have been.

There was a lot of business to do before she died, bills to pay and so forth, and who should have what. She wanted Edna to have the little silver tray and so on, Chris was in charge of all that. Everybody got their farewell messages. And every day she admonished me to behave myself when she was gone.

'You must put away all wrong thoughts forever,' she wrote one day. Another time it was, 'Promise me Calmness with the patients, no gush — no familiarity. Do your job kindly and be quiet.' But my patients liked a bit of a joke with the treatment, anyway how could I change my ways at that age, I was forty-six! She didn't tell the others how to behave.

People kept asking about our brother Stan. Mother said there was no need for Stan to come, it would only be sorrow for him.

I said again, 'Shall I ring up Mrs Sheppard, I mean Mrs Lovell-Smith?'

'No,' she said. She might have been sad. 'She won't be far behind me.'

Funny how Kate Sheppard turned into Mrs Lovell-Smith. She was lucky, Ken's father was a sexy man! But who emptied Mother's bed-pans, who washed her hair, eh? It wasn't the famous Kate Sheppard, it was me. I had my uses. Mother got the pip with a lot of people in her time. Anyone who didn't see things her way, Mother cut them off and that was that, but at the end she went a bit soft and buried the hatchet. But she'd never hear a word against Kate Sheppard or against Chris.

Whenever Chris turned up Mother's eyes would follow her round the room as if she'd never seen her before, her own daughter! Chris would stay for hours holding her hand. And later I would find this sort of stuff on the pad: 'Bliss! You! I just love to look at You!'

That made me mad. I hate all that soppy stuff. Awful! I'm glad nobody else saw it, they'd think Mother had lost her marbles.

I sorted out the bills that needed paying and Roy came in to do her will. He brought two people from the office as witnesses.

'When you're dead, get a message through to me!' said Roy. 'Send me a telegram!' He thought life after death was a great joke. Mother couldn't laugh any more but she didn't mind his jokes.

She said she was going to leave me a special legacy for looking after her in her sickness. I would have done it for nothing! Sometimes Chris came and gave me a break but I hated being away from her. Chris was hopeless. Every time she saw Mother she came out with her eyes red and her mouth all wobbly. Oh, she was wet all through. I was always the strong one.

Mother said my legacy would have been more except she had paid for all my business down in Dunedin. That cost a lot, staying in the Refuge, it was years ago but still it cost her a lot.

Chris said we should have an essay competition in her memory on the subject of International Goodwill. Mother said to use that favourite verse of hers:

> *Ring out false pride in place or blood,*
> *The civic slander and the spite.*
> *Ring in the love of Truth and Right,*
> *Ring in the common love of good.*

She said Stan and I had to give eighty pounds each for the prize fund and Chris and Cos should only give twenty pounds, I suppose because they were married women, they didn't have their own earnings.

Every few days Dr Simpson came to see Mother. He was more and more amazed.

'I've never seen anything like it,' he said to me out in the kitchen. I always gave him a cup of tea. I was starting to feel more at home with him. He never mentioned the kid and nor did I. 'She says she feels no pain at all, and she sleeps. Is that true?'

'Ten hours a night,' I said, 'and a bath every day.' That was my biggest job, giving Mother her bath. 'Am I looking after her all right?'

'You're giving her excellent care,' he said, surprised. 'I did offer her the deep X-ray treatment but she put me in my place! Said she preferred to be like David, and fight with the weapons she knows.'

'Mother says we could've beaten the cancer if we'd got it soon enough. I should have known it wasn't just constipation.' I didn't like to say so outright but it was my fault she was dying.

'She's so calm!' he said. 'So happy!'

'That's because she's going to meet her boyfriend,' I said. That made his eyes pop! 'Not Father,' I giggled. 'St Bede! He's her guardian angel.' She was longing to meet Bede in Spiritland and I wished her luck.

Once late at night I peeked in and she was sitting bolt upright staring at someone across the room. She held out her arms and looked so happy! Her head was wagging around and her eyes were lit up and laughing. Then she lay back on the pillow with a smile on her face and I went and tucked her in.

'Mother,' I said, 'what happened?' I wanted to be in on the joke.

For once she wasn't cross with me at all. I gave her the pad and pencil.

'Granma was here!' she wrote. 'Don't cry!' I was not crying, she must have been going blind. 'Granma was singing! I said, "Why do you sing?" "I sing," Maria said, "because it's jolly." '

'I didn't hear the music, and I was right there at the door.'

'The Music is all around us but our ears are stopped,' said Mother with her pencil.

'I want to see Granma!' I said.

She wrote to me, 'You will! Listen! I shall always be near you.'

That was the best fun I had with Mother in her illness.

Three weeks went by. All the people on Mother's list had been to see her. The last ones were Mrs Ballantyne, Mrs Edmonds, Miss Vincent and Miss Bundersea. Mrs Black wanted to come again but Mother had had enough. She wrote me a note last thing at night: 'I want Dr Simpson tomorrow evening.'

My heart nearly stopped. He never came at night, not usually.

I rang Dr Simpson and told him, 'Mother says tomorrow night.'

He just said, 'Very well, Bim, I'll be there.' He knew what she meant.

I asked Mother if I should tell Chris and she said no, Chris wasn't strong. But when Chris came out of the sickroom she was dead white so I think she knew anyway. She didn't go straight home. She went into my bedroom and lay flat on her face for half an hour. In the end I gave her a good shake.

'Go home and sleep on your own bed!' I said. That made her move. She got up and grabbed her coat and nearly ran out of the house. She couldn't control herself.

When the doctor came I listened at the door.

'Bim has been good to you,' he murmured. And after a while he said, 'She is so faithful.' I knew Mother was writing something and I wondered what it was. I hoped she was writing, 'Yes, she is a good girl. She does a lovely rub,' or something like that.

Dr Simpson gave my hand a special big squeeze when he left the house. He had friendly eyes. 'It will be some hours, Bim. She'll drift off to sleep and she won't wake up tomorrow.'

I giggled, I don't know why. I couldn't help it.

'Are you all right on your own?' he asked.

'I'm used to it!' I told him.

'I could easily go and get Mrs Twyneham.' I shooed him out the door as fast as I could and went back to Mother. I didn't want anyone else there. I was glad to be the one, I was proud.

'Will you stay with me to the end? I won't be much trouble,' Mother wrote. And then she wrote a whole lot of other things, all her last instructions before she left.

'I long to be proud of you.

'A Lady would be quite a good beginning.

'Do all in your power for The Boy and those who have befriended him in his loneliness. You will then wipe out a great debt here and now.

'Don't show all your feelings.

'You are growing for another Life.

'Think of your Grandmother who was poor but left a great memory.

'Bring no more Dishonour on the family.'

She had a lot to write before she fell asleep. It was all

278

things I'd heard before, but it looked more serious on paper.

As soon as she dropped off I looked through the pad at the things she wrote to the doctor. 'I think Bim is becoming kinder,' said one note. Well! What a thing to write! 'Like the convolvulus. It is faithful too.' That was a funny one. 'I am weary. Let me go. Let me go. I want to rest. I am nobody.'

The doctor was right, she slept deeply and she didn't wake up. I kept popping in to look but she slept on. Finally I got a few hours' shut-eye and when I woke up it was morning. I hurried in to Mother and she was dead.

I didn't stop to think about it, I just rang up Dr Simpson like he told me to. As he told me to.

Mother didn't want a tombstone because she wouldn't be dead. The essay competition was instead of a tombstone. Archdeacon Haggitt took the funeral service. There were a lot of flowers in the church. A lot of people too. And obituaries in the papers. But Kate Sheppard didn't come.

A few days later Roy read the will. She was as good as her word. I've got a copy, I'll read it out. She left a legacy of 'TWENTY-FIVE POUNDS to recompense my daughter GUINEVERE ALICE CECILE for the care and attention she has given me during my illness.' I was proud to hear those words and they got my name right too. The next bit went like this: 'I refrain from giving to my daughter CHRISTABEL MARY any specific legacy to reward her for her kindness and attention during my illness because I have already caused to be placed to her credit the sum of ONE HUNDRED AND FIFTY POUNDS as a token of my gratitude.' Well! That was a surprise! I asked Roy what was the difference between 'care' and 'kindness' and he didn't know. And what about 'recompense' and 'reward', why was that different? I don't know, Roy didn't know. I thought recompense sounded sarcastic but she wouldn't be sarcastic in a will, that's silly, that just shows I'm no good with words, not like Chris.

But she's been a good sister to me. Mother thought the world of Chris, of course she did, I did too. She was so clever. She had a lumpy sort of face but she was kind. So was I! No, it's not Chris who got my goat. Who wants to be kissed and cuddled anyway! But look here, Kate Sheppard, she didn't go to the funeral. All right, she sent some roses but I chucked them out. Mother didn't want flowers. Mother was only sixty-nine and Kate Sheppard, I mean Lovell-Smith, she was eighty-five. If Mother had been sick for a few more years we would have been great friends, people like it when you nurse them, you get quite close. Kate Sheppard was a useless old woman, she could hardly walk. The wrong one died. Otherwise Mother and I would have been great friends. But it didn't work out like that. No. She had euthanasia and bang went my chance. Still, she was only thinking of me.

Mother left our brother Stan ten pounds for his travel expenses so he could come to the funeral. After the bills and the legacies Roy divided the money between the four of us and we got £384 2s 1d each.

So that is the story of my famous mother.

I think I'll finish up with some of her favourite sayings.

'Give to the world the best you have and the best will come back to you.

'The living body has the power to heal itself.

'The world is a mirror. If you see chaos and confusion there, the fault lies within.

'Love beats at the heart of things.'

Oh, that's enough! She had a lot of sayings.

Chapter 32

A few days ago I thought I'd finished telling the story of Ada Wells. But I forgot to say how Mother came back. She wasn't dead at all. I knew she wasn't dead, she said she would still be near. But I never guessed what message she would send me.

I was very unsettled after she died. I used to go to the Spiritualist Church. There had to be a message, it wasn't fair to leave me in the lurch like that without a word. Finally it came.

'We have contact with a spirit,' said the medium. 'The message is for her daughter. There is a young man in Oamaru she is very concerned about. He is in grave danger.' Oh! I knew who that was all right. I tried to put it out of my head but the next week, same again:

'She must go to his aid. It is a matter of life or death.'

I couldn't go on ignoring it but I wasn't particularly pleased. I'd gone to all that trouble to get rid of the kid and I might as well not have bothered. Mother never approved of my cutting him off and now she was dead and still telling me to look after him. She didn't even send her love.

I wrote to the Fergusons and found out where he was. I had that money from Mother so I went down to see for myself, he was working on a poultry farm, a good outdoor life, but it didn't agree with him. I bowled up to the farmer and said, 'Have you got a young boy working here? I'm a relation and I've come to see him.'

The chap was pretty surly I must say. He pointed at a shed down in a gully beside the big long fowl-houses. They must have had two thousand hens at least. So I went down the hill and looked inside this shed. Well! There was the kid picked clean as a chicken bone. It turned out he was only seven and a half stone, and he was six foot two. He was just slumped on the floor, not doing anything, just sort of dozing.

'Wake up kid!' I said, and I yanked his ear same as I always did. He just looked blank. He was in a bad way. I don't think he even recognised me! 'So that's what happens when I neglect you,' I said. 'You can't look after yourself can you?'

Well, I helped him up the hill, had to half-carry him. Then I made that farmer drive us back into Oamaru. We didn't go near the Fergusons. It was all their fault, they didn't care! We got on the next train back to Christchurch and I made him a bed in my flat and nursed him back to health. I rubbed him and I fed him up. He was there four weeks and gradually he put on a bit of condition. Then I didn't know what to do with him. I can't say we got on very well, we never did and we never will. Anyway, he went off to look for another job and that was that.

He went to the war and I didn't see why I should write to him or anything. But after he got back he started coming to see me, bothering me, and he's never stopped. I don't know why he comes.

I feel just a bit tired after telling this story. I've gone right through Mother's life! Right through from beginning to end! Wouldn't she be pleased! At least I think she would. Chris could have done it better no doubt but Chris isn't here, she's dead.

Now what'll I do with myself? Go back to the wireless I suppose. But I've got in the habit of talking into this thing, I've just sort of fancied I was talking to Biddy or someone. I must get Stan to take it away, there's nothing more to say about my mother.

Stan came in yesterday afternoon. I was just lying on the bed, I was so tired.

'Hey, what are you doing there?' he asked.

'Having a rest,' I said. I thought that was pretty obvious.

'I think you need a nice hot bath,' he said.

'Not on a Thursday,' I said. 'Saturday night's my bath night.'

He took the blankets out of the bath and started running the water. The cats were yowling and he gave them some tinned fish. I heard him open the hot water cupboard and say oh dear oh dear. Then he took me to the bathroom and sat me on the stool. Put my nightdress and housecoat on the peg and left me to it.

'Wash behind your ears!' he said with a silly grin.

'Don't boss me round,' I said. But the bath wasn't too bad.

I didn't want to put on my night clothes but it turned out my dress was damp and it didn't smell very salubrious. He made the bed with fresh sheets while I was getting dry.

'It's not my bedtime is it?' I asked.

'So you think it's Thursday do you?' He gave me a funny look.

It was hard to tell.

'It's Saturday,' he told me. 'I think you've been out of it.'

I got into bed, it was the easiest thing to do. I went over and over it in my mind. How could it be Saturday?

'If it's Saturday, what about my chickens?' I suddenly remembered. 'They'll be hungry and thirsty! The poor little things!'

'I'm sorry to say they are dead,' said Stan. 'That's bad luck. I've buried them in the back yard.'

I love animals! I wouldn't hurt them for all the world. My poor chicks were dead! Now it started coming back to me. Just lying on the bed and feeling sort of funny. I remembered going to the WC and I remembered getting a drink of water but that's about all.

'Oh dear oh dear!' I said.

He made some scrambled eggs and decorated them in that tarty way with bits of tomato and parsley, and brought it to me on a tray. I felt awful, lying in bed when it was still light outside. Being waited on!

'I saw the builder's account on the table,' he said after a while. I felt hot all over remembering that bill and my ears started roaring. 'It looks a bit much.'

'It's daylight robbery!' I said.

'I'll have a word with him if you like,' he said. 'See if I can talk him down a hundred dollars.'

'You!' I laughed in his face. 'He'd eat you for breakfast! Here, take this away. I can't eat that toast, it's burnt.'

'I'll talk to him all the same,' he said. 'If I can't get him to knock a bit off I'll pay half of it. You haven't got that sort of money to throw around.'

'I don't take charity!' I yelled at him. He took the tray away and I said to myself, 'I didn't ask for a son like you.' So lanky and pale with that awful ginger hair like Father's. I like big muscly men with black hair on their chests. He came back and sat by the bed. He looked me right in the face with those pale blue eyes of his. They're exactly the same as mine. It was like looking in the mirror, me looking back at me only back to front.

'And I didn't ask for a mother like you,' he said. He never dared say such a thing to me before. That's what you get when you're old, I thought. 'When I was a boy I called you the Queen of Scorn.'

'I never asked to be odd!' I said, I couldn't help it.

'It's all right, Bim, we're even now,' he said. That was his idea of a joke, ha ha.

I never was good at numbers. Mental got me flustered every time. I lay back and numbers whizzed through my head. Two thousand chooks. Thirty thousand women. They're all dead now for sure. So where are all the souls?

'In the war, think of all those people killed!' I said.

'All around me,' said Stan. 'And dying on the march.'

'But not you! How could that happen?'

'All those people are only a lot of ones and twos,' he said. 'They just add up, that's all. Don't let it worry you.'

'Mother had rules that worked for everyone in the world,' I said. 'But I can't work it out.'

'Why should you?' said Stan. He went into the kitchen. I think he was cleaning out one of my cupboards. The cheek of it! 'Clean out the dark unwholesome corners, condemn rubbish of all kinds.' Mother wrote that. I thought and thought about her life and my life too. It was like in the hall of funny mirrors, you saw yourself but all funny shapes, not right. I was going to be all right, I was one of the elect, but what about all the others?

Well, one of Mother's last words came back to me. 'It's like muddling over a sum — muddling! You must get it right sometime.' I dozed off again and woke up with a jump.

'What's wrong with me? Eh?' I said out loud. I forgot he was there.

'Nothing, Bim,' said this voice from the kitchen. He came in wearing my pinny. 'You did all right. I wouldn't be here without you.' I did all right! Only Gran would say something like that. 'You saved my life, you did it twice over.'

'Only because of Mother. She made me.'

'You gave me holidays from Hell.' He was never in Hell! 'And now everything is perfect. I've got my pigeon pair.'

'How can it be evolution if they're adopted?' I said.

'I just wish you'd let me do things for you, that's all,' he said.

What a peculiar thing to say!

'I can do for myself,' I said. 'I don't need any help from you. You of all people! You might as well just stay away.'

Then he went out for a minute and brought me a cup of hot milk and honey. He just stood there looking at it. And I just lay there in the bed looking at it. It was in the red cup and saucer that my Mother left me, the big one. I could smell it.

'Well?' I said. 'Are you going to give that to me or are you not?'

'Not if you don't want it,' he said.

'I can take it or leave it. Suit yourself,' I told him.

So he gave it to me. I dare say he wanted me to say thank you but I wasn't going to kowtow to him.

'Goodbye then, Bim,' he said. 'I'll come by in the morning if you like.'

Acknowledgements

I would like to acknowledge the many people who have helped me in my research, especially my late mother Celia Taylor, my father David Taylor, and family members Jill, Robyn and Graham Nuthall, Des and Betty Twyneham, Edna Milne and Stan Wells. Judith Devaliant generously shared her exhaustive knowledge about Kate Sheppard. I was given assistance by the staff of the Canterbury Museum, the Christchurch Library, the Christchurch City Council and the Alexander Turnbull Library. Others who have helped include Rod Alley, Elizabeth Baker, Cheryl Cameron, Janet Carter, Lynley Hood, Pamela Jones, Margie Lovell-Smith, Donna Malane, Erin McGifford, Michael Noonan, Libby Plumridge, Andreas Ries, Gwen Somerset, Margaret Tennant, Jane Tolerton, Hetty Turner and the Lower Hutt Theosophical Society. If I have omitted to mention others I hope they will take this as a personal acknowledgement.

During the writing and research, Michael Smither's support and understanding has been crucial. Geoff Walker and Mary Barr provided intelligent feedback on the style and structure of the book. Finally, a grant from the New Zealand Literary Fund helped pay for the supply of electricity to my writing shed, without which this book would not have been written.